Pleasures of the
FORBIDDEN VALLEY

Pleasures of the
FORBIDDEN VALLEY

Diana Mercury

AVON

An Imprint of HarperCollinsPublishers

PLEASURES OF THE FORBIDDEN VALLEY. Copyright © 2009 by Diana Mercury. All rights reserved. Printed in the United States of America. No part of this book may be used or reproduced in any manner whatsoever without written permission except in the case of brief quotations embodied in critical articles and reviews. For information, address HarperCollins Publishers, 10 East 53rd Street, New York, NY 10022.

HarperCollins books may be purchased for educational, business, or sales promotional use. For information, please write: Special Markets Department, HarperCollins Publishers, 10 East 53rd Street, New York, NY 10022.

FIRST AVON PAPERBACK EDITION PUBLISHED 2009.

Designed by Rhea Braunstein

Library of Congress Cataloging-in-Publication Data
Mercury, Diana.
    Pleasures of the Forbidden Valley / Diana Mercury.—1st ed.
      p. cm.
    ISBN 978-0-06-145095-2
1. Women anthropologists—Fiction. 2. Himalaya Mountains—Fiction. I. Title.
    PS3613.E73F67 2009
    813'.6—dc22

                                                    2008036710

09 10 11 12 OV/RRD 10 9 8 7 6 5 4 3 2 1

For my girlfriends

Acknowledgments

With gratitude to the divine muse,
who often comes through when asked nicely.

Pleasures of the
FORBIDDEN VALLEY

Chapter 1

꒳

After completing some postgraduate field work in anthropology, I took a couple of months off to travel and explore the world. When I found myself in Asia, in the shadow of the Himalayas, I decided I would try to find the Lost Valley.

Nobody I knew had ever been able to locate it, and some said it didn't even exist, that it was a myth or a hoax. But that only made me want to reach it all the more. I believed in it because I *wanted* to so badly. From the time I first learned of the Lost Valley, I longed to go there.

My search took me from Kashmir to Katmandu, to a tiny village somewhere in the most remote reaches of the Great Himalayas. For three days I talked to people in the village, asking about the Lost Valley, but nobody seemed to know what I was talking about.

I finally decided that the whole idea of a "lost" valley was ridiculous anyway, and to drop the whole thing. I would leave in the morning. But that night, in the bar below the room I was renting by the week, the innkeeper—a toothless old man who had denied any knowledge of a lost valley—suddenly appeared at my side and said he would help me.

It seemed he'd finally decided to trust me.

"A man will come tonight," he said. "To meet you."

"Is this man going to take me to the Lost Valley?" I asked.

"Nobody like you go to Lost Valley," the old man replied. "Not ever. Not allowed."

"Nobody like me? What do you mean?" I asked innocently. But I knew exactly what he meant. I glanced at the folding screen by the doorway and saw my own image reflected in dozens of octagonal mirrors set into the sandalwood panels. I was a young woman, blond, tending to the curvaceous. *Plump*, by western standards. I had large green eyes with expressive dark brows that I didn't pluck often enough because I lived out of a pack most of the time. In my own country, men seemed to find me reasonably attractive, but during my travels in other lands, I sometimes found myself an object of intense fascination to men who apparently found me exotic. A friend had explained it to me. "It's the ivory skin, golden hair, and jade eyes," he said. "Even the part of you that might be considered excess in your culture is desirable. You're a goddess to these guys."

But I was beginning to think being an exotic goddess wasn't necessarily all that advantageous. It certainly wasn't getting me what I wanted. The whole mystique around the Lost Valley was that it was *never* open to outsiders.

"So who is this guy?" I asked the innkeeper. "If you don't think he can get me into the Lost Valley, why should I meet him?"

The old man shrugged. "He is some kind of an official of the country. He lives there. Maybe you can bribe him." He grinned, exposing his toothless gums, to show he was joking. Or not.

I was thrilled with the excitement of it, but I felt a creep of uneasiness as well. So the myth *is* real after all, I thought. The Lost Valley really did exist. And I realized I hadn't completely believed in it myself. Maybe I still didn't.

The moment I met Hama, I could see that he was not someone who could be bribed. He was a commanding, authoritative figure. He wore a beige khaki military uniform, high boots and a sash over his broad chest, and his trim waist was cinched by a heavy leather belt. His bearing was proud, his manner courtly and noble.

We had instant chemistry, sexual and otherwise. He was an interesting conversationalist and had quiet power, exerting it as he did his influence over what I wanted so badly—access to his country.

He had been traveling abroad, he told me, and stopped in the village to take care of some official business. He would soon be off again. In a day or two.

"So you are on your way home to the Lost Valley?" I asked.

"I am on my way home," he replied, smiling enigmatically.

"A day or two" became several. A week passed. Hama and I became friends, spending evenings together in the hotel café, or at one of the other places in town he had introduced me to. We talked of everything imaginable, except for what interested me most—the Lost Valley. He would just laugh when I brought it up, and change the subject.

Hama's English was excellent. He also spoke Hindi, Cantonese, some Mandarin, and fairly good French. I tried to get him to teach me some words of his native tongue, but he would say things in his dialect only after a couple of drinks of the strong local brew, and only when I cajoled him enough. I would repeat the strange words, which sounded like a cross between Sanskrit and Portuguese, and he would laugh. He wouldn't even bother to correct me.

He knew what I wanted, and I never gave up. But for a long time he wouldn't confirm that he was actually from the Lost Valley, or that it even existed.

Hama blamed the local bureaucracy for its failure to move things along more quickly so he could complete his business in the city and be on his way. I didn't doubt the slow pace of the bureaucracy, but I began to suspect that he was actually staying for my sake. He didn't want to leave me. Not unsatisfied.

I had worn him down, at least partway. He was no longer pretending the Lost Valley was merely some wide-eyed American woman's overwrought fantasy. He did not deny that he lived there and was soon to return. But when I pressed him, he'd shake his head and say it would be impossible for me to come with him.

"What if you were to just—smuggle me in across the border?" I once suggested playfully.

He smiled and shook his head. "And nobody would notice you, after you had crossed this 'border,' would they?"

"So there's nothing?" I asked plaintively. "No way you can think of, to get me in? No special visas, permits—*nothing*?" I moved closer. "Hama, let me come with you," I murmured. "I'll do anything you ask."

He grasped my hand so hard it hurt and said hoarsely, "You shouldn't play with me, little girl."

I pulled my arm away, shaken. There was a dark sexual power in him that vied with his tame gentlemanliness. I wondered if the gentleman would always control the dark power.

For the rest of the evening he was silent, brooding. He seemed to be thinking something through.

I felt triumphant, certain I was getting closer because this time he hadn't completely and flatly denied me. But I felt scared. Like I was playing with fire.

The day he told me he would bring me with him, I couldn't hide my excitement from him.

"But hear me out first, Diandra," he said sharply. "There is a price." I felt his dark-eyed gaze traveling over the swell of my breasts beneath my T-shirt. "And I'm not sure you'd be willing to pay it."

"Hama," I said with a burst of laughter. I would pay *any* price. I almost said it, but I bit back the words.

Let him think I had a choice.

"Okay, so what is the price?" I asked.

"You," he said softly. "*You* are the price."

Chapter 2

⁂

You are the price.

He let the words resonate in the air.

Hama Rulan was gracious and polite, a naturally shy man whose business dealings had compelled him to learn how to be at ease in international company. But there was something of the animal about him too, something dark and earthy.

Suddenly I felt vulnerable. Yes, I had made the offer. But was I willing to pay the price?

I thought of a particularly intimate dinner and conversation we had shared one evening in the corner of a dark café. Afterward, on our walk back to my hotel, Hama had pressed me against the mud brick wall of a building in a narrow, deserted alley and kissed me.

I felt the cool wall against my body, and his warm body against me as well, and then he was turning me toward him and we were face-to-face, his hands on me, his strong arms around me. I turned my head and felt his warm mouth grazing over mine.

It was too dark to see much, and I let myself melt against him for a moment. I felt his hard warmth and a suggestion of cock, like a jut of bone. I indulged in the contact for a fleeting moment, then gently pushed Hama away. He pulled me along through the alleyway, holding my hand.

I became guarded afterward. The heat was still there between us, but I turned it down to a simmer and put the lid on, knowing I had to concentrate on my objective. Hama seemed to accept the gentle rebuke with grace and good-natured disappointment, which he communicated with humor and the implication that he would keep trying. I countered that I too would keep trying—to reach the Lost Valley. He seemed to find this amusing, and so did I, or I would have if he hadn't gotten me so worked up.

I had no moral qualms about being with a man I desired. My vagabond lifestyle and adventurous spirit had led me to experience many brief but passionate intimacies with men I had encountered on my travels, and my motto was always to go for it when things felt right. But in this case, my frustration in denying Hama sexually was akin to his own frustration, as the representative of his government, in denying me entrance to his country, his community, his culture.

He had no choice, apparently. *Personally*, he told me, he would have liked nothing more than to bring me home with him to his village and entertain me there, to introduce me to his family and friends and make me familiar with their ways. He said he wouldn't even mind if I "studied" them.

"I would be a particularly fascinating specimen for you to examine beneath your anthropologist's microscope," he'd said, and wasn't entirely joking.

"Cultural anthropologists don't usually use microscopes," I told him. "We use our eyes, our ears . . . our hands . . ." I ran my fingers over his arm, deliberately trying to get a reaction from him. He stared at me, and I knew he was longing to possess me.

And he knew I was longing to get into the Lost Valley.

But it was impossible, he had said. He would not, *could* not, yield to me.

He told me how it went against the soul of his people—this lack of hospitality to strangers. But such measures had become necessary to protect them from invaders, both political and social. "Those who would bring unwanted changes to our way of life."

"I don't want to change your way of life," I insisted. "I want to immerse myself in it. To become part of it."

"I only wish you could," he'd murmured.

And so the Lost Valley had become for me a personal Shangri-la, a fabled and inaccessible place that I was determined to reach at any cost. I was relentless about finding a way to get through the mountain pass that would take me there.

Hama wanted to help me. He became my advocate and began to work tirelessly to find some sort of loophole to get me what I was after.

It seemed he had found the loophole.

But he wasn't going to offer it to me for nothing.

You are the price.

Hama lifted his hand slowly. Reached out to me.

For days we had flirted, brushed against each other, let our eyes meet, longer than necessary. But he'd always been respectful. Except for that one moment in the alley, he had never taken liberties. Until now. The well-shaped hand settled in a friendly way upon my shoulder, as it so often did. But now he let it move down over my arm, fingers trailing along the edge of my breast, sending a shudder through my body.

You are the price.

I heard my own voice, surprisingly dispassionate. "Are you saying that if I have sex with you, Hama, you will take me to the Lost Valley?"

He snatched away his hand and a funny look crossed his face. "Of course not," he said. "If it were that easy, then—I think we would have been there long ago!" He hesitated before speaking again. "I have wanted you since I first met you. You know that. But no, that is not my meaning. And it would do you no good in any case."

"Then what *is* your price, Hama?"

"The price is not mine, Diandra. The only way you would ever be allowed into my country would be to become one of us. And, there is only one way for *you* to do that . . . by marrying into us. Do you understand? You would have to submit to the legally binding marriage ceremony of my people and obtain the proper legal documents."

Hama looked alarmed as I began to laugh heartily. Why hadn't *I* thought of that? Where I came from, in California, there was a joke among my girlfriends about how guys wanted to marry us for the legal status. Why not turn it around?

"Shall I marry you, then, Hama? Are you volunteering yourself?"

"I am offering." That hungry look came over him again.

He was serious. He was offering to marry me. And that meant I would finally get my passage into the Lost Valley.

And I would get to fuck him.

At that moment, with the vibration of his fingers against the edge of my breasts still humming, I wanted both very badly.

Chapter 3

I wasn't in love with Hama. I doubted I ever could be, though I did like him very much. He was handsome enough, and politely witty. He looked good in his uniform, and he had all the social graces. He seemed like a nice guy. And yet for me, there was something missing. Some heart and soul connection.

But he had a great body, tall and lean, and he moved like a lion, with deliberate, muscular grace. He had intense dark eyes and a wild cat's feral gaze, which he fixed on me like I was his prey. He was one of the few men I thought I could freely fuck, just for fun, and not fall for.

Marry him? Sure. Why not?

"Well, we can always get a divorce, right?" I said. "I mean, if things don't work out." I said it jokingly, but it was a real question for me. Because of course this marriage would be temporary.

He looked at me with a serious expression.

"You *do* recognize divorce in your country, don't you?" I asked sharply.

"Divorce is easy enough," he said. "It's the terms of marriage I wonder about, with you, little American girl."

"What terms? Why? Do you keep your women locked up or something?"

"No, in fact in certain ways our women have more freedom than you have in your American society. That is what concerns me."

"*More* freedom?" I scoffed at that.

"Indeed. I am not so sure you could adapt to the freedoms allowed you as a wife in my country—"

"Give me a break, Hama. You're fucking with me, right?"

He shook his head and looked at me soberly.

"Well, freedom means freedom to do what you want—or to *not* do what you *don't* want, true?"

"Yes," he said. "I suppose that is true."

"So what have I got to worry about?"

"With freedom comes responsibility," he said gravely.

"All right. What kind of responsibility are we talking about?"

"The normal responsibilities of a wife to her husband."

"Are we talking about sex, Hama?" I said.

He seemed almost embarrassed by my direct words. "Our ways are different than yours, Diandra."

"Oh, like what? Kinky, you mean?" I smiled. "That's okay. I'm cool with kinky."

He did not respond to my humor.

"Listen," I said. "All joking aside, what I want to know is

this: Am I free to leave? *Any* time? Whenever I want? As far as assurances go, that's all I need."

"I'm not sure that *is* all you need."

"Why don't you just tell me what your concerns are, Hama."

"We are really a very simple people," he said. "But there are those who might take some of our cultural practices and sensationalize them, or even try to legislate against them. If you agree to marry me and come live with me, you will become one of us. You will then make up your own mind about how things are. But I will not talk about our ways with an outsider—that is what we would call you, 'an outsider.' I am sorry, Diandra. If you cannot abide by my conditions, I will understand."

What *conditions*?

"I'm an anthropologist, Hama. I *want* to immerse myself in a culture that's different than my own. That's what I'd be going there for. All I need is a guarantee that I can escape if I need to."

For a moment a look of hurt passed over his well-formed, strikingly dark features. I regretted having used the word "escape."

"Of course," he replied coolly. "You would always be free to leave, anytime."

So I agreed to Hama's "conditions."

He told me we would have to wait another couple of days for some local official to return to his office so he could witness the signing of the papers.

"Do I get an engagement ring?" I quipped after we decided.

He had soberly clinked my wineglass with his, and that was it. We had made an agreement.

"We don't do that," he said curtly. "Nor do we observe the practice of exchanging wedding rings. Those are customs we consider superfluous. Of course, ordinarily the bride would be bringing in a dowry, but that requirement will be waived."

"Oh." Of course. *A dowry.* Still a very common requirement in much of the world. "Hama, if you need me to pay something—"

"No. It will not be necessary. My estate is quite well situated."

We made out a little before parting that night. He took me into his arms with solemn authority and kissed me on the mouth. I was sorely tempted to get naked with him, now that my goal was in view. But prudence warned me not to let go just yet. If I was going to sell myself, I'd better make sure I got the goods first.

Then again, I thought, if he were to press for it, I could easily see myself being persuaded. After all, we were engaged now. I was rather curious to see what I had signed up for.

Surprisingly, though, he didn't press it.

Chapter 4

✗

We sat in a tiny, stuffy office, and I tried to understand what Hama and the man behind the desk were saying to one another as they spoke in a rapid-fire dialect I could not follow. I tried to read the papers we were signing, but they were written in a language that looked less familiar than Greek to me. Uneasily, I affixed my signature to the document.

"So I am free to enter the Lost Valley now?" I asked when they told me we had finished. It was the only thing I cared about.

Hama and the other man exchanged a few words. Hama had translated my question, and the official seemed to hesitate before giving the answer. "Yes," he said. "You may now legally enter the valley—provisionally."

"Provisionally?"

It was explained that although we had entered into agreement, we were married only by proxy. The legality of the marriage would be ratified after the paperwork was complete.

I now had the freedom to enter the country, a tiny sovereign nation "beyond Nepal and Tibet," the official said portentously in English. I did not understand what he meant by that, but I'd find out where the Lost Valley was soon enough. So I would be allowed to enter, but I would have to leave if the marriage was not made final and the paperwork completed within a short time.

"So what must we do to make it . . . complete?" I asked, a touch impatient with all the legal talk.

"It's a mere formality," Hama assured me. "We will get the required signatures in my village, once we are home."

Home. He was talking about the Lost Valley. In my excitement, I didn't press my questions regarding the legal issues.

Hama and I had dinner together in our favorite cafe and walked through the town to my hotel.

Well, so it's my wedding night . . .

I was surprised to find I felt a little down. I suppose, like most girls, I had ideas about what my wedding would be like. And this wasn't it.

I tried to get excited about the fact that I had finally achieved the legal right to get into the Lost Valley. Instead I found myself yearning for a little human connection. But Hama seemed less available to me tonight than on the first night he'd come to my hotel.

I thought he might take my hand, but he seemed preoccupied. I also thought he might take me back to *his* hotel, which was somewhat grander than where I was staying, but he steered us straight to the old inn.

At my door, I paused and turned to face him.

"So . . . " I grinned at him. "Are you going carry me over the threshold?"

He frowned. "What?" he said.

"Never mind."

He bent down to kiss me. A quick nudge on the cheek.

Then he straightened up, smoothed his uniform, and stepped away from me. He was far less sensual with me than he had ever been before.

Maybe he was nervous.

I leaned back against the door and gazed up at him innocently. *Come on, big boy. It's all yours.* That was the deal, right?

He stared at me, at my breasts, lingering on their curves. He had always seemed fascinated by my breasts. I made the slightest movement toward him, and he came at me, knocked me back gently against the door and fell on me with kisses. He kissed me on the top of my head, my eyebrows, cheeks, and lips. Surprisingly tender kisses for this strict military man. Tender and sensual, erotic with longing. He kissed me, but not deeply. His tongue never penetrated my mouth, and his generous erection pressed against me only by accident, as it was difficult to avoid. He seemed to be maintaining a deliberate chastity—though his vibe was anything but chaste.

I was definitely getting mixed signals.

He actually picked up my hand and held it tightly when I started moving it down over his fly. The instruction was clear: *We're not going there.*

At the same time, he was panting, obviously hot for me.

He's afraid, I thought. He's nervous.

Well, great. Whatever.

Too bad he smelled so good and had such a great, big, hard body and that sexy macho he-man thing going on. All fake? The very thing I'd thought we would definitely click on appeared to be imaginary.

Well, who cares? I thought. This would make my job all the easier.

I invited him in, finally, being as blunt as my pride would allow, but by then he could probably hear the exasperation in my voice. He politely and nervously declined, mumbled something about having some official letters to write, and left me at my door.

$\mathcal{I}$got into bed and turned out the light.

But Hama had gotten me so worked up it took me a long time to settle into sleep. When I heard a noise down in the yard, I jerked awake. I knelt in bed and looked out the window.

Ami, the innkeeper's son, was dumping the trash. Ami, with his white drawstring pants and his ready smile. He worked in the kitchen, washing dishes and chopping vegetables. With his back toward me, his ass was small and tight, shining in the moonlight. Footsteps echoed in the alleyway and the dark hulk of another man appeared below. I recognized Yuri, a regular in the tavern. A huge, heavy guy, he never said much, liked to sit by the arched doorway between the tavern and the inn and stare into the kitchen.

I was about to understand why.

Ami glanced back at him, then turned away, seemingly paying Yuri little mind as he finished his task. He bent over slightly, letting the thin white fabric of his pants cup his ass cheeks and expose the bulge of his genitals between trim, muscular thighs.

Big Yuri slowly moved up behind Ami. His movements were silent, stealthy; furtive, somehow. For a moment I wondered if he was going to hurt Ami. I actually thought about calling out, to warn the smaller man. But Ami was almost doubled over now, and I suddenly got it. He was presenting himself to Yuri.

Yuri stepped up close to Ami and ran his hands over his white-clad buttocks, filling his hands with them. Both men groaned loudly as Yuri kneaded Ami's flesh through the fabric with his large, strong fingers.

Yuri's hand slipped between Ami's legs, and soon Yuri's arm was moving rhythmically.

I shouldn't be watching this, I thought. But I couldn't stop myself.

Suddenly, Yuri pulled his hand out and yanked down the tight white pants. Now the bare white naked ass was exposed and Ami was on all fours, waiting eagerly. Yuri loosened his own trousers and brought out a thick cock quivering with excitement. He pressed it against the small, sweet ass, and in one or two violent strokes he was buried inside. Ami bit his own arm to keep from crying out. Yuri made no effort to stifle his grunting as he rammed his cock into Ami's ass.

Ami was practically lying prone and his face buried in the dirt of the alleyway by the time Yuri finished, collapsing on top of him.

I left my window, crawled back into my bed and fingered myself to orgasm for the third time since I'd left my new husband at the hotel room door. This climax was full and shuddering, heated by the primal scene I had just witnessed in the alley. But when it was over and I lay panting, alone in my bed, I did not feel satisfied.

I cursed Hama for that.

Chapter 5

❧

We set off several days later by yak train, a very slow way to travel, but Hama seemed in no hurry. Now that I was actually moving toward my goal, my impatience was mounting to an almost unbearable pitch. My impatience to see the fabled Lost Valley, and my impatience for something else.

A real wedding night.

But Hama refused to touch me.

I take that back. He would touch me, yes, maddeningly and confusingly, erotically and sensually—but he would always hold back in the end and leave me alone in my tent.

It was beginning to upset me. I began to question what I had done. He had hinted about some sort of strange sexual requirement in marriage, but I never thought that would mean celibacy. Or was Hama just a prude? But even if he was, we were married now. Why weren't we having sex like normal married people? I was *sure* he wanted it; he exuded a potent heterosexual sensibility.

On the other hand, he seemed so methodical, so businesslike. Maybe the smoldering sensuality was just another language he had learned to speak to get what he wanted. But then, what *did* he want? Why had he suggested this marriage and agreed to it? And then not even take advantage of it, when it happened? Why did he sometimes look at me so calculatingly, as if planning every action one step ahead of me? Was I just crazy to be embarking on this vague, suspect journey?

Yeah, maybe I was.

I knew nothing about the people we would be living with; I hardly believed they could be real. I tried to get Hama to prepare me for what I was about to face, but he did not respond in any depth to my questions.

"Hama," I said to him finally. Simply biding my time had not achieved the unfolding of the answers to this mystery, so I just put it out there. "What is it?" I asked. "Is this marriage to be on paper only? I mean, that's *okay* with me, but just tell me. I'm a little confused here."

"You must be patient," was all he would say. "Wait until we get home."

Home!

*T*hough he never lost his polite solicitude, as the days passed and we traveled on our slow journey, Hama seemed to grow cooler toward me. I tried to relax and enjoy the spectacular mountain scenery.

We had gone through terrain of amazing diversity, from tropical rain forests to moonscape regions that reminded me of Mustang, the arid region at the end of the Kali Gandaki beyond the

Annapurna and Dhualagiri ranges. There, in the ancient King-dom of Lo, language and culture is almost purely Tibetan, unlike Lower Mustang, where the people are related to the Manangis. I recognized the Tibetan influence, but there was something different about this land I had never seen before.

I realized I did not know what country we were in anymore. I wasn't even certain if we were on the south draining side of the Himalayas or the Tibetan side. The land forms and the location of villages, even the narrow road we traveled—none of it conformed to anything I had ever found on a map. In fact, I had never seen the Lost Valley on any map—and I'd looked for it. That struck me as strange, of course—that it wouldn't be noted—since the official who had approved the marriage told me it was a sovereign nation.

Villages thinned out. Days passed with no trace of human habitation.

Finally we came to a small mountain hamlet. It was like a place I had never heard described except in fairy tales, a strange and beautiful mixture of influences. Prayer flags were flying from the terraced hillsides, but the architecture and culture, while very much of the Himalayas, seemed to hearken back to medieval Europe. The Dzong—the center of government—was built on the hillside in the usual way, but along with the Tibetan, Nepalese, and Indian influences I might have expected, it had Romanesque arches topped with pointed towers and flying buttresses like a Gothic cathedral.

I peered at the architecture, astonished to find such a thing in this remote place. And I was even more surprised when I noticed the intricate carvings around the windows and eaves of the building. I had seen depictions of the sexual act on temples before, but you generally didn't see them on buildings that looked like high Gothic churches. In one particularly evocative bas relief, two naked men sandwiched a woman with perfect orbital breasts on which the man facing her was bringing his mouth down to suck. The man behind her was arching his back and looking quite rapturous, and it was clear they were fully conjoined.

Looking away, finally, I noticed one of the yak drivers who traveled with us, a sinewy young man who liked to flirt with me using only his eyes as we walked along the road together. He was watching me, and I knew he had seen my fascination with the sexual carvings.

I made sketches in my journal of the architectural whimsies, as well as the beauties of nature, which were just as compelling. All around us rose enormous mountain peaks, colossal ice monsters, and glaciers poured down into the valleys, the lower ridges fringed with forests of pine and cedar, with the occasional emerald meadow shining in the sun. I began to think I might find Yeti, or the Abominable Snowman, in a land like this.

We passed a group of men working by the road, and when they caught sight of me, they became excited and started chattering wildly among themselves, staring at me, dropping their tools. The closer we came to our destination, the more I was struck by how beautiful the people were. They appeared unlike any other I had ever encountered, and yet in a strange way, it seemed that anyone of any race might find something familiar in them. With lofty, noble bone structure, smooth coffee cream skin, huge gemstone eyes, and flowing hair, these workmen exemplified the type. They wore tunics and high leather boots like storybook knights.

Their style went along with the strange architecture, as if the characters and the castle had been illustrated by the same hand.

I was startled, but not really frightened, when one of the men reached out to touch my hair as I walked by.

My flirtatious young yak driver stepped between the workman and me, speaking sharply. The mason dropped his hand, grinning and waving us along good-naturedly.

I heard one word over and over, which I later learned was to be translated as "made of gold."

I felt flattered by the attention of these men. Maybe more flattered than I ought to have been. My husband watched me speculatively. I grew angry.

Why should you care? I asked him silently. *You don't want me.*

*O*ne night, someone spoke softly outside my tent. My valiant young yak driver. I recognized his voice, and my instincts were suddenly on alert. I knew why he was there. Apparently, it had not been lost on my other traveling companions that my husband left me alone every night and went to his own tent as if he was afraid of turning into a pumpkin.

The young man spoke hurriedly, quietly. I called out to him but couldn't understand his reply.

"Come in here," I said.

He slipped inside my tent. By the light of the lantern, he seemed to be made of golden light and oily darkness. I could almost see the horns and tail. His eyes were large and moist-looking. His trousers were full, his thighs slender and supporting a decided pyramid. Our eyes locked, and I thought of how he had lately taken to looking at me with a sideways smile as he walked along with his big animals, moving rhythmically, like a dancer. Having him around had definitely made the long days of walking more pleasurable.

I let the blankets fall away and wished I was sporting something other than my well-worn ANNAPURNA: A WOMAN'S PLACE IS ON TOP T-shirt.

But he just stared into my eyes, and I must have somehow given the go-ahead, because suddenly he was straddling me, sinking slowly to his knees on my sleeping bag, letting his weight settle into my body. It was almost a shock after so long without a lover, feeling the pressure of the man's weight, the pain of his cock hard and pressing against my thighs, grinding now through our clothes; almost as an afterthought, he kissed me, his mouth wet and tangy-tasting, his hands on my body squeezing too hard. It felt great.

I became conscious of the fact that I was technically a married woman now, and this man was not my husband. I tried to push him away, but he had felt my hungry response a moment earlier and he did not take my efforts seriously.

God, he was so strong. I guess you would have to be, to handle yaks. He squeezed me with his thighs, his weight heavy on me, and began to suck my nipples through my T-shirt. I bucked up against him and felt the cock harden and pulse against me. He was sliding his hand down my boy shorts now; he found and began fingering my clit.

Where had he taken that lovely warm bulge?

Ahh . . . there. His fingers felt good, but he was impatient too. His cock was big, pushing at me. Without undressing me, he opened a way through my clothing. He entered me suddenly, huge and hard, and I felt him fill me. Deeply. Thrusting. As he fucked me, I let a moan escape, then remembered, somewhere in my mind, that anybody nearby could hear us.

I almost didn't care. I was mad with the need of him, with the weeks of sensual teasing and deprivation by Hama culminating in this *gotta have it* moment with a yak driver whose name I wasn't even sure of. I was getting fucked by a man, and that was everything I wanted right then. If the experience was tinged with shame and a sense of desolation, that was something I would feel only later.

Now he was ramming his narrow hips against me and unconsciously jamming my head against the side of the tent with each thrust, and I was loving it.

He didn't wait for me to come, but erupted inside me, finishing off with one or two last stiff thrusts. He pulled out, rolled over on his back and lay there panting. I was too overcome with sensation to worry much about how abruptly it had ended. But I was decidedly unfinished, and I lay beside him quivering.

After only a few minutes he sat up with a huge erection poking out of his open pants, pushed me over on my back, mounted me, and did the whole thing over again. Only this time he undressed me as he fucked me, and he took a bit longer to complete his satisfaction, and so I had enough time to get mine.

Chapter 6

I had no fewer than three different lovers during that trip to the Lost Valley, not counting my husband, who doesn't count, because he wasn't one of them.

One night we stopped in a tiny hamlet situated on the edge of a mountain so steep I was amazed that anybody could live in such perilous circumstances. Outside a doorway, a sheer drop of thousands of feet. How could you live in such a place?

The dwelling we visited, no bigger than a small apartment, was the home of an entire extended family, father and mother and an old aunt, and two full-grown brothers, cousins of our host. These two handsome fellows, who were probably in their late twenties, spent most of the evening speaking in low voices together and sneaking glances at me.

We were invited to spend the night. To my surprise, Hama and I were given a room with the two brothers—and there was only one large bed in the room, which we were all meant to share.

"It's done all the time," Hama explained, whispering in my ear, seeing the expression of panic cross my face. "People share beds. It means nothing. It's only that bed space is precious."

I shrugged, trying for nonchalance. I'm an anthropologist, I thought. I do weird shit like this.

It was a large enough bed, after all.

That night I lay there for a long time without sleeping. Between my husband and two other men. Soon they were all breathing deeply. I thought longingly of my clumsy but passionate yak-driver lover, who was sleeping out in the stables.

I dozed off for a while, then came awake to the sound of Hama's snoring.

I sat up a little and found one of the young men, a chiseled-featured beauty with soulful black eyes and black ringlets, propped up on his elbow, staring at me. I stared back. He pulled me into his arms.

Silently, we kissed and melded, and I became like water swimming against him. It was like falling back into a dream. I felt enveloped in a deep bliss. It was a strange and unusual experience, and I began to wonder how he managed to accomplish it. Then I realized I was actually being caressed by *two* male bodies as four hands roamed over my flesh, two mouths kissed and suckled me, two cocks rubbed against me, four legs tangled up with the two of mine. The sensations of their lips, and both their tongues on my nipples, was so intense I felt in danger of being shot out of my body. They crawled around beneath the woolen blankets on the big bed, trading off positions. While one of them licked and poked his tongue into my cunt, one of them fucked my mouth. He had a small, uncircumcised penis that I could almost take all the way in up to his balls. It was delicious.

I prayed my husband would not awaken, though part of me fantasized that he would, and that he would suddenly find his carnal desires unstoppable, and join us in a foursome. Like golf. But he continued to sleep on, or pretend to, anyway.

Just before one of my young lovers was about to come, his brother—who was almost identical, with the eyes of an Egyptian god—pulled his cock out of my mouth, glistening wet, and the next thing I knew I was in a sandwich between them. Just like the carvings I had seen on the temple.

They held themselves still a moment, not entering, just there, letting me get used to the idea of being full of them, and then they began to work it. Slowly, excruciatingly. I felt their two cocks entering me at the same time, one in my cunt, one in my ass. Slowly, slowly, slowly. So skillfully. Whenever I thought I'd had enough, they waited, getting me accustomed to the extreme sensation that was so close to pain until it became pleasure and I did not want them to stop.

They moved into me relentlessly, just gradually enough so I didn't freak out and scream and shove them off me. They kept me in just enough scorching bliss that I could handle the overwhelming sensation of being split apart. They had obviously done this before.

For me, it was a first. Thank God brother number one had a small penis. After a moment of intense pain—okay, a long moment—I began to wonder if I hadn't died and gone to heaven. And after a while I was driving it. We hit our stride, one shoving in, one pulling out. I began to urge them in deeper, both at the same time. I wanted to be full of them, as deeply as they could be. By the end of it we were thrashing and clawing at each other to deepen the connection.

We shared a shuddering climax that had the mattress slamming against the wall.

Still Hama did not awaken.

It was a strange journey, wearying yet exhilarating, and I began to worry about running out of my stash of condoms before I even arrived at my destination.

One day we came to the edge of a deep canyon. I could see the track continuing, skirting the edge of the canyon wall.

"This is it," Hama said to me. "We leave the yak train here. They will unload and return to the city. Our own porters will come for the loads and take them from here."

"How close are we, then?"

"Just a little ways."

"Why don't we have them take the loads all the way?" I asked, glancing over at my sexy yak driver, who was standing in the shade with his shirt stripped off and draped around his neck. I loved the deep dark color of his skin, and the texture of it, so smooth. I was not yet willing to part with him.

"No," Hama said. "The trail is too narrow ahead, and yaks cannot cross the rope bridges over the river." He sounded impatient with me. "And beyond that, no strangers are ever allowed in the valley. No outsiders at all. For any reason."

"Right." I almost laughed. As far as Hama was concerned, even a Himalayan yak driver was an outsider.

* * *

"*W*hat are you doing?" Hama hissed in my ear. He was evidently quite annoyed with me.

"I'm helping unload," I stammered, unaccustomed to him speaking to me in such a tone.

"I can see that. You know I have asked you repeatedly never to go near the men when they are loading or unloading the animals."

I dropped the strap I had been trying to untie and looked up at him, bewildered. "I know, but I'm not going to get in the way. I know enough about the process now that I could be of help. It's not rocket science."

I thought he would protest that it was my *safety* he was concerned about, but to my surprise he seemed to be on the edge of losing his temper. Hama *never* lost his temper or his control in any way. But he was close to it now. I could see it in the clenched muscles of his face, hear it in the tightness of his voice. "Whatever possessed you to do a thing so demeaning of me?" he demanded.

"What are you *talking* about?" I snapped back at him, feeling my ire rising. But I damped it down at once, sensing that I'd stepped on some macho code of honor, perhaps something peculiar to Hama's isolated mountain community. Instantly, I was in anthropologist mode. Curious. Analytical. Objective.

"Please come with me, Diandra," he said. "I would speak with you in private."

He walked away, and I was clearly meant to follow, but I lingered a moment as my yak driver lover loosened a rope and watched me from the corner of his eye. "You lower yourself for me," he said in a husky growl, half approving, half disgusted. "This makes me want you even more."

Interesting, I thought.

As I walked past him, he reached out and grabbed my arm. He hauled me against him and kissed me, deeply and soulfully. It was the best kiss he ever gave me.

I was sad to see him go. As the yaks and their drivers descended the hill, I stood and watched them all fade away around the bend. Just before he disappeared, my lover turned, lifted his arms to the skies and called out a farewell to me in his own language.

Slowly, I wandered back into camp, where Hama was waiting for me. I had thus far avoided "obeying" the command he had issued to me—to follow him. But I could avoid being alone with him no longer.

"*It*'s not enough that he has you every night!" Hama said, his voice low and trembling with rage. "But you must add the ultimate insult? To help a man of his station with manual labor! What could you be thinking, woman?"

We stood apart from the remaining porters, who were organizing the luggage and supplies the yak drivers had left behind. Hama was transporting a number of large, mysterious bundles. Goods, he had told me, from Europe and the Americas.

Goods! That's all he would say. I was tired of his enigmatic answers to all my questions, questions about our destination, questions about the country we were traveling through, and even the contents of his epic luggage. And I resented the slow pace we had kept because of that luggage. I wanted to *get there.*

He didn't ever come near me anymore, not even in a friendly way. And now he was giving me some shit about packing or unpacking animals. My professional objectivity cracked a little. This guy was from a different culture, but it didn't mean he wasn't an asshole. Or completely nuts.

Like the smart chick who put herself into this situation. Once again I had to wonder what I'd gotten myself into.

I was glad the other men were nearby and within earshot. Something about Hama frightened me a little.

And he was no longer pretending he didn't know what I'd been up to with the yak driver.

"Hama," I said in as kind a tone as I could. "I'm sorry I've upset you, but . . . *you* don't seem to want me, so do you really mind if someone else does?"

His face went through a thousand contortions. He took a deep breath. "Dear God," he murmured. "How can you think that I—" He stopped. "Of course. I should have realized!" He actually laughed. "You are, after all, a woman."

I let that slide.

He spoke thoughtfully now. "Perhaps your behavior has been somewhat understandable, given the situation you do not fully understand . . . I can forgive you many things, Diandra."

"Good to know."

"But if I ever again catch you loading or unloading a pack animal . . ."

"That's the deal breaker, huh?" I tried very hard not to laugh.

So having sex with another man—or men—was bad enough, but loading a pack animal, for*get* it. Let's call the whole thing off.

I decided to approach the question very clinically. Just as I had been taught in school and in my admittedly scant previous field experience. "So," I said. "I tried to help with the loading . . . just what does that signify for you?"

"It signifies that I am not enough of a man to keep you, my new wife, away from the necessity of doing *that* sort of work."

"*That* sort of work?" I said. "And what sort *is* that, exactly?" I was curious how this particular taboo might extend into other areas of life and work. Would I be forbidden to wash the dishes? Reprimanded for doing laundry? One could only hope.

He shook his head. "You truly are from somewhere else, aren't you? It is going to take some getting used to, this arrangement. We must not forget that."

He was a completely different person than the one he'd been just several minutes earlier, when I glimpsed something malevolent in him. He went off, smiling, to give instructions to the two porters who were coming with us. Apparently *they* were not outsiders.

I began to question my ability to stay objective, given the situation. How was I to do a field study on my own marriage? Of course it was impossible. Then again, I didn't believe that anthropologists could ever be completely objective about the cultures they studied.

I had always wanted to travel to a place so remote that I

would have to learn to rethink *everything*. My entire cultural paradigm. I was certainly getting what I asked for, and it seemed that rethinking my cultural concepts of marriage was part of the deal I'd struck to get where I wanted to be.

Chapter 7

After several more days of arduous travel, we reached the pass. I had no idea where we were. Hama would only call it "the pass." It seemed to have no other name, and nobody knew how high it was. But from the effects of the altitude on my body, I knew it was as high as I had ever been.

As we had climbed, the rocks and cliff faces had grown to otherworldly proportions, and I felt very small. Miniaturized.

We came around a giant rock on the trail and suddenly a waterfall appeared, but it was silent and uncanny, completely frozen.

The porters left their loads and gathered in a circle. I watched them perform a strange ritual I had never seen before in my travels. They chanted and danced, as one of them beat on a drum, a hypnotic heartbeat. It was strangely beautiful, these big taciturn men suddenly doing this odd, graceful thing together.

They finished and went to sit in the shelter of the rocks. We waited by the waterfall for what seemed hours, and it began to snow. I was wearing layers of clothing and still felt like I was freezing, but the porters did not seem particularly bothered. Finally there was some inexplicable signal and we were off. We headed straight into the canyon wall near the waterfall, where a passageway suddenly appeared, a narrow cleft in the vertical wall.

The way was steep and narrow and I felt sick and dizzy. Higher and higher we climbed—I felt it in my legs, my lungs, and my throbbing head—but the air was so full of snow we could not see anything beyond ourselves. We passed through an impossibly narrow cleft of rock and then, after what seemed hours, we began to descend. I felt it in my legs, in my breath. Snow lay everywhere and fell thickly through the air. A strange light shone through the snowflakes that whitened the sky. I began to feel very cold.

A man emerged from the swirl of white, riding a dark horse. The hood of his fur-lined cloak fell back, and long curly black hair tumbled down over his wide shoulders. His face was friendly and handsome. He looked at me and grinned.

"Excellent choice, Hama!" he called out in a booming voice, then galloped away to shout something at several horsemen who had followed him.

He returned with a riderless horse and indicated I should have it. Hama lifted me up onto the back of the small black mare, which was clothed in long flowing robes of fur-lined velvet finished with tassels and sewn with hundreds of tiny mirrors and beads. The horse's bridle was also embroidered with colorful patterns and encrusted with beads.

A hooded fur cloak was tossed over my shoulders and instantly I felt warmer. A horse was produced for Hama too, and we were off. Several more porters had joined us. Some of them were following up the rear, bearing the supplies. Some went on to pick up the bundles Hama had cached on the other side of the pass.

We traveled downhill through a tight crevice. The walls of rock were so narrow in places that my legs brushed against them and I had to lift my legs to the horse's withers to avoid getting scraped. Above us I could see nothing but the moving patterns of white. Darkness fell and soon I could hardly see in front of my face.

At length we arrived at a small hut where we were to bed down for the night. We shared a meal cooked in the stone fire pit in the corner of the single small room. Apparently it would be at least another day's ride to the village. Hama kept assuring me that we were almost there, but another day had gone by and we had yet to reach our destination. I was weary of traveling.

But I liked the newcomer to our party, Gazer of the black eyes and the black and curly hair tumbling down over his well-shaped arms and back. He was a delicious hunk of male, a fact that intruded into my thoughts even as I tried to maintain my anthropologist mode. Peering over my journal with pen in hand, I found myself contemplating the man's biological characteristics rather than those of a more culturally relevant nature. Tall, broad across the shoulders, lean through the hips. Perfect. He seemed to like the look of me too; he kept sneaking quick looks from across the room.

Once again I reflected how, in California, I was just a healthy, average-looking young woman—but here I turned men's heads like a golden idol. Then again, lately I *was* looking pretty hot, even by western standards. The days of endless walking had melted away some of my more abundant curves, and my skin was golden brown from traveling in the sun, setting off my green eyes and enhancing the brightness of my hair. Once, catching sight of myself reflected in a mountain pool, I thought for a moment I was someone else.

I felt energized, vigorous, and sensual. My body seemed to be in a state of perpetual heat. I warned myself that I had better start thinking—and acting—like a married woman.

After the meal, the hut had settled into silence. We were crowded, for the space was tiny. I felt men's bodies warm around me. We were all pressed together on a single large pallet on the floor, which was necessary just to keep warm enough. This was the coldest night of our entire journey. I felt certain there would be no threesome tonight. The vibe was ultrarespectful and hands-off, even if the sexual undertone of the situation was palpable. I felt Gazer's attraction and Hama's strange jealousy.

We were just dozing off when a heavy rapping sound woke us all.

Voices called, deep male voices. Gazer got up, lifted the latch on the door and let in a large, serious-looking man who was accompanied by a smaller man with the air of a servant, carrying a pack. They were dressed in furs and dusted white with snow.

Gazer and the large stranger grasped each other in a friendly bear hug as the porters looked on.

"What the hell?" Gazer was laughing. "You said you would not come."

"How could I resist?"

Hama got up from his pallet and was pulled directly into the embrace. The three of them spoke excitedly in a language I could not understand. They were obviously very close and delighted to be together again.

"So. What do you think?" Hama asked the question in English.

The men all turned at once and looked at me.

Hama, Gazer, and the big stranger surrounded me, and Hama held out his hand, helped me up from where I sat on my bedroll. Even after I stood, they seemed to tower over me, as if I were in the center of a ring of giant redwood trees. It struck me what big men they all were, and how unusual that was, to find men of such size in this part of the world—or anywhere, for that matter. I thought of my hot threesome with the two slender young cousins, and couldn't help but wonder what sex might be like with three big guys like these.

I chided myself at once, for losing my discipline as an anthropologist. Or as a wife. To be thinking of men, men, *men*, all the time! All I wanted to do was fuck.

And that was not what I was there for, I reminded myself.

I was there to immerse myself in another culture. To learn the ways of the people I had come to live with, to become one with them, so that I might take the insights I'd gained and bring back a new perspective to my own culture, to share an increased understanding. . .

I was already composing my paper in my head.

What a coup this will be, I thought. To have an intimate encounter with the culture of the Lost Valley of the Himalayas. I would be published for sure. They'd be clamoring to hear about this . . . This experience could make my career.

"Diandra," Hama was saying to me shyly, taking my hand. "Allow me to formally introduce you to these two fine fellows. This is Gazer; you have already become acquainted with him. And this is Rafe."

"You're Hama's brother, aren't you?" I said, suddenly seeing the resemblance. Rafe was even bigger than Hama, but he had the same slender, broad-shouldered strength, the same big brown eyes with the same serious expression. Rafe was not as polished as Hama, however. There was a forceful, blunt directness about him.

"Yes, I am Hama's *elder* brother," he said in a rough but playful voice. He enhanced the world "elder" with some primitive meaning. He reached out and took my hand from Hama, who did not object.

"I am your new husband," Rafe added.

I stared at him in shock. I turned to Hama, who was waiting quietly for my reaction.

I turned to look back at Hama's brother. Well, this was a novel idea!

I felt a bit annoyed, to have it sprung on me like that. But frankly, I didn't care which one of them I was married to, as long as the marriage license gave me passage into the Lost Valley.

True, it was *Hama* I'd been eager to bed for so many weeks. But I had my concerns about Hama, and what it might mean, being tied to him by the bonds of matrimony. The lack of sex after the legal proceedings had been rather off-putting—though now it was beginning to make a lot more sense.

Anyway, this other guy *was* rather interesting looking, I had to admit. Perhaps this would be better anyway. We would be starting fresh. After all, I had never cheated on *Rafe*. At least not knowingly.

"Bait and switch, huh?" I said.

Gazer didn't seem to understand the joke, but Hama and Rafe started laughing. Rafe's smile was a flash of white against beautiful dark skin.

Sure, I thought. This could work. Rafe would be my husband instead of Hama. Why not?

I noticed Gazer looking at me almost sadly. He had a way of shyly stealing glances at me as if he'd never seen a pretty woman before. I felt a wash of heat rush up my thighs.

I turned my attention back to Rafe. His black hair was cropped short, but I supposed long showy curls would get tiresome after awhile.

So this was my husband.

"She'll do, Hama," he said.

The men seemed pleased, and I felt a sense of happy relief among them. Hama was watching me for my reaction.

"Okay, Hama," I said in a low voice, grabbing his arm and pulling him close. "What the hell is going on here? You totally led me to believe I was marrying *you* when I signed those papers."

"You *did* marry me, Diandra," he said flatly.

I shook my head, confused.

"And you married my brother, Rafe."

"I . . ."

"You married us both."

Huh. I stood there, stunned. Then I started giggling like a teenager.

Oh, I thought. *I get it.*

"Polygamy," I said.

"Polyandry, to be precise."

"Ah." I nodded, duly impressed. I had noticed Hama liked to show off his vocabulary. Polyandry—the marriage of a woman to more than one man—is extremely rare, even less common than polygyny, the marriage of a man to more than one woman. But as an anthropologist, I should have been aware of this possibility. I had heard this type of marriage was still practiced in remote areas of the Himalayas.

"In your country," Hama said, "a woman marries one man— *one at a time*, at any rate." He raised a brow. "For us, it is different. According to our ways, one woman marries all the brothers in a family."

I nodded, proud of my composure, finding this utterly fascinating. "Fraternal polyandry," I said. "It's a way of keeping the resources of the family intact." I had learned about these arrangements in school. But I had never seen such a system in practice.

Hama seemed to relax a little, finding me so calm and unruffled by this development.

"You might have told me before," I said.

"No. We do not share this with outsiders. You can imagine the sensationalistic way it could be interpreted by those in the West."

"I'm not cut off from the 'West' just because I married you, Hama," I said. "And what makes you think it's such a secret, or that I would keep it a secret if it were?"

"You are one of us now. You will carefully consider before you make any moves."

"Yeah. I guess." I felt a prick of unease. The main reason I wanted to find this valley and explore it was so I could write about it. So I could share what I had learned with the world—or at least with my colleagues and anyone else who might be interested. My motives were partly altruistic. I loved sharing knowledge with people. But my ego was a rather large factor as well. I was an anthropologist, but I had the soul of a journalist. I wanted to get the scoop. And I wanted to be admired and praised for getting it.

"I know you must have many questions," said Hama, "and I am prepared to answer them. You have wondered why I have withheld my passions from you, even after the marriage was legal. This is the reason. My oldest brother has first rights with you. I would have violated the law—not to mention his honor, and yours as well—had I made love with you before my rightful wedding night, which must be only *after* his."

"I see. Well, I appreciate that. And Hama, I'd like to . . . I want to apologize for my . . . uh . . . indiscretions."

His expression darkened. He took a breath and said quietly, "It was understandable, I suppose. I am sorry you thought you were not wanted by me. Believe me, you were. You are. At any rate, you and I will be truly committed only once we have had *our* ceremony, and our wedding night. After that takes place, I will expect you to be a faithful wife."

He said this humorlessly, solemnly.

"So when does this . . . *ceremony* take place?"

"Your first night will be with Rafe, because he is the oldest. It is for him to decide when to ask for you. But I do not think he will wait long. Then, as the second son, it will be my turn and we will have our nuptial rites. And then, it will be Gazer's turn, and—"

"Gazer!"

"Of course. He is our younger brother."

Chapter 8

ð

We rode down through the clouds, crossing an enormous, ethereal snow bridge over a raging, churning river, finally breaking into sunlight. We lost elevation quickly and passed through several different ecosystems, from the snow-covered pass through the empty barren rocks of the high mountains, descending through evergreen forests and into the woodland hills.

I had a strange feeling we were not where we should have been, as if transported to another part of the world, or even to some other world entirely. Nothing made sense. The set of the stars at night, the direction of the sunrise in the morning; the flora, the fauna. I puzzled over it. Trees too large to be growing at that altitude. Bright splashes of strange flowers in the shadows of the glades. Glimpses of animals and birds that should have been somewhere else, in another place and time.

Giddy with excitement, I was wondering what sort of photographs and samples I might bring back with me when my time here was done.

Through a parting in the mountains the valley appeared below us, neat groves and dazzling green fields, a psychedelic vision of color after days in the stark highlands, jewel tones of emerald and garnet, and the river gleaming sapphire.

On a hill above the valley was the charming building-block village nestled below the Dzong. Most Himalayan valleys with populations of any size were graced with these stone or brick structures housing the religious and civic affairs of the local people. I had noticed the medieval European influence in the architecture as we drew closer to the Lost Valley, but here, the combination of Tibetan, Indian, and Gothic elements was even more striking and unusual. In fact, the Dzong was a Romanesque stone castle with occasional high Gothic flourishes, pointed arches, and flying buttresses. But it also boasted a beautiful turquoise onion dome and minarets. I wondered if it would be decorated with erotic stone carvings like the ones I'd seen before.

Dropping down farther in elevation, we had to cross the great river again. Here it was no longer thrashing and crashing through the canyons, but wide and deep. A ferryman took us and our horses across on a barge. As we crossed, I was overcome by an odd feeling, a strange sensation of dislocation, as though I were truly entering an otherworld. Probably just the effects of getting some oxygen into the brain again, I thought.

I recited to myself, over and over, Hama's promise that I could always leave at any time. Not that I was vaguely inclined to turn around—quite the contrary. But I had a strange foreboding that somehow I was venturing into a place that might not be so easily escaped.

As we approached the village, people turned out to greet us. The narrow streets were lined with colorfully dressed villagers, all grinning faces and waving hands.

The inhabitants of the valley were of that same stunningly beautiful race I had noted as we drew closer to the pass.

Rafe, who was far more loquacious than his brother Hama, told me that hundreds of years ago a handsome, adventurous Russian lord with a touch of Gypsy blood had come to the valley, bringing with him a wife of French and English heritage, as well as his lovely Chinese-Indian mistress. Their offspring had thrived and merged into the local population, which was itself a mixture, producing a strange and unusually beautiful people, with lovely, warm coloring, graceful bodies, and expressive eyes.

"It is more than genetics, though. There's just something about the air here." He grinned. "It's good for breeding. Big, beautiful specimens. Sheep, goats! Big, plump squash."

He winked at me, and I mentally unpacked my birth control pills.

"Seriously. The animals, the crops—this place is an oasis. You will see. Spend a month here, and you will find you have never felt more alive! Stay a year, and you will never go back."

The villagers were chanting as we rode our horses slowly up the cobbled road through an arched gateway into the walled town. The sound, like Sanskrit prayer, had a mesmerizing effect. Banners streamed from the ramparts; drumming and flute music filled the air. I felt like a princess arriving with my prince.

My princes. Three of them!

Like a castle keep, the Dzong dominated the village at its feet, a collection of tiny houses butted together in a small, whitewashed village. Hama informed me that his estate, one of the largest farms in the area, lay on the other side of the village.

The beauty of the place was enhanced by the surrounding meadows, lush cultivated fields, orchards, terraced highlands, and the incredibly high and immense mountain peaks, just visible through halos of cloud. The sunlight was shining gold on the highest crests when we finally stopped in the village square and dismounted our horses. I had never seen anything so dramatic and literally breathtaking.

A young woman came forward and greeted Hama warmly. She then embraced Rafe and Gazer. At last she turned—almost reluctantly, it seemed—and regarded me. She performed a stiff, perfunctory greeting, which I awkwardly returned.

She was slender, a little older than me, with gaily colored clothes, head scarf, and a pretty face, but a sour expression.

"Diandra," Hama said to me, "I present to you Gaja, your new sister-in-law."

My new sister-in-law?

Uh-oh, I thought. I've got a sister-in-law. Hama had never mentioned her. Then again, he had never mentioned his brothers either, let alone the fact that I would be marrying any of them. Or rather, *all* of them.

Gaja did not seem pleased to be meeting me. Given the warm

reception I'd received from all the men, I hadn't anticipated this.

But before I had a moment to ponder this new development, someone else stepped up and we were being introduced. And then someone else, and someone else. I saw no more of Gaja for the time being.

That night there would be feasting and celebration for the safe return of Hama to the folds of his community. The wedding ceremony was to take place the next day.

Rafe, I was told, had "asked" for me.

Late in the evening, after much eating and drinking and music, a healthy contingent of the village population formed an impromptu parade to accompany the Rulan brothers and their new bride home.

It was about a half-mile walk—or in my case, a ride on a horse—from the gate of the walled village to the twin stone pillars that marked the turn into the Rulan brothers' estate. They told me that had it been daylight, I would see the house on the slope rising above the town. But now all I could see around me were the cheerful faces of the villagers shining by the light of the torches they carried, and so many stars above me that I did not recognize the sky.

We made our way slowly up the hill and at last the entire procession passed beneath a stone archway and entered a stone-paved courtyard.

The men tended to the horses and supervised the porters unpacking the loads, except for Hama, who removed his attention from his "goods" somewhat reluctantly, took me by the hand and said, "Allow me to show you around your new home."

I sensed he felt somewhat guilty for keeping from me the true nature of our marriage, and I was secretly glad it was no longer all on me to be the contemptible one. I might have been acting like a slut, thinking I was supposed to be a faithful wife to him and yet fucking other guys, but it turned out *he* was pimping. For his brothers.

It's not so much pandering as it is matchmaking. I heard Hama's voice in my head, justifying the situation in his bureaucratic, calmly inflected English.

"I'll give you the short tour of the place, Diandra," was what he was actually saying. "Tomorrow you can peruse the grounds at your leisure. Here we have the stables, as you can see, and down the pathway there is the barn. But you can examine all of this later. I am sure you are tired."

I felt his thumb gently pressing and stroking the palm of my hand, a sensual reminder. *Patience.* There was a keen promise in his expression.

Perhaps he really intended to fuck me after all. I felt an undeniable sexual thrill, a stirring of eagerness for him, though not as strong as it had once been.

From the stables we walked across the courtyard to the main house, entering a large open room with a huge stone fireplace. The room was comfortably set with classic, well-made western furniture, chairs, couches, and small tables, as well as a divan of Indian origin and large flat cushions for sitting on the floor.

"The common room," Hama said. "We spend most of our evenings in here."

It was a pleasing room, almost circular in shape and dome-like, with exposed timbers meeting at the top of the lofty ceiling, giving the space a peaceful and communal feeling, like a large tepee. The tepee effect was enhanced by the lack of windows, and I found it odd the space did not feel dark and oppressive, but rather comforting and protective, womblike.

The architecture, in keeping with the medieval spirit of the place, was rustic, but the stone floor was spread with luxurious rugs, and the low couches were draped with wonderfully rich and lushly decorated textiles. Graceful lamps hung from the beams and cast a glimmering golden light that was picked up in myriad tiny mirrors, beads, and crystals sewn on the fabrics draping the surfaces of the room.

My eye caught on a stunning curved sword hanging on the wall above the mantel.

"That belonged to my great-grandfather," Hama said, noticing my interest.

"What a beautiful thing," I said.

"Beautiful and deadly. My father once told me that his grand-father killed seven men with that blade."

I wanted to hear more. In what context had his grandfather killed seven men? Self-defense from marauding bandits? A jealous rage? But there would be plenty of time for family lore. Hama was already ushering me into the kitchens, a series of smaller rooms off the common area. One room contained stores of grain, honey, and dried provisions, another was for milk and cheese. And there was a large storage closet for vegetables and fruit. Hama told me that in his society most of the cooking was done by the women of the household in the common room, in the fireplace, which was hung with a big copper kettle and had several roomy niches, like a pizza oven. There was yet another small room for washing dishes that opened to the courtyard outside.

"We're lucky enough to have a well in the courtyard," he said. "You won't have to go far to fetch water."

Just beyond the well, he told me, was the bathhouse, in its own small building, with tile walls and floors and a fireplace for heating water.

"I'll take you there last," he murmured, "as I am sure you will be wanting a bath."

"God, that does sound heavenly," I agreed.

"In fact, I should warn you, the bath you will receive tonight will be like none other you will ever experience."

"Really?" I said, intrigued and a little alarmed. "How so?"

"Will you wait and see?"

I shrugged. "Sure. Of course."

"Are you adventurous, Diandra?"

"Well, *obviously*," I replied with a laugh, wondering what the hell he was getting at. "Come on, this isn't fair."

"The bath is part of the marriage rite. It's a sort of purification ritual, if you will. And a sort of test."

"A test!"

"Don't worry," he said, and his voice hardened a little. "You will pass."

Chapter 9

❧

I was ushered into the bathhouse, where water had been prepared for me in a huge copper tub and several young women dressed in nothing but short muslin shifts were waiting to attend me. The water was hot; I could see the steam rising in a curling mist. I was a little afraid of what might happen but meekly submitted to the ritual. If it was part of the marriage rite, I would go ahead and participate. What better way to experience another culture than to be part of its customs?

I was in too deep before I realized the implications of this ritual. Though I had suspected something interesting was up, given Hama's odd warning, the dangers of the soft, caressing hands of the young women who attended me did not at first alert me. Slowly, they undressed me, helped me into the tub, and began to bathe me. Some of them shed what little clothes they wore as well. It seemed sensible at the time. Why get their dresses wet?

But after a while I knew something wasn't quite . . . right.

It wasn't quite right, the way they leaned their bodies into mine as their hands massaged me. The way they smiled at one another, as if they were sharing a joke. The way they let the tips of their breasts brush over my arms.

From the beginning of my time in the Lost Valley, no matter how academic I attempted to be, no matter what kind of objective stance I struck, I felt somehow that merely by entering this secret and almost inaccessible place I had also entered some kind of altered state, like a dream, a drug induced vision, and I had only to wait it out. I would come back to myself eventually, somehow.

That first night I was drunk on fatigue, culture shock, and something akin to jet lag. Yak lag. I lay there passively while the women poured warm water over me and soaped me up and rubbed me, swirls of sensation all over my body. They rinsed me and splashed the clear water on my skin. I hardly noticed it when they began to kiss me. There must have been seven of them, seven young women touching me all over with their fingers and their lips and the softness of their breasts, beautiful young women, some of them naked, some of them in wet muslin dresses that clung to their strong dark bodies.

How had I come to find myself lying in a tub, naked, with seven women massaging my body, tonguing me and sucking on me, on my lips and neck, my nipples?

One of the girls slipped into the tub with me. Her thin shift ballooned up around her and she shrugged herself out of it and reared up, naked, and I was enthralled with the sight of the water dripping from her small, full breasts. With her smoldering eyes locked on mine, she lifted my hips out of the water with her hands firm beneath me, pushed my legs apart with her fingers and bent down over me. I felt her tongue on me, parting the lips of my sex, then dipping inside me, her teeth like pearls gently pressing against my clit, while the other women leaned over the rim of the tub, feeding on my breasts and kissing my neck and the soft skin of my thighs.

I wanted to protest but I was squirming in ecstasy, bucking against her mouth. All at once I let out an involuntary cry; I shuddered and let go, throbbing against her soft lips.

They brought me to orgasm again and again, until I could take no more and I begged them to stop. For a while I just lay there, stunned. I had never been with a woman before. Let alone seven of them at once.

As they helped me out of the tub, they smiled and looked at each other triumphantly, as if they had accomplished an important task. They chatted together in their native dialect, which I was already beginning to pick up, a few words and phrases, but I didn't need to understand the language to get what had happened. They had been "testing" my sexual response.

It seemed I passed the test.

So that's what Hama had been talking about. A sexual responsiveness assessment. No wonder he hadn't doubted me.

I could hardly stand on my own my legs, they were so rubbery. The women dried me, draped me with blankets, and led me from the bath into a room with a bed piled high with furs. They laid me down and tucked the blankets around me. They each kissed me on the cheek, one by one, and went away. The room was dark. I closed my eyes, wondered briefly where my husbands were, and fell asleep for many hours.

* * *

I woke the next morning feeling refreshed. As soon as I began to stir, a woman appeared and greeted me in decent if heavily accented English. She was not one of the girls who had bathed me and pleasured me the night before. I had met her at the feast in the village but couldn't remember her name. She was about my age, with curly dark hair and large, heavy-looking breasts. She wore a long embroidered gown and lots of heavy, colorful jewelry. Her black-fringed eyes were the color of chocolate and her lips were full and red. She looked at me appraisingly, taking in, I was sure, the bruised and bitten flesh of my neck and shoulders, and the marks on my breasts, which were exposed when I sat up and the blankets slipped down.

"I trust you slept well," she said.

I nodded. "Very well, thank you."

"My name is Shani," she said. "I am a friend of the family. Hama asked me if I would check in on you." She spoke in a deep, soft voice with a strong local accent and had an air of purpose and authority, which seemed somewhat out of alignment with her pretty, soft appearance.

I drew the blankets up over my breasts, though I knew she had already seen me in my disheveled, naked state. I was a little paranoid, wondering if she might suddenly hop into my bed, spread my legs apart, and go down on me with gusto. If there was going to be a repeat performance of last night with *this* lush lady, would I object? I wasn't sure. I could hardly think straight anymore.

But she had other things on her mind. She opened a trunk and pulled out some clothing, indicating that I should get dressed. I relaxed a little.

"You can choose from these dresses," she said.

"Where are my things?" I asked. Then I saw that my pack had been placed in the corner of the room.

"Your belongings are all there, but you will need something suitable for the wedding ceremonies. Gaja and I have collected some clothing for you. One of these dresses will do for now. Later you will change into your proper wedding attire."

Still filled with languid sensuality, I let Shani dress me. Her hands were warm and strong and expert with all the ties and draperies of the lovely costume with which she was adorning me. It was like an ornately decorated sari made of flowing, colorful silks, only fitted to the body with a corset that laced up the front. Again I had the feeling that I'd stepped into some medieval crusader's fantasy.

"Very nice," she said, looking me up and down when I was dressed. She was pleased with me so far, but I could see that she was not yet finished.

She put my hair up in an elaborate pile of braids and twists, wreathed my neck with ropes of beads, and slid bangles onto my wrists.

"Now," she said, "I will be guiding you through your day. If you have any questions about what is going on, please ask me."

We were about to go out the door when another woman appeared and blocked our way. It was Gaja, my new sister-in-law; slender, a little older than us, with a pretty face but a sour expression. She looked at me and said in perfect high-brow British English, "So Sleeping Beauty is finally awake, is she?" I could not mistake the hostility in her tone.

"Diandra," Shani said to me. "You have met your new sister, Gaja?"

"Yes. I've already had the pleasure," I said.

"So," said Gaja. "I am ready to do my duty." She looked me up and down in my fancy clothing. "Oh," she said to Shani, "I see you have already dressed her. But that's *my* job, you know, as the sister of the bridegroom." She feigned a look of exaggerated indignation.

"I thought you might appreciate my help," Shani replied mildly. "And remember, I have been through all this myself, when my brothers married Rena."

"Just as well you stepped in, I suppose," said Gaja. "I've never been good at this sort of thing anyway." She looked at me and said dryly, "Shani always knows what to do for every occasion."

They stopped, alerted by something in my expression.

"What?" they said together.

"Nothing. Forgive me," I said. "It's just . . . your English. It's so . . . fluid and so . . . easy. So perfect."

"Of course," Gaja said with a shrug. "We are not backward, as you might have expected. Most of us speak several languages."

"I know Hama studied in New York," I said. "Is that a common practice for the people here, to send their children to universities abroad?"

"For people of a certain class, yes," Gaja said. "My brothers and I have studied at universities in the United States and Europe. So you see we have the benefit of your western education as well as that of our own."

"I hope to acquire the best of both myself," I said defensively. "Which is why I have come here."

"Ah, so *that's* why you came, then," Gaja said sarcastically. "To study. You did not abandon your old life for *love*."

I hesitated before answering. "No," I said truthfully. "I'm an anthropologist. I wanted to experience the ways of the people here. Hama convinced me this was the only way I could do it."

"*Hama* convinced *you*?" She sounded skeptical. "And Hama understands your motivations?"

"Yes."

"And you made your feelings clear to him?"

"Yes, I believe I did." Her interrogation irked me. "But why don't you ask *him* about it?"

"I did. He told me what you just told me. I wondered if you thought you were deceiving anybody."

"It was never my intention to deceive anyone," I said. "We both went into this arrangement with our eyes wide open. And I have accepted the terms of marriage. All of them."

Gaja smiled, and I swear she looked downright evil. "Good," she said. "Because you will shortly be asked to live up to those terms."

Chapter 10

꿈

It was an exhausting day. I had met dozens of people, changed clothes several times, and let myself be escorted through numerous rites, rituals, and ceremonies, which everyone seemed to understand but me. They were all quite nice about it, though— all except for my new sister-in-law, who kept up a simmer of hostility toward me.

Hama and his sister and brothers were orphans; they had lost their parents—their mother and their two "fathers"—in a blizzard years earlier. But there were plenty of aunts and uncles, cousins and friends, all flocking around, intensely interested in me. The women dressed me and undressed me, adorned me with scarves and ropes of necklaces, and rearranged my hair; they laughed uproariously at comments I did not understand. They fed me delicacies and made startled hissing noises whenever I was about to make a misstep. I felt like a confused dog with a half-dozen well-meaning trainers all snapping their fingers at me, making sure I obeyed all their commands.

When darkness fell, I was led in a colorful procession to the Dzong, where I was taken to a raised stage that was dominated by a large, low mattress and festooned with colorful draperies. Behind the mattress, dozens of torches stood blazing. A thin muslin curtain separated the stage from the curved rows of seating where spectators were already gathering. I wondered what sort of performance we were about to see.

I stood just offstage while Shani and Gaja and several other women put the finishing touches on their proud creation, which was me. They had done so many different things to my face, my dress, and my hair that I did not recognize myself when I saw my reflection in the mirror. And what I saw in the mirror looked rather odd to me—overdone, heavily padded, too richly made-up and gilded. But apparently by their standards I looked absolutely gorgeous. Even Gaja grudgingly admitted this was so.

Among the women there had been a lot of giggling and joking—lewd, sexual joking, playful pinching and winking, as well as a certain amount of half-envious, half-pitying glances directed my way.

Standing by the stage as the audience filled the benches beyond the curtain, it suddenly hit me.

My wedding night was to be a spectator sport.

"No *way*," I said out loud when the light bulb went on. I had read about such nuptial traditions, but it hadn't occurred to me that I might be facing such a rite myself. Polygamy was one thing, I thought—ritual exhibitionism quite another.

"Now just wait a minute, here," I said to Shani and Gaja. "I am *not* going to—you can't expect me to—"

Gaja was looking at me with a malicious half smile. "Oh yes. You and my eldest brother must consummate your wedding union right here, tonight, for all to witness."

"No chance."

"It is required. It is our way of ensuring a marriage is sanctified. And *legal*."

"Fuck legal and sanctified."

Her stony expression brooked no objection. I suddenly remembered my solemn pledge to Hama—that if I agreed to come here, I agreed to abide by the customs of the land. All the customs. Particularly the marital customs. Or—I could leave. Simple as that.

I could leave.

I was certainly not going to leave. Not yet, not after coming so far. I was just beginning to scratch the surface of this fascinating culture. Fascinating in ways I had not even imagined.

"But I can't do it!" I whispered. "Not in . . . not in *public*."

"Really? Are your sensibilities that fragile?" Gaja looked at me knowingly, and I wondered if she knew something about what I had been up to, sexually speaking, for the past few weeks. She might have known, if Hama had told her anything, or if the yak drivers had talked to the porters, or if . . .

"It is not so terrible, Diandra," Shani said soothingly, running her hands over my arms, petting me. "You will do it behind the gauze curtain, with the light of the torches shining behind you. Everyone can hear you—you are supposed to be very *loud* about it, you know. But the people watching see only your shadows."

Like Indonesian shadow puppets, I thought.

I found myself wishing that Hama was to be my partner that evening. At least he was familiar to me. I knew very little of Rafe, except that he was rather big and brutish, and I was terrified at the idea of having to perform with him behind a thin curtain for the entire village to witness.

But I had no choice in the matter. My partner in this outrageous dance was to be Rafe. I caught sight of him on the other side of the stage, flanked by his brothers, dressed in a colorful jacket and leather trousers, looking as nervous as I was feeling.

As it happened, I needn't have worried so much. The whole ritual was carried out with such playful reverence that it was impossible not to be overcome by the pageantry and sheer sensuality of the experience, so that by the time he actually penetrated me, it seemed almost natural and certain.

The fact that I was given a mug full of some extremely potent liquor hadn't hurt either. The effects of the intoxicant, combined with the music, the chanting of the crowd, and the sensual power of Rafe's body, ensured that when the time came for me to do what I had to do, I was completely uninhibited and ready for him. And after all, as a woman, *my* part of the show was easy.

A bell had chimed and we were pushed out onto the stage together like prizefighters entering a ring. I heard the sound of cheering like a faraway waterfall as Rafe pulled me down on the mattress and began to kiss me and hug me against him. He was all-powerful, a massive male animal with no thought but to ravish this female to whom he was now legally and socially bound. It was almost violent, our coupling, and very quick. The crowd would not have seen more than a quick shedding of clothes—his large hands pulling on the shoulders of my ceremonial dress, nearly ripping the strong, embroidered fabric—and the silhouette of an enormous, thick cock, briefly exposed. We came together with me on my back and Rafe above me, straddling me, and for half a minute or so we were one grunting, writhing mass, a pulsing union—and then a collapsed heap.

For a moment he throbbed inside me, and then I felt the sticky liquid trickling down my thigh. He pulled out of me and lay there panting and unapologetic. He was like my sexy yak driver in his single-minded pursuit of his own satisfaction . . . only he was even more massive and powerful.

I sat up and gathered my clothing around me as the crowd cheered. I didn't think it was necessarily a good thing for my new husband to be hearing applause for that sort of performance, but they didn't seem to be rating his sexual prowess in the usual way. They just seemed happy it had been accomplished.

"It's good luck," Shani told me later. "The faster and fiercer it happens, they say, the better for the crops." She grinned at me mischievously. "Looks like we're going to have a very good year."

It was all very inelegant and not at all what you'd call *satisfying*. As in sexually satisfying. Still, I found a terrifying pleasure in remembering the few but violent and deeply penetrating thrusts my number one husband had subjected me to on our first wedding night. Subsequent marital encounters with him proved similar in nature.

* * *

$\mathscr{I}$t turned out the customs of the valley didn't seem to be terribly novel or unusual when put up against the varieties of behavior in human culture. Given all the hype about the Lost Valley and Hama's reticence to give me any specifics before our arrival, I couldn't help but feel a little disappointed when all was said and done. Even the bundles of mysterious "goods" Hama had brought into the valley turned out to be nothing more than everyday supplies that any insulated people might import from abroad. But I kept up my optimism. Okay, so maybe I was no Margaret Mead. But in the region of the Great Himalayas were some of the last places on earth that were still isolated and for all intents and purposes inaccessible. I felt honored and lucky just to be there.

Chapter 11

≈

At night I was subjected to an endless treat of male attentions. By day I was employed in various jobs to help support the community. I especially enjoyed the gardens and the animals, and was often given work in the stables, tending to the shaggy mountain ponies used for transportation and farming. I was wary, careful lest I violate any important social codes, but I soon learned it was perfectly acceptable for the lady of the house to feed or curry the horses, as long as I did not stoop to loading pack animals.

Though I had never intended my stay to be permanent, as the weeks passed, I began to feel more and more at home. When I started out on my journey, I had thought I would probably be gone a couple of months. Now I began to think I might stay even longer. I was enjoying my life immensely.

Having been raised by an elderly aunt who had long since passed, I had no close family in the United States, and my few

good friends were scattered around the globe. There was nothing pulling me from my Shangri-la; indeed there was everything
to keep me there. It was the most beautiful place, scenically, I
had ever experienced in all my travels, a fertile river bottom surrounded on all sides by the precipitous snow-covered mountains
rising up thousands of feet from the valley, the peaks sharp and
spectacular, the views always changing with the time of day and
the weather.

The people were happy and friendly, always singing, even
while they worked. They accepted me with surprising openness
and simple friendship. I had satisfying employment that kept me
challenged and occupied, and still enough leisure to devote time
to my field study, which I thought of as my real work. I was always thinking about how best to filter my intimate experience of
the Lost Valley through the scientific lens of an anthropologist's
eye. My notes, I was sure, would someday be transformed into
an interesting and prestigious project attracting the attention of
the elite community I wished to impress with my startling and
original portrayal of a heretofore unknown people.

But as time went on I found myself more content for that anticipated success to be realized sometime far away in the future.
No hurries.

I was immersed in a strange and unfamiliar culture, just as
I'd always wanted to be. I was healthy and fit, in the best physical
shape I had ever been in my life. To top it off, I had the kind of sex
life most women could only experience in their fantasies.

The beauty of multiple husbands, I found, was that I didn't
have to worry about one husband having, or being, "it all."

Though he was a boorish and self-centered lover, I could

appreciate the sheer animal brutality of Rafe's powerful thrusting when he fucked me with his enormous cock. And when I say enormous, I mean, like, *jumbo*.

Hama turned out to be very cerebral about sex, very focused on *my* pleasure, and he fixated on my orgasm almost to the point of annoyance. I say *almost*. It's very difficult to be annoyed with somebody who is determined to have you come. Again. And again. With Hama, I knew I would always achieve my release.

That first time behind the curtain, Hama undressed me slowly, sensually, peeling off my jewel-studded jacket, then his own, untying the laces of my blouse, and then those on his own colorful, billowing shirt. Like Rafe, he had a strong, powerful body, but Hama was more elegant than his older brother, and more controlled. He kissed me almost chastely as he drew the fabric over my bare shoulders and exposed my breasts.

I had once thought I would be completely ecstatic when I made love with this man, but when it finally happened, I almost didn't care anymore. And I certainly wasn't pleased about the setting in which it was taking place. Exhibitionism had never been my thing. But to my great surprise, I discovered that the presence of the watching crowd actually fueled my lust.

I grabbed Hama's head in my hands and made him kiss me deeply. His hair felt thick between my fingers. When I felt his tongue wrestle mine, my legs buckled beneath me and he caught me easily and gently let me down on the mattress.

When he had me half naked on my back, his mouth sucking on the tender skin of my neck, my legs parted for him beneath my skirts. He lay on top of me, sucking my breasts. Pulling at each nipple in turn, watching my response.

He reached beneath my skirts and I felt his finger warmly poking about near my clit. I surged against him.

"You're so wet," he murmured.

He was right, which surprised me. I was really getting into it. The first time, with Rafe, I hardly had time to be aroused, but during this, my second wedding ceremony in as many days, my body was actually getting into the spirit of the occasion. Hama fingered me until I was whimpering, ready to explode. Then pulled his hand out and loosened the ties of my skirt.

"I thought it was supposed to go a lot faster," I teased him in a low voice, breathing hard.

"Are you getting impatient, my love?" His fingers on the ties stumbled with the increased urgency of his movements.

I was naked now and he was nearly so. He hurriedly pulled off his tight leather breeches to expose himself.

The head of his penis was wet and glistening, and I thought with disappointment that he had already come. But the liquid was clear. He saw me looking at it and reached down, squeezed the tip of his penis, fingered a drop of the stuff and brought it up to smear on my lips.

It tasted sweet and salty and musky, and my own response was liquid.

He moved down over my body and thrust his silky head between my thighs. His tongue was like a warm wet sponge, stroking and teasing and penetrating. Once again he brought me close to the edge and then pulled away.

He held himself over me, naked, erect, his strong muscular arms like columns supporting his body, his thighs like the bodies of huge snakes, constrictors closing around the captive prey. I wanted to suck that big penis, taste that sweet clear nectar again, but he was suddenly fucking me. It seemed to happen so fast, without warning, strangely—he was in me and I let out a gasp and the whole audience responded with cheers. He filled me, wholly and generously. Then he pulled it out of me and thrust it in again. And again. In relentless rhythm.

I don't know how long it lasted. I know it was not that long, but it was long enough.

He waited until I was up and over the edge, my body throbbing and singing with orgasms, and then he spilled himself a river. My thighs were drenched afterward.

God, he was good. Almost worth the wait.

But Gazer was probably my favorite lover of all the brothers; he was sort of a combination of the other two, gentle and considerate and yet headstrong with passion, always erect and ready at a moment's notice. Sometimes overly hasty in his enthusiasm, he would then display a charming contrition and make it up to me with his magical mouth.

Gazer was young and slightly crazy, not terribly deep, but fiercely loyal to those he cared about, and he cared about everybody. He fell in love with me after a few days and some fantastic sex. He made me little animals out of clay and sang to me at night with his guitar, making up songs about the two of us soaring off somewhere together on a flying carpet, or walking on the beach in Tahiti, just to hold hands. He was cute and funny, and when he smiled, he smiled wide, his whole face crinkling.

With Gazer, I sometimes broke the rule about taking turns with my husbands. Often in the darkness we would come together when everyone else was asleep, even if it happened to be

Rafe's night or Hama's night. It was easy enough to get away with it, given the living arrangement. Most of the rooms in the main house were built around the central hub the entire family shared, where we cooked and ate and gathered socially. Off this large common room were various add-on apartments. Gaja had her own apartment, as did each of the brothers. Rafe's suite was the most spacious, with a patio opening into the garden. The room I was given was very nice as well. Gazer's space was little more than a closet, but it was big enough for a bed, and for the two of us that was all that mattered.

It wasn't difficult to slip from the apartment of one brother to another without anyone the wiser. On the other hand, given the intimacy of our situation, nobody was ever really fooled.

I wasn't in love with any of my husbands, but I *was* quite fond of them all. And as we grew closer as a family, our appreciation for each other increased. If Gaja could have been happy with the situation, everything would have been perfect. As it was, she seemed to accept the arrangement, kept to herself for the most part, and left me alone.

I sometimes thought, rather wistfully, that it was just too bad I had a deep-seated wish for one deeply felt romantic love. I had found a situation that was ideal in so many ways, and yet so lacking in that particular thing.

Maybe I would never love like that. Maybe that kind of love didn't even exist, I thought, at least not for me. But on some level I cherished the ideal of true love. The old-fashioned kind. A one man, one woman, forever kind of love.

But I pushed such thoughts aside. After all, I had it made. I had three good men at my beck and call, great sex and plenty of it—and yet it was easy for me to stay detached enough that I didn't have to worry about getting unduly emotionally involved with any of them.

Life was good.

Some days I even entertained the idea of staying there in the valley forever, living the good life with my three sexy husbands.

The situation was ideal, I told myself. With no complications.

And then Yeshi returned.

He rode headlong into my life on a white stallion, with the wind whipping up his cape and blowing through his long dark hair. I will never forget the day I met him. Or the day I learned of him. They were one and the same.

Yeshi is coming.

Yeshi is coming!

"Who is Yeshi?" I asked innocently.

Shani looked startled. "You mean nobody told you about Yeshi?"

It was as if she had said the pope was popping by for a visit and I didn't know who the pope was.

"Well, I mean, I've heard his name mentioned, I think," I said. "I've heard the guys talk about him. At least I believe it was him. I thought he was just some friend who was away, studying abroad or something."

"Well, he *has* been away, studying abroad," Shani said. "But he's not just 'some friend' of your husbands. He's their youngest brother."

Youngest . . . brother?

"My God," I breathed. "*Another* one?"

I didn't know if I could handle another husband. Between the three I already had, I was very fulfilled—and tired.

I was a faithful and happily married woman. I had no need of any other man. Or woman, for that matter—and none of the young women I had known so intimately on the day of my arrival tried to initiate another such session.

"Please tell me he's the last," I said.

She laughed. "Yes. There are four of them. That's all."

"That's *all*. I can't believe there's another one. And I can't believe that nobody told me about him before."

Shani looked down. "I suppose nobody wanted to be the one to tell you about Yeshi because . . . well, Yeshi's complicated."

"How so?"

Her voice went faint and faraway. "He is not so likely to be happy about this marriage as the others, you see."

"Why is that?"

"Well . . ." She hesitated, obviously unsure of how much to tell me. "Yeshi has a woman of his own. He is very much in love with her. He had hoped to bring *her* into the family as wife for all the brothers."

"Then . . . why didn't he?"

"Perhaps he felt it wasn't time. He wanted to complete his education. When he returned . . . He had hoped when he returned . . ."

Great, I thought. Some grand love affair had been torn asunder, and it was all because of *me*.

"Who is she?" I asked, thinking of all the village women I knew. Nobody had ever mentioned anything about any of this.

"It is not my place to say, Diandra," Shani said quietly.

"Why not?"

"I just can't."

Apparently she didn't know the answer, or didn't want to tell me if she did.

"So it's a secret?" I said, a bit caustically.

"Well, you have to understand our ways. Someone like Yeshi would have to be very discreet about his feelings for a woman, or risk his chance with her for the future. If he truly cared about her, he would make certain that very few people would even know it. You see, nobody minds if a young man has an affair or two, but it isn't really . . . *proper* for the youngest son to bring a *bride* into the family, because that is the elder brother's prerogative, you know. But it often happens; a younger brother will show a preference, and in so doing, will inadvertently choose the bride. That's all right as long it is done properly, and the eldest approves her, and weds her first . . ."

The way Hama had done with me.

"So . . . does Yeshi even *know* about me?" I asked. I was beginning to feel more than a little alarmed by what she was telling me. Apparently I was married to a man who wanted to be married to somebody else!

"Oh yes, he knows all about you. Rafe sent word on the day of your marriage rites."

"But I thought the brothers had to *agree* on a wife."

"No. They don't *have* to agree. Only Rafe, as the oldest, must approve. It was his decision alone. When Rafe agreed to take you as wife, his choice was final. Yeshi must accept you as *his* wife, too."

Yeshi must accept you . . .

The words struck an ominous note, and I had the feeling it might not be as easy as all that. Something in her voice warned me it would not be so simple.

"Come," she said. "He will be here soon."

Chapter 12

✴

The people always knew when someone was descending the pass en route to the village, and by the time Yeshi emerged from the cloud road, the gates were open and the way was crowded with foot traffic, bicycles, and donkeys—the entire village had turned out to greet him.

I heard the roar of welcome before I saw him. I was protected by a small entourage, as the women in the village had decreed I was to be presented to my husband formally. I was pretty sure I hadn't been presented formally to any of my other husbands, so I didn't know why they thought I should be with Yeshi. But Tara, the little maid who tended to the menial duties of our household, had thrown a silk veil over my hair and draped a shawl around me. I laughed and asked her what she was doing.

"Until your wedding night, your charms are to be concealed from him," she explained in dialect, which Shani translated, though I was picking up the language and understood what the girl had said.

Hama, who was strolling through the room, reached out and passed his hands over my silk-draped hips. "Try and hide it away if you like," he grinned. "You can't conceal the beauty of these curves."

I shivered, wondering what Yeshi would think of me. And I wondered what *I* would think of Yeshi.

$\mathcal{V}$isitors to the valley were rare and always caused a stir, but usually we had more notice when a newcomer was traveling down from the pass. Yeshi was too fast for the usual announcement of arrival, and so we were only hastily prepared. I know I certainly had questions left unanswered about this latest husband they had suddenly sprung on me.

Tara had bundled me up so well I felt about as shapely as a sack of grain, and when my fourth husband appeared, suddenly and powerfully present, I wished I too were mounted on a horse so that I could meet him eye-to-eye.

Looking up at him, I took in the magnificently caparisoned horse, the silver-white color of its coat and the striking dress of the rider, dressed in black from head to toe, his dark cape whipping behind him. His skin tone was rich, a true bronze, and when he greeted the crowd, he flashed a grin that was blazing white. His topaz eyes, shining fiercely, trained down on me with a laser focus.

What I saw in those fierce, tumultuous eyes the first moment we looked at one another pierced me and left me shaken. I felt his mockery and anger, even hatred, yes—but also desperation and sadness. He must have seen a jumbled mixture of emotions in my expression too.

The half-wild horse he rode suddenly reared up, scattering the crowd. The man clung effortlessly to the stallion's back as if he and the horse were one thing.

I glared at him. There were children underfoot who might have been hurt, and I was certain he had compelled the horse to rear like that, just to show off some macho display of power. I turned with disdain and walked away through the crowd, my silk draperies snapping in the air behind me.

But I couldn't help breaking into a smile when I was sure I was finally alone. My newest husband's nose was somewhat off-center. Perhaps it had been broken sometime in the past. It was the imperfection that made Yeshi perfect.

I did my best to pretend the sudden presence of this powerful man had not rattled me. During the feasting in the square, I ignored him, as he ignored me. I cast my eye across the crowd, wondering if Yeshi's lover was present. I watched the people around him; he was certainly popular and everybody wanted to welcome him home, men and women alike. Plenty of the women were young and pretty, I noticed, and several of them shot curious looks my way, watchful. But I couldn't single out any one of them as a likely candidate for being *the one*.

As soon as I was able to gracefully escape the crowd, I made my way alone across the fields to our farm. When I arrived, I checked on the animals and pumped water for the garden by the kitchen. I breathed deeply of the violet evening air. Summer was in full richness. I felt alive and excited, and also apprehensive.

I hid myself away inside my own room as darkness fell, waiting for the family to return. I was glad to be alone in my own space but still felt quite agitated. Uneasy with the knowledge that there was another Rulan brother, another man who was supposed to be my husband. Another man I was supposed to surrender to. To take into my body. To fuck. Every third night—no, every *fourth* now.

Whether either of us *wanted* to, or not. I felt a certain indignation, wondering if and when I would get the summons from Yeshi, as I had received it from each of my other lawfully wedded mates.

Your husband is asking for you . . .

On edge, I waited. It had never taken long before.

*T*he summons did not come that night, but I had not expected it then. Nor did it come the next morning.

By midday I was wrung out with anxiety, wondering what would happen.

He was all I could think about.

I had heard his voice outside my window that morning. He was up and out of the house early. He set off somewhere on horseback; I had peeked out of my screened window and watched him clatter out of the courtyard. He rode bareback, with only a hackamore to guide the horse, dressed in an old pair of Levi's jeans and a colorful woven tunic of a type that was prevalent in the valley. He wore no cap, as the men usually did when they were outdoors. His hair in the breeze was like a rippling of black silk.

Apparently, unlike his brothers, Yeshi had not been affected

by the excesses of the night before. They all got up later, one at a
time, dragging themselves into the common room for breakfast,
grumpy and puffy-eyed, and I realized something. Last night I
hadn't slept with *any* of my husbands. Strange!

And definitely a first.

I tried to be unconcerned, but I could not help wondering.
Where is he? Where is Yeshi?

Maybe he just—rode away, I thought. Never to never return.

Bareback? With no pack?

I hoped. All day I hoped. And I worried.

I worried and I hoped.

Late afternoon. I tried to remember what I would ordinarily
be doing at that time of the day. Mending, I thought. Here in
this remote valley, we did not simply toss things out and go get
something new at a department store. Clothes were made by
hand, and when they wore out, were patched and worn again.
I wasn't a very good seamstress, but I could sew buttons and
mend tears.

I went to find Gaja.

With a jolt I realized I was beginning to enjoy the after-
noons when my sister-in-law and I would sit together in one of
our apartments to talk and do the hand work on the clothing,
table linens, towels, and blankets for the household. The two
of us had been spending more time together, and although I
couldn't claim she was warming to me, or I to her, we seemed
to be developing a guarded understanding and respect for one
another. Gaja's sharp wit made for some entertaining sessions,

though often the joke was on me. She found my ignorance of her culture amusing, and it was clear she enjoyed every hugely funny faux pas I happened to commit. Through her, I was getting a particular take on the culture, and I tried to be grateful for that.

Shani often joined us, for which I really *was* grateful. Shani wasn't as clever or as sharply observant as Gaja, but she loved to laugh and joke around, and she was kind. She was always nice to me and seemed eager to help me adapt to the ways of the valley. If Shani had a fault, it was that she could be *too* nice. Sometimes I felt her big chocolate eyes fixed on me with such soulful compassion, felt her warm, rounded body pressing so lovingly and close with affection, I just wanted to push her away. She could be cloying. But then I'd feel guilty for not being more welcoming of her obvious good-heartedness.

I found Gaja with Shani in the common room, huddled together, talking in low tones. They seemed startled to see me.

"Don't we have some work to do, ladies?" I said.

They stood, looking a little guilty, smoothing their dresses. Beside the sharp, slim Gaja, Shani looked soft and almost matronly, though she was only in her late twenties.

They were about to follow me down the hall when we heard the sound of hoofbeats on the stone flags of the courtyard. We moved to the window, all three of us together, and looked out to see Yeshi, flinging his leg over the back of his horse and jumping down to the ground with a rugged, tensile grace. He led the horse to the water trough, slipped off the tasseled hackamore and let the horse drink unfettered. When the groom came out of the stable, Yeshi greeted him and flashed a smile so brilliant it left me feeling weak. Using only his hand on the long mane, he led the horse into the stable himself, chatting with the old groom, and when he disappeared through the open door, I felt like something had been taken away from me.

Chapter 13

An hour passed, maybe more.

"He's not asking for her!" Gaja's voice was low but intent. She sat in the window seat of my apartment, gazing out through the carved rosewood screen into the empty courtyard. Shani sat on my small couch, nervously gnawing her fingernails, her needlework forgotten on her lap.

I folded a length of silk and laid it in a basket. "Don't talk about me like I'm not here," I said.

The room was growing dark. Tara would be in soon to light the oil lamps. Shani had been attempting to show me an embroidering technique that was used to decorate clothing and textiles. Gaja was working on her own piece, a gorgeous dress collar studded with tiny mirrors, but she seemed even more sour and preoccupied than usual.

"By now he should have asked for you, if he will be wanting

you tonight, Diandra," Gaja said in a tight voice. She was probably thinking about the elaborate preparations that were supposed
to take place before each wedding ceremony, many of which fell
on her to carry out.

"Well," I said acidly, "perhaps he's still tired from his
long journey." I remembered how exhausted I had been when
I first arrived in the valley. My husbands had let me sleep for
a long time before I was expected to face my first wedding
ceremony.

But they certainly would have been asking by now. . .

"Yes, maybe that's it," Shani said, with a glance at Gaja. But
they did not look convinced either.

Tara peeked her head through the slit in the draperies over
the doorway. "Your husband is asking for you, memsahib," she
said to me.

I looked at the other women, who were suddenly acting flus-
tered, neglecting their needles. Shani lost several stitches with
her carelessness, very unlike her. They certainly were affected, I
thought, which was strange. Neither of them had acted that way
before, with any of the other brothers.

Or *had* they? Maybe I was simply unaware.

"Should I go to him, then?" I asked, rising tentatively from
my cushion.

"Go?" They looked astonished.

"No, no—stay right where you are!" Gaja snapped. "You
should know by now that once your husband asks for you, you
are not to see him until you are to . . . to meet in ritual."

But it was a false alarm. It was Hama who had sent for me,
not Yeshi. Shani and Gaja had thought Yeshi was announcing his

wedding night, in which case I would not have been allowed to go into the men's quarters. This was customary during the time of preparations for the ceremony.

Finally they let me go. The sun had set completely, and this was the strict cut-off point of decision, legally and by tradition. The wedding, they said, would not happen that night, which was fine with me.

I found Hama in the stables, where he was talking with one of the grooms, who was mending a piece of tack. When the groom went out and we were alone, I asked Hama what was wrong. He looked anxious.

"Yeshi's not pleased," he said, pacing a little. "I was afraid of this."

"Hama . . . " My heart jumped inside me. *Yeshi's not pleased.* My face burned scarlet, I was sure, because my cheeks suddenly felt so hot.

So he's not attracted to me!

"I can't help but feel somewhat . . . *guilty,*" Hama was saying. "It was *I* who brought you into our home, and—" He stopped, unable to finish what he had been about to say.

"Well," I said glumly, "*he's* not to be blamed. I guess the odds of four brothers all wanting to marry the same woman aren't all that great."

Hama turned to me with a stricken look. "We had always talked about how it would be someday, when we brought a woman into our home. The four of us. We made a pact."

"A pact?"

"Yes. And I . . . I did not . . . I did not honor that."

I searched his face, wondering what the hell he was telling

me now. "Okay, so . . . you're saying you broke some sort of agreement with your brothers when you brought me here?"

He paced away.

"Hama, *did* you? You had an agreement with all your brothers that—what? That you would all agree on the woman you would marry?"

"Yes, it was something we swore to one another . . . we agreed the woman who became our wife would be someone we all liked."

"Gazer didn't honor the agreement either, then," I said. "Or Rafe. And he would ultimately be the responsible one, because it was *his* choice."

Hama's voice dropped, and it sounded throaty when he spoke, as if confessing a terrible sin: "It's not Rafe's or Gazer's fault, Diandra. I let them both believe Yeshi had given his blessing on this union. I told them I had contacted him when I was in the city and he had sent word that if everyone else was agreed, he would give his go-ahead."

"So Yeshi didn't even know?"

"I sent word to Yeshi, but only after Rafe had his first night with you."

"But I thought . . . " I shook my head. "Why?" I was bewildered. "Why would you do that?" I was surprised. I knew how much Hama valued his family. And his honor, as a man. I thought this sort of betrayal was out of character for him.

"Why? Why did I do it? Because—" Hama grabbed my arm. "Because I *needed* to do it. Because of *you*." His breath was hot on my ear. "My God," he whispered. "You don't even know . . . "

I was stunned by this passionate outburst from Hama, who was usually so controlled, so cool.

But his innate sensuality seemed to overpower his self-possession. He pushed me up against the cool stone of the wall and kissed me hard, his hands roving over me, pulling at my clothing, loosening my blouse so he could fill his hands with my full, heavy breasts. I felt his cock nudging against me, felt his attempt to part my thighs through our clothing.

This was exciting stuff. Hama had *never* broken the rule against having me on another brother's day.

Except for once . . .

It had been Gazer's turn. I remember that. And come to think of it, it was Hama who made the first move that had led to what happened that night.

We were sitting together outside after dinner, listening to the snap of the dying fire in the pit. We had cooked outside. It was early evening, and a beautiful one, clear skies and stars already speckling the firmament. Gazer pulled me down into his lap and began fondling me a little more erotically than he should have, given the presence of his brothers. I think the fact that Gaja happened to be away, assisting at the birth of Shani's sister-in-law's baby, made him a little more daring that night. And it was his turn; everyone knew he was going to have me—at least once! Quite often he didn't even wait until nightfall. He would grab my hand and lead me away before evening set, if he could get his chores finished in time.

And so he had that afternoon as well. He'd cut me away from whatever it was I was doing—I think I was chopping vegetables in the kitchen—grabbed my hand and pulled me toward his room. But we didn't even make it that far before he was apparently so overcome with lust that he couldn't take another step without fucking me first. He pushed me down on the cool stone floor and in moments had taken brutal possession of me and was riding me hard. Anyone could have walked into the room and seen us there on the floor, going at it.

But in the evening, after dinner that day, Gazer was clearly ready to get busy again. I felt him high and hard beneath me as I sat on his lap. His hands crept up beneath my blouse and cupped one of my breasts, his fingers lightly rolling the tips of my nipples.

I gasped, tried not to giggle, and moved in his lap, unintentionally grinding against him. He was like an iron tire rod beneath me. I tried to get away, but he held me tightly. He was a bit of an exhibitionist.

"You're pushing it, pal," Hama said, gazing at us from his place beyond the fire.

There was a curious tension emanating from Hama that night. For him to use American colloquialisms in his speech signaled something serious.

Rafe, who hadn't been paying attention, looked up.

Gazer blinked. He was a simple man. He was the only one of the brothers who had not yet traveled beyond the rim of the valley, and he wasn't especially inclined to strike out on his own. He liked the valley, was proud of the farm, and enjoyed his work. He didn't analyze; he was always present in the moment. It was obvious he hadn't seen it coming, but he now understood that Hama was angry about something. He wasn't sure what it was, and he didn't really care. He just wanted to maintain peace in the household.

Gazer had an innate intelligence with creatures. Animals. Other men. He had a way of getting along with them. "Hey, bro," he said softly. He smiled his winsome, totally disarming and sweet smile. Nobody could stand up to that smile. "You're not gonna pull the older brother switch on me tonight, are ya?"

Hama looked bewildered for a moment, long enough for the ferocious thing that had risen in him to lose its grip, and suddenly he was just Hama again. Powerful, virile, but in a distant, militaristic way.

"What's the 'older brother switch'?" I asked.

Rafe cleared his throat. "The older brother switch. That's a technical term." He grinned.

"Yeah?"

"Yeah. It's when one brother asserts his right as the eldest to claim possession of wifey for the night."

"But—that's against the rules! Isn't it?"

"No. Taking turns with the wife is not a *rule*. It's only a convention of politeness. The actual authority over who *may* claim her is based on the will of the brother with the most seniority."

"And I suppose *she* has nothing to say about it at all!"

"She only has the say of yes—or no."

"I guess that's something," I grumbled, slipping out from Gazer's sensual arms. I stood and began pacing around the fire. I was wearing a deep-cut gown and a cape one of the men had draped over me earlier. My hair was curling softly down over my shoulders. I felt beautiful that night, daring and dark and adventurous. I had the keen attention of all my husbands—or so I thought. I had not known about Yeshi at the time.

Gazer picked up his drum and began thumping out beats in time to my body's movements, and I in turn began to undulate and step in response to his rhythms.

"Yes," Hama said, his voice higher than usual. "Maybe I *should* claim precedence."

He stepped up to me and pulled me roughly into his arms. There was something strange about him that night. Like he was tired of always being a gentleman and wanted what he wanted. *Now.*

I felt the length of him hard against me, the pressure of his body forced against mine, the feel of his mouth hot on my neck. He tried to kiss me on the mouth but I turned away from him. He was too much for me, too arrogant and overpowering. I felt my own body respond to his male urgency, but I felt a little afraid of him too. As I turned away from Hama, I found Rafe right there behind me—

"Brother, step aside," Rafe said. "After all this talk, I do believe *I* shall claim precedence myself."

I cried out softly and felt Rafe's arms encircle me and pull me from Hama's grip.

Rafe was holding me tightly now. Though he wasn't quite as feverish as Hama, he was unabashedly smashing my breasts against his chest and pressing an imposing erection against my belly. "Oh, yeah," he said. "You do feel so good, my wife." He held me tightly and danced me around the fire.

Gazer's drumming kept time to the rhythm of our movements. Rafe's body was grinding against mine, and I let myself melt into him, though I had to resist self-consciousness, knowing the other men's eyes were on me. Rafe enveloped me, arms and legs, the two of us entangled, and our dance was an erotic, sensual enactment of the mating ritual. As I glanced down at Gazer, sitting on a cushion by the fire, he met my eyes with his own, which were glazed with lust. The intensity of his drumming increased with the intensity of Rafe's caresses of my body.

Rafe was breathing hard and I could feel his cock hard beneath his pants, jabbing between my legs as he bent to get low enough to rub himself against me. I caught sight of Hama, who stood a little ways from the fire, legs spread, watching us with a strange expression. His heaving chest told me he was breathing hard, aroused, or perhaps angry, as he watched.

What happened next I only remember as I would remember a dream. One of the men—it had to be Hama—came up behind me as Rafe held me close and began humping against me. They were both rubbing their bodies against me now, and I felt them rough and hard through my dress.

They pulled me down on the ground and Rafe went first, thick and hard and furious. As usual he was only inside me for a very few strokes before he exploded. He grunted when he ejaculated, thumping against me. Hama pushed him off me, climbed on and plunged his cock into me, and with far less control than usual, fucked me hard until he too suddenly gave a spasm and came violently, grasping my hair and my arm tightly and crying out. There was none of his usual attention to detail.

The drumming stopped. Gazer stood above us, waiting. Hama rolled off me but continued to survey what was happening, watching carefully as Gazer mounted me and began to do all the things he knew I liked. Kissing my mouth and sucking my tongue, sliding up high on my body and teasing my nipples with the tip of his penis.

I remember Hama's expression most of all, the way he watched with what seemed like veiled anger as his brothers took their turns. It was then that I had my first inkling that Hama was not necessarily what he seemed to be. Calculating, yes. But cool? I was not so sure.

I had to admit the dark passion in Hama raised a response in me that might have already died away if not for the unexpected shot of sensual power. Just when I was getting bored by what sometimes seemed his forced attentiveness to my needs, he would lose his wits and abandon himself to mindless rutting. I felt it again in the stable that evening, the night after Yeshi's arrival, and I wondered if Hama was about to throw caution to the wind and bend me over right there against the feed bin.

"You don't even know," he was whispering. "You have no idea how much I need you, Diandra. I need you so much I was willing to screw over my own brother just to make sure I got you."

A soft clanking sound just outside the door had us jumping away from each other.

I was just pulling my blouse closed when Yeshi entered the stable.

Chapter 14

He was the youngest brother, but Yeshi was the tallest, the broadest of shoulder and the fullest of thigh—though he gave an impression of lanky slenderness. His hair was black and silky, long enough to sweep down over his forehead but not quite long enough to touch his shoulders. His neck was strong, the line of his jaw so beautiful it might have been considered delicate had it not been so powerfully built.

He glanced unconcernedly at Hama and me, lifted the saddle blanket he was carrying and slipped it over a peg on the wall.

"Little brother!" Hama cried. His recovery was admirable. He arranged his posture to hide the enormous erection straining the front of his trousers. He slapped his brother across the back and pulled him sideways into an embrace that Yeshi only half-heartedly returned.

I knew that Hama's affection for his younger brother was sincere. But he had betrayed him anyway. And that bothered me. And it bothered me to think he had essentially hidden from me the fact that this younger brother even existed. As he tricked his brothers into believing Yeshi had given his approval of me.

"With so much going on, I feel I haven't given you a proper welcome," Hama said.

"Not at all," Yeshi said coolly. His English sounded more casually American than that of his brothers, and yet was slightly British, as was theirs. "It is *I* who has not given a proper welcome . . . to your *beautiful bride.*"

"*Our* bride, bro," Hama said with a nervous laugh.

"*Our* bride." Yeshi stepped toward me. "We shall see."

We shall see. The way he said it, like an actor exaggerating a line, gave the words layers of meaning. Sarcasm and amusement and skepticism. I realized then that my marriage to Yeshi was not a done deal.

He stared at me with the same fierce eyes as when he had looked down on me from horseback, though they were even more disconcerting now that I was seeing his face up close—the high, exquisitely molded cheekbones; a mouth that was somehow snarling and sensual at the same time. His nose was narrow and slightly crooked, and this rugged, broken imperfection gave his beauty a devastating masculinity.

As he took in the sight of me, disheveled, breathing hard, veil fallen, my breasts practically spilling out of my partially unbuttoned blouse, Yeshi's lips hardened into a sneer.

"Hama," he said softly. "Will you leave us a moment?"

Hama hesitated only briefly before bowing to Yeshi. "Of course."

I wanted to cry out to Hama not to leave me, but he had already turned and gone out of the stable.

I stared up at Yeshi, terrified. I could not go anywhere; I was standing in the corner between the tack room and the first stall. I felt trapped. Panic rose in me.

He came closer. I breathed in the faint scent of leather, a vague suggestion of spice, and the earthy essence of a healthy man. He was forcing me to look into his eyes, which were the color of smoky topaz, darkly lashed, grave and mesmerizing. I felt his hands on my shoulders, a sudden, tight grip, pleasurable and painful, and he stepped closer and brushed his mouth down on mine—a brief, rough kiss, angry and yet strangely gentle at the same time.

A thousand thoughts went through my mind in that split second. My first, self-protective impulse was to fight him, but he had taken me by storm, and it took me a moment to catch up. I was too late. He was already ending it. But then—it was as if he couldn't help himself, he had to linger there a little longer. He subtly deepened the kiss, and my resistance melted away.

He was huge and powerful, and he made me feel slight and vulnerable, like he could pick me up and break me in half without effort.

As he kissed me, his tongue slipped between my lips. His hands were sweeping alongside my breasts, his groin deepening against mine; the feel of his large, hard cock was shocking, and somehow very different from the way Hama's had felt, pressing against me only moments earlier in a very similar way. This was more than mere localized sensation.

With this man, the erotic connection seemed to blast all the way down through my legs and into the earth, up into my belly and through my heart.

My head lolled back as he ended the kiss at last, and I felt his mouth on my neck, sensual and bruising. Involuntarily, I arched up against him and my legs opened slightly to the pressure of his body, the subtle movement of his thighs parting mine.

He was kissing my mouth again, and I felt the thrust of his tongue, and his arms were encircling me, holding me in an embrace that I felt I would drown in.

My emotional state seemed to echo the tumult in my body. Because for all the sudden and undeniable heat between us, I felt his animosity, stronger than ever. He communicated it in the arrogant plundering of my mouth and in the way his skillful hands tested me like I was some new acquisition, which I supposed I was. A new toy he hadn't wanted.

I was set against this man, knowing he was already set against me. I wanted to fight him, to resist him, but my body was somehow in thrall to his, and my mind and heart seemed strangely connected to my body's demands. I had known Yeshi for a matter of hours—moments, really—and he had become the most powerful force in my universe.

Abruptly, he let go of me as if releasing handfuls of hot coals and moved away.

"Well," he said. "It is no longer a mystery to me, how you managed to insinuate yourself into this household." He spoke as if to someone else in the room, with a ragged catch of breath. "But know this . . . " He turned back to me, in possession of himself

again. "I will *not* bed you, woman. I will *not* be your husband.
You may have bewitched my brothers but you won't have the satisfaction of me. *You will never be my wife.* And mark my words,
fair lady. You will *never* survive here. You are out of your depth.
You are out of your league. You are out of your mind, if you think
you can make this work. You will be gone before the Dry Wind
Moon."

And with that, he was gone himself, turning on his heel and
striding out the door.

I huddled, shaken, by the chimney, until my breathing had
returned to normal.

I slept alone that night.

Again.

Several days passed, and Yeshi did not come near me. Neither
did any of my other husbands. I was a bit annoyed about that,
since I had worked myself up into quite a frenzy, my mind and
body replaying Yeshi's hostile kisses and caresses over and over.
I thought perhaps one of my other husbands would quench the
strange fire kindled down deep inside me the moment Yeshi and
I first met.

But they didn't. I'm not sure they *could* have, but they didn't
even try. In fact it seemed my husbands were all avoiding me.

I was completely mystified.

Finally I complained about it, in the most subtle yet unam-
biguous way I knew how, to Shani and Gaja during one of our
afternoon sewing sessions. Gaja frowned and looked troubled,
but I couldn't help notice that Shani seemed delighted. She was
obviously pressing back a smile on her plump, flushed lips. A

heavy pendant on a beaded chain seemed to dance on her heavy, rounded breast.

"What?" I demanded, looking at her.

"Forgive me, Diandra," she said. "I don't mean to make light of your situation. I just think men are so—*adorable*."

"Adorable? How so?" I asked crossly.

"The brothers, you know, they're just awfully . . . *loyal* to each other. They don't want to break the rules or dishonor each other in any way."

I thought of Hama's betrayal of Yeshi in bringing me there but decided not to mention that. "What do you mean?" I asked. "Dishonor each other how?"

"Well," she said, "the reason they aren't coming near you is because Yeshi hasn't had you yet. They can't take their turns until—"

"Who cares if Yeshi hasn't had me yet?" I interrupted. "If *they* want me, then let them have me. He can have his girlfriend! I don't *care*."

Gaja spoke up, something she rarely did unless it was important. I paid close attention to whatever she thought about any given subject. "It's more complicated than that, Diandra," she said gravely. The bones of her face were so close to the surface of her tanned skin, she looked like a carved idol. I realized with a guilty flash she had lost weight since I had arrived. The sleeves of her tunic hung off her skeletal shoulders. "The wife is a very powerful figure in the family," she went on. "She must be in right relationship to all. When all the brothers in one family are married to one woman, it is very bad luck when one brother is not . . . not in a proper relationship with his wife. It affects the entire family, and the entire community as well."

"So this other woman, the one Yeshi wanted for his wife—the mystery woman—she must not like *me* very much, if she thinks I took over the place she thought would be *hers*. But I don't see anybody shedding any tears. Where *is* this girl?" I demanded. "And why is it nobody will tell me who she is?"

I had asked around about this mystery woman, and though nobody actually denied her existence, no one could—or would—tell me her name. I knew most of the women in the village now, and there were many lovely ones among them who might have been Yeshi's lover. But they had all treated me with friendliness and welcome.

"Come on," I said. "You *must* know who she is."

Gaja said, "It does not matter anymore who she is, Diandra. *You* are the wife now. The past is past." She sounded angry, as if she was only calling it as she saw it, not how she might have preferred it.

Shani looked at me with a helpless shrug, and I had the feeling she would have helped me if she could. What sort of constraint was on them, not to tell? What sort of taboo? Most of all, I wondered: Who was she?

Who was she, this mysterious woman that Yeshi loved?

*W*hoever she was, she had a powerful hold on him. Yeshi seemed determined to honor his vow never to touch me. Never to be my husband. Never to take me as wife. But he and I had to live together. We couldn't avoid each other. We couldn't ignore each other, though at first we tried. We definitely tried.

Yeshi's presence continued to be an invisible, impermeable wall that separated me from my other husbands. The seething sexual caldron I had been living in before his arrival had simmered down to a household of simple brotherly affection. And brotherly affection only. I resented this and thought it unfair. After all, if Yeshi had another lover, why shouldn't I have my guys, my rightful husbands, the ones who wanted me?

I was obsessed by the idea of this other woman that Yeshi loved and whom he had wanted to bring into the fold of his family. Once again I went over all the women I knew in the village, tried to fit them to Yeshi, tried to imagine them as his passionate lover. But somehow none of them seemed quite right for him. There were those I thought might do well with Hama, Rafe, or Gazer, but when it came to Yeshi, I couldn't picture him with just anyone. He would need someone . . . *unique*. A woman who was not only beautiful and charming, but smart and subtle. And sensual. Very sensual. Because he was obviously a sensual and *sexual* man, judging from that hot kiss we had shared.

I found myself watching for clues. As friends and neighbors came in and out of the big farmhouse where we lived, or when we mingled with people in the village, I noted the pretty girls who made their way to Yeshi's side, and there were more than a few who did. It seemed that his presence on the farm encouraged many visitors, old and young, and yes, many women. But he rarely offered any of them more than a polite and friendly greeting. If it was his intent to be discreet with his love, he was succeeding.

I was sure he must be seeing her, if she was a woman of the valley—and from what I could wheedle out of Shani, she was. But when did he see her? Yeshi was almost always on the farm. When he did go into the village, one of us usually went with him. Though I kept track of who came and went, my curiosity found no satisfaction.

I thought the mystery was about to be solved one evening when I went out to the barn to check on an ailing ewe. As I walked down the path, the sounds of laughter and music drifted out from the main house. We had a crowd of friends and family visiting that night, celebrating Hama's birthday. Shani's family was there; all her brothers and her sister-in-law, and some other people from the village, were staying over. It would be dark soon, and I hurried to take advantage of the last of the dimming light. My feet were silent as I entered the barn.

I stopped short as I heard someone moaning pitifully, a sound that tailed off into a soft, heartrending cry, then—thumping. Rhythmic, accompanied by grunting. A woman's voice, pleading. A low male growl in response. Muffled but close, inside the barn.

I crept around the corner and peered into an open stall.

Shani lay in a bed of straw, her hair down, her legs spread and bare, long and creamy naked. I had never seen her looking so beautiful or so wicked. Her face was contorted, as if she were in pain. Her skirt was up around her waist and her fingers were buried in the dark hair of a man, a married friend of her brothers, who was licking her between her thighs, his tongue long and supple, teasing into her folds, which he held open with his fingers. She was the one emitting the moaning cries, while he was groaning with eagerness, humping the straw while he nibbled and licked.

He hoisted himself up over her, knocked a bit of straw off his cock, which was hanging stiffly from his open fly, and roughly plunged himself into her.

She accepted him with a grunt, and spread her legs wider to accommodate his small, pounding hips.

A movement on the other side of the barn caught my eye. Someone else was in the barn, seeing what I was seeing.

I ran outside, drinking in the fresh, clear air, hoping it would clear my head. I heard footsteps following me out of the barn and I turned.

"Oh, you there . . . " It was Hama. He grabbed me, pulled me hard against him and began squeezing me, his hands roving up and down my body, as if he couldn't believe it was really me. "Oh, you," he said again. "I have missed you."

"Did you see them?" I asked him.

"Oh, yeah. They're doing what *I* want to be doing."

"Hama, is that common among your people? Having sex with someone else's spouse?"

"Not any more common than it is among *your* people."

"Touché."

"My little brother has to have his turn with you, and soon," he said, panting. "I can't stand this."

"Let's just do it," I begged. "Fuck me, Hama," I added in a whisper. "Take me into your room and let's just do it."

"No. No, I can't." He shook his head and shoved me away.

I stared at him, startled and hurt.

"I have already done enough damage," he said. "Just to have brought you here. Do you understand that? I will not make it any worse."

He turned and stalked out of the stable yard.

Chapter 15

Days passed into weeks. The pressure mounted.

I knew Yeshi was feeling it too. His brothers desperately wanted him to fuck me so they could get back on their regular schedule. But Yeshi wouldn't budge. He refused to ask for me.

Not only did he refuse to ask for me, but he went out of his way to shun me. Aside from the hot, lingering kiss in the stable the night we met, his behavior toward me consisted of studied indifference. When he was forced by circumstances to look at me, it was with a cold expression, and when he had to speak with me, it was only in the most laconic terms. I wanted to attribute this treatment of me to a nasty personality, but Yeshi, as I came to learn, was actually a decent man. He was gentlemanly and pleasant to everyone in the village and in his family, though I couldn't help but notice he seemed somewhat reserved with Hama.

Only with me was he biting and sarcastic.

I told myself I didn't begrudge him the choice not to have me as wife, but in fact I was secretly hurt by his vehement rejection.

Over time, as we were forced to live and work together, Yeshi became less sullen and more outwardly antagonistic. Our way of relating became a pattern of sniper-fire exchange, using spiteful, witty repartee as ammunition. Yeshi was quick-witted, perceptive, and a master of the cutting remark. But I could hold my own in *that* game, and give back as good as I got.

A strange physical intimacy developed between us too, which consisted of the both of us scheming to find ways to express hostility through touch—without ever resorting to actual violence.

Since I had never been one to get off on either the sadistic or masochistic acts, I was a appalled at the glee with which I came up with "harmless" ways of inflicting torture on Yeshi, as he did on me. It was the kind of pinching and poking and shoving and bumping that feels hot when you're playing with the right person. Or the wrong person, in the right circumstances. And I knew that in a strange way he was enjoying me as much as I was enjoying him.

We were engaged in a grown-up version of the boy dipping the girl's pigtails in the ink well game. It didn't take a degree in psychology to figure out there was a raging sexual attraction running beneath our outwardly warring behavior, but I often went to bed feeling guilty for my own part in our feud, and bewildered by some of the things he did—and said—to me. What got me most was when he would say—"jokingly"—that he was counting down the days until I left the valley, because my departure was inevitable.

This only made me more determined to stay.

Now that the household was complete, a new dynamic had come into play. I didn't know how much of the change had to do with the presence of Yeshi, or the presence of Yeshi combined with *my* presence and the strange family politics that had ensued. However it all mixed together, the outcome was exciting and strange. Life for me in those days was endlessly fascinating.

I would have thought that living in the constant presence of a man who resented me so intensely would be disturbing and difficult, and it was; but I also found it strangely exhilarating.

Since we had a tacit agreement to dislike one another, I found myself annoyed whenever Yeshi did anything that made me less inclined to dislike him. And there were small moments that threatened my resolve.

One night I was sitting in a doorway, looking out over the courtyard, watching Gaja teach her dance class. She had a group of about ten young women working on a traditional dance. I had to admit she was quite graceful as she demonstrated a spin.

"And the winds came in and lifted the grain and swirled it through the world . . . " Gaja's voice, ordinarily so flat and dour, was charged with music and energy.

I laughed when the girls copied her, half of them using the spinning as an excuse to topple to the ground.

Two men sat near the dancers, one playing the flute, the other on a drum. Yeshi was on the other side of the courtyard, working on the exterior wall of an additional room the brothers were putting on the house. They all wanted their own rooms now that they were married. Since Yeshi had returned, he and Gazer had to double up.

It happened that I was sitting on Yeshi's pallet—his bed, where he slept—because it was near the open wall and had the best view of the dancers. It was neat and comfortable, with a fur-lined mattress and colorful woven blankets.

I could feel the vibrations of Yeshi's pounding and thumping as he worked. He was a pretty good carpenter and mason, with nice tools; he did everything with old-fashioned hand tools, saws and hammers, chisels and planers.

The ritual dance Gaja and the other young women were rehearsing drew me in with its story. It was apparently a story everyone there had heard many times. Everyone except me. I noticed the drummer, sitting across the courtyard beyond the dancers, staring at me. As I got more involved with the dancers' play, I snuggled deeper into Yeshi's bed, drawing up his warm blankets and nestling into his pillows. After a while he came through the doorway and passed by me. I think I made him a little nervous, being in his bed.

"Do you want me to move?" I asked.

"No. What are you watching so intently? What are they doing?"

"They're doing the ritual harvest dance."

"Ah, yeah, that's a good one. I like all the spinning."

"Me too." I waited for him to say something sarcastic, but he just stood there a moment, watching the dancers with me.

Yeshi went back to work. I lay in his bed, feeling the warmth, feeling my body stretched out on the soft mattress. Night had fallen and he was working by torchlight. I cast my glance through the open doorway for a glimpse of him in the little adjoining room. His body was lean and muscular, long and graceful. I was fascinated by the line of his shirt draped from his shoulders to his hips. The fullness of his slender thighs. The hang of his thick cock in his jeans.

He worked tirelessly. I wished he would look at me the way the drummer did.

I grew sleepy and burrowed into Yeshi's pillows, pulled the furs higher. I was so comfortable, I could doze off. The dancers had taken a break, so I closed my eyes.

The noise of construction was closer now. I opened my eyes and sat up a little. He was in the room with me, doing something around the doorway.

"Now don't run away," Yeshi said. His voice was gentle and commanding. I curled up in his blankets again and lay there feeling supremely comfortable and very nearly content.

What was it, I wondered, that had changed for me? I felt new. Reborn. Revitalized. Life was good. Life was *always* good, but now it was better.

I knew what it was. It was him. Yeshi brought a breath of youth into the lodgings, a high energy, a sense of merriment and fun, and yet at the same time he instilled in the others an attitude that only the highest standards in everything would be tolerated. The household itself, from family to servant, was on heightened vigilance now that he was in residence. I had realized after a few days that though Yeshi was the youngest of the men in his family, he was looked upon as the leader.

This was why he could get away with not carrying out his marital obligations, and why his brothers were so adamant that he should. But still he refused to ask for me.

"Hey."

I opened my eyes and looked up eagerly, expecting Yeshi, but he had disappeared.

It was the drummer. Big teeth, unruly curls, a sweet, sad expression in big brown-gray eyes, nice hard body. I hadn't even noticed that the drumming had stopped.

"Why are you not out there dancing with them tonight?" he said.

"Oh, I couldn't. I would need the beginner's class," I replied with a laugh.

"No, I don't believe it."

"Well, it's true."

"I saw you dancing in the village square once. You were like the wild long-haired antelope with your steps and your grace."

I smiled at the compliment. He reached out and touched my hair, curling a strand of it around his finger. Yeshi appeared in the doorway at that moment and saw us together. The drummer was leaning toward me, one knee bent and resting on the edge of the pallet where I lay. His attention was focused on me and his expression had become avid.

I expected Yeshi to go back into the room where he was working, but instead he moved out farther so he could see better, and, I sensed, be seen. But the unruly drummer did not notice him standing there, watching us.

"Your hair is the color of gold," the drummer said in English, leaning a little closer. In my ear he murmured something in his own language, thinking, I'm sure, that I would not understand the rough dialect he spoke. "And is your hair *down there* golden as well?"

"The dancers are waiting for you," Yeshi said to the drummer, speaking softly. "You'd better get back to it."

The drummer gave a start, stood up straight and glanced at the dancers, who were milling around the fountain, drinking water and chatting.

The two men faced each other awkwardly, as if the space they occupied was suddenly too small for the both of them. I could sense some male territorial vibe coming from Yeshi. Unruly Drummer backed off accordingly. He saluted with a rather sad face and walked back to his drum.

Yeshi went back to work and did not look at me again.

Chapter 16

꼭

As time went on with no change in the status of things, Gaja passed along to me the grumblings of her older brothers, subtly blaming me, I felt. As if *I* could have done anything about Yeshi's stubbornness. After all, it was all about *him* "asking" for *me*.

I was willing.

I tried to make light of it, to bring the issue out into the open. One evening as we were all finishing dinner, I bluntly brought up the subject. It was just the immediate family that night, and Gaja had gone out into the courtyard. I was alone with all my husbands. It seemed the perfect opportunity to speak up.

"You know what?" I said. I waited, making sure I had their attention.

They all looked at me. "What?" Gazer finally asked.

"I don't see why everyone doesn't just chill, you know?" I

said. "Yeshi can do whatever he wants to do, all right? He's a grown man. He can have his . . . *space*." I decided to keep the word "girlfriend" out of the conversation. But certainly they all knew what I was talking about. I was sure of that. "Really," I went on, a little nervously now, because they were all so silent and still. "It's okay with me. Yeshi can do as he pleases. And the rest of us can go on as before, okay? Yeah?" I looked at each of them.

There was a long uncomfortable silence. Yeshi stared out the window, refusing to meet my eyes. Rafe toyed with the food on his plate, thoughtful. Hama was shaking his head. Gazer looked confused.

"What any of *you* may choose to do is of no interest to *me*," Yeshi said. He got up and left the table.

One by one by one the other brothers took up their forks and began eating again. It was as if nothing had happened.

I talked to Hama about it later.

"Well, Diandra, I find it difficult to explain." His voice was patient. He had grown to accept these huge gaps in my cultural understanding. "But until you and Yeshi are wedded, *none* of us is. We can't just pretend."

"What do you mean, 'none of us is'? I thought when you and I put on that show for the village it meant we were married."

"Yes, but the papers don't get signed until all the brothers consummate the union. Until then, it will not be official."

I'd had a feeling something like this would happen. I was well aware that we had never signed any papers since our arrival, but I didn't really give a shit about papers, as long as nobody hassled me about being there.

"It didn't seem to matter before, when he wasn't around," I said. "You were all happy to take your turns then. Nobody questioned the legality of it all until *he* showed up."

"Well, certainly, it was all right when he was out of the country, but now he's here, and it's just . . . it's awkward. There are legal issues."

I shrugged. "So we live in sin," I said with a touch of irony, thinking fondly of my old auntie and what she would have had to say about the whole arrangement. "Who cares?"

He said seriously, "If you don't consummate the marriage with Yeshi, the entire contract will become void after a certain amount of time . . . "

"How much time?"

"I don't know, exactly. There are different time frames for different circumstances. But now that we are all here, it has to be done. Soon."

"Soon, you mean, like in Himalaya time?"

He smiled nervously. "I suppose so."

"Well, then," I said lightly, "there's no hurry. Hey, I just want everyone to be happy. I honestly don't care if the marriage is legal or not."

"Well, I do care." Hama's voice was quiet. "And if we are not legally married, you will have to leave the valley."

Shit, I thought. I wasn't ready to leave yet. I still had work to do.

Yes, there was my field study, which was incomplete at that point. But I also wanted to find out what made Yeshi tick. And the last thing I wanted was to prove him right by leaving. Or give him the satisfaction, if I was forced out.

"How about if *I* ask for *him*?" I said one day to Shani and Gaja, only half joking. "Would that work?"

They shook their heads, glancing at one another uneasily. "No, Diandra," Gaja said. "It doesn't work that way . . . here."

"As women, we have to wait until *they* ask," Shani explained.

Their voices were low, and I felt strangely privileged. They had finally admitted to me one way in which their culture might have been behind mine in regard to women's autonomy.

*T*hough he was too subtle to let on, I knew Yeshi was aware of the pain he was inflicting upon his loved ones. He was too shrewd to be oblivious to what was happening around him. I thought he was actually enjoying the discomfort the two of us were causing the others, until one evening he approached me privately and said, "Diandra, I would speak with you about this marriage business."

He had appeared in the alley of ancient cedars behind the house when I was walking alone early one evening. The sight of him on the path above me had my heart jumping up in my chest and my cheeks burning. He was so graceful, like a stag, proud and shy. He stirred me.

"All right," I said with a shrug, eyeing him warily as he approached, already hoisting my armor in anticipation of a battle. "Speak."

"Because I have yet to initiate the required wedding ceremonies, it seems I am the cause of much grief to my brothers, and a source of gossip for the whole village." He looked at me steadily. His eyes looked almost green in the twilight. "Do you understand what I am saying?"

I nodded, suddenly feeling very self-conscious. "I am well aware of the situation, yes," I said.

"So . . . " He stepped closer to me, and now I felt terrified.

"Giving in at last, are we?" I said.

He stared down at me with a look of hatred. He closed the space between us with one easy stride and grabbed both my arms, his fingers digging into the flesh, and shook me a little. "I told you the day I met you I would never have you as my wife. That's a pledge I intend to honor. I will *never* make love with you."

I yanked myself from his grasp and stepped away from him, rubbing my arms, trying to maintain my cool expression, but I was breathing hard. I told myself what I felt was anger, but the anger was all churned up with the heat of lust.

"Here's the thing," he said, and I couldn't help but notice he was breathing hard too. "If we give the people what they want, they're happy, they leave us alone, so we're happy. Do you follow me?"

I didn't answer.

"So we give 'em what they want."

He let that hang in the air a moment.

"Are you agreed?"

"You're sending me mixed messages here, Yeshi."

"I say we give 'em the show. Let them see what they want to see."

"But—"

"A *show*."

"You mean, like, put on a mock . . . display? Behind the curtain?"

"Exactly."

I started to laugh, but he just scowled at me.

I looked Yeshi over. I remembered the fear I felt the night when he'd forced that violent kiss on me. I still felt a sort of fear, but it was different now. I knew the rough way he handled me was a symptom of physical frustration and was the only way he could justify touching me as he wanted to touch me—the way I wanted him to touch me. Though he sometimes pretended to be brutal, his touch was always sensual, and we both knew it was calculated to arouse us both.

Ironic, I thought, how sexuality was the most powerful force between us, and the very thing he did not let himself express.

I knew from living with Yeshi that he was a gentle man at heart. He was kind to the old ladies and great with kids. Men looked up to him and respected him, and all the women were at least half in love with him. I tried to keep up my wall of dislike to match the one he had for me, but in truth I actually liked him better because of his scorn for our situation and his refusal to play along with his society's rules.

And yet there were times I wished he would let down his hostility and talk to me the way he talked to the others, instead of pretending to ignore me. I wished he would smile at me instead of turning one of those rare, cold, windswept glances of his on me, so sad and mournful I was always left bewildered and wondering what was going on inside him.

But now he was looking at me with a playfully sly expression. This was a side of him with which I was not personally familiar. "So what do you say, Diandra?" he asked.

"You want me to *pretend* to . . . to perform the marriage rites with you. Is that it?" I decided not to use the cruder words that came to mind.

"Yes," he said.

"Well . . . I appreciate the altruistic motive involved, and the sheer ingeniousness of the plan, but I'm just not sure I'm a good enough actress to pull it off."

"Leave it to me. I'll do the acting for both of us."

"Your girlfriend won't object?"

He turned away, holding his head high and haughty, as if he hadn't heard the swipe. "Do you agree or not?" he asked.

I realized he was serious. He meant that we should do it. It seemed implausible to me, but he was staring out at the woods with a solemn expression, waiting for my answer.

The silence stretched out so long he turned and looked at me again.

"I don't know, Yeshi." My voice was troubled. "To pretend like that? It seems . . . wrong, somehow. Deceitful."

"You were hoping I would suggest we do the real thing?" He moved close to me again, but his voice was so cold the vibration of it rippled in icy waves through my body, making me shiver uncontrollably.

He pulled me roughly against him and began rubbing his hands up and down my arms and back as if to warm me. He murmured against my ear, still playful, but with an edge of spite: "My three brothers aren't quite enough for you, are they?"

My God. He was right. I *wasn't* satisfied with his three brothers. I wanted *him* too. And as much as I had desired Hama back in the early days, it was nothing to the way I wanted Yeshi. As painful as it had been for me in the beginning with Gazer, lying awake in the middle of the night, hoping he would sneak into my room and fuck me even though it wasn't his night—and as much as I had desired my passionate Yak driver—this aching, throbbing heat of longing for Yeshi was incomparable. Especially right at that moment, when his body, hot and hard and very obviously male, was jammed against me.

And I had the feeling he was dying for me to snap, to break down and admit it. *Yes. I do want the real thing. I want* you.

Maybe then he could break down and admit he wanted *me* too.

But his scorn for me was too much to bear. I would not be humiliated by my own desires. Maybe it wasn't too late to hide from him what I was feeling. Grasping at my dignity, I pulled away from him; but seriously—and he knew it—every nerve in my body was screaming to stay locked in his arms.

I held myself proudly and said, "Actually, no, I think a bogus wedding ceremony is just the ticket. A mock marriage would suit me fine."

Was it my imagination, or did he flinch a little at my words?

"It's brilliant, really," I went on. "A phony wedding night."

"Right. After all, what could be more appropriate?" he said. "A phony wedding night for a phony marriage."

His words hit me like a blast of wind down from the pass. I shivered and hugged myself, hoping he would want to warm me again, but he walked away without even looking back at me.

The next morning he asked for me.

*   *   *

*B*y now I knew the drill. Dress for morning and break my fast
on the hearty fare provided by my sour-faced sister-in-law. Then,
the ritual preparation. Bathe, exfoliate and remove unwanted
hair, while at the same time contemplating spiritual cleansing,
psychic shedding of the skin, and emotionally plucking out that
part of the persona that might be impeding the smooth contact
of soul on soul, or skin on skin. That, I had gathered, was the
general idea.

Luncheon, a salad made of seven different kinds of fruit
and grain, each with a separate symbolic and nutritional com-
ponent designed to enhance the wedding night ritual. A rest in
the afternoon, then a relaxing massage, lying prone beneath the
skilled fingers of the young unmarried women. No need for a
"test" this time, but the massage was heavenly anyway.

By now I was just one of the girls, and it was great fun. Or
would have been, had I been more relaxed. I drank more of the
intoxicating brew than I ever had before in preparation one of
these occasions. But it wasn't enough to make me forget what I
was doing. Or would be doing, very shortly.

I felt strangely apprehensive, though I should have thought
it would all be old hat to me by now. Especially given the plan:
Yeshi and I weren't even going to actually do the dirty deed.

Shani seemed to sense my uneasiness, and she took me
aside. "So what's going on here?" she asked anxiously. "Are you
okay?"

"Yeah. It'll be okay," I said. For some reason, I felt I needed
to reassure her. "And soon it will be all over with."

"It concerns me," she said. "I know it has been difficult between you and Yeshi. I suppose I am just a little confused as to why the sudden change of heart."

I said to her in a low voice, "We're not *really* going to do it. We're just going to pretend."

The chocolate eyes went large and her mouth made a perfectly round *O*.

"Yeah," I said. "So don't worry about it," I added a little sharply.

I wished I could convince *myself* not to worry about it.

I reminded myself I had no reason to be afraid of Yeshi. He was just a man. And I had three other men of my very own! What did it matter if the fourth one wasn't interested in pleasing me? He could live his life the way he wished. I couldn't blame him, and I certainly didn't want to cramp his style any more than necessary.

But truth be told, I was in awe of Yeshi. And if I wasn't exactly still afraid of him, I was afraid of what I was feeling for him.

I didn't want to admit it, and I certainly didn't like it. I wasn't happy about it, but I couldn't lie to myself, even if I had managed to lie to him.

I wanted Yeshi. Despite—or because of—every conflicting thing I felt for him, I wanted him. I wanted him badly.

I only want him because he doesn't want me, I told myself.

It didn't matter. I still wanted him.

At first I had found the idea of a mock ceremony rather humorous, but now that we were about to carry through with our plan, I was dreading it. I was feeling too emotional about the whole thing—my heart was oddly engaged. I realized my feelings could be horribly stepped on and crushed if I went through with this sham wedding.

But what else could I do? I had agreed to it. The equilibrium of our family depended on it.

Chapter 17

❧

The thin gauze curtain dropped down between the stage and the audience. A hush fell over the night. Then the chanting began.

I stepped onto the stage, where Yeshi was already waiting. God, what a handsome man. Potent. Muscular, lean, and graceful. He wore the ceremonial beaded jacket and leather trousers. His eyes were huge, and his beautiful, sensual mouth was set in a hard, unyielding line. He reached out and grasped my hand.

I let out a little gasp, feeling his touch like an electrical connection.

This was the moment when Rafe had grabbed me—not just my hand but my entire body—and threw me down on the low bed.

Hama had taken my hand reverently and held it; he had leaned in and kissed me tenderly, with an edge of passion.

Gazer had joyfully scooped me up in his arms and twirled me

around, kissing me in midair, setting me down on the mattress only sometime later.

Yeshi just stared at me, his expression strange and mournful. A moment ticked by, and it occurred to me that maybe neither one of us could go through with this charade.

"You want a rain check?" I asked softly, pulling my hand away.

"I'm not running out," he replied in a whisper. "But *you* can if you want to."

"I'd just like to get it over with."

"Okay, so . . . here goes." He moved his head close to mine. "I guess first we let them think I'm passionately kissing you." He placed his hands on either side of my face and let his head fall against mine, and we lingered there, our cheeks touching. He smelled so good. I had to stop myself from deeply inhaling his essence.

"Not very convincing," I said in a low voice. "About the passionate part, I mean."

He seized me, his hands fisted around my upper arms, and bent me back with the force of his kiss. Fake kiss. His mouth pressed against the side of mine. I stumbled and nearly fell backward, but he slid his arm around me like I was a stem of grass and pulled me up tight against him. I cried out with surprise and pleasure, feeling his hard warmth against my body.

"Go ahead, baby," he whispered. "Make some noise. They want to hear you."

The next sound I meant to let out was one of protest, but it came out sounding strangled and throaty and full of the desire I was fighting not to feel.

Our lips were millimeters apart, our eyes locked but out of focus. He leaned into the warmth of my breasts. His hands moved down over my body, over my back and arms, just barely touching me. His mouth had dropped to my neck, and I felt his teeth lightly scraping over my throat.

We had agreed that actual touch would probably be necessary during this production, but we had also agreed to keep it as minimal and "professional" as possible, like two stage actors playing a love scene. But I noticed right away that Yeshi was touching me more than strictly necessary to fulfill the illusion of lovemaking. And my own body betrayed me as well. It seemed to be out of my control, in how it responded—I couldn't help arching against the man and somehow opening to him.

With a swift, skillful maneuver, he lifted me down onto the mattress, and lowered himself on top of me.

I felt the weight of him like a delicious burden. He was heavy and warm and his smell was something I wanted to drink up. He buried his face in my hair, and I felt his hot breath on my neck as he whispered in my ear, "Now I'm going to have to undress you. You might want to make it easy for me."

The feeling of his breath on my neck and his cock pressing against my thigh through our clothing made me want nothing more than to make it *very* easy for him. But I scoffed softly and tried to wriggle out from under him. He wasn't supposed to be pinning me down so hard.

He held me tighter, and I struggled even more. And the more I struggled, the more passionately he responded; my resistance seemed to fire up in him some instinctive urge to possess, like a cat's compulsion to pounce on the prey that tries to flee, and he easily held me fast beneath him. He began to pull apart the ties of my clothing.

I realized then that I was powerless to stop him. He *would* have me shed my clothes. The crowd was going wild. I heard the cheering and shouting, muted by the draperies that separated Yeshi and me from the people who were watching.

It might have been a sham wedding, but Yeshi was really undressing me. And though I did resist him, he was so much bigger and stronger that I was completely in his power. The ties on my blouse and skirt were no match for his strong fingers.

Like a proper romantic hero, he ripped the front of my gown open in one motion, and there I was, the romantic heroine, writhing half naked beneath him, my nipples peeping out of the tatters of my embroidered bodice.

With another swift movement of his hands, he opened my skirts, and I felt completely exposed though my sex was still protected by a thin sheaf of silk. I felt young and vulnerable, and instinctively squeezed my thighs together and covered my breasts with my hands, my arms crisscrossed over my chest.

He rose on his knees above me, looking down on me appraisingly. He gently pulled my hands from my breasts.

"My God, you are magnificent," he said. I was sure it was for the benefit of the crowd, but the overdone words thrilled me anyway.

He was looking pretty magnificent himself. I could clearly see the outline and bulk of his erection through his tight leather trousers, like a cylindrical column of concrete.

As if he couldn't help himself, he suddenly reached out and

trailed a finger lightly over one of my bare breasts. The sensation of his finger traveling over my erect nipple had me gasping with lust and indignation.

"No," I cried softly. "You promised . . . "

"I never promised you a thing," he replied in a low voice.

I tried to protect myself from him, curling away from him, clutching my ripped clothing, pulling the edges of tattered fabric back together over my nakedness, but he did not allow me to retreat. He gripped my shoulder and pinned me back down, holding me captive with the weight of his body on mine. Parting the remnants of my gown, he stared down at my bare breasts. Then he bent down to take one of them in his mouth, but seemed to remember himself in time and only just touched the full flesh with his breath. He appeared to be suckling me, but in reality he was only teasing me unmercifully.

I lay there panting, feeling so overcome with sensation I thought I might faint.

He sat up and with theatrical deliberation pulled off his own jacket and then the shirt beneath it, so that he was naked down to his hips. In the candlelight, the muscles of his arms and chest were carved and gleaming. The color of his skin was deep and rich, the texture of it like caramel, smooth and golden brown and buttery. And now that I was finally touching him, really touching him, I found that he felt as good as he looked. The striking proportions of his body had never been more apparent—the broad, well-defined shoulders, the slenderness of his waist, the hard ripples of muscle from his chest to his groin.

He leaned over me. "Now," he murmured in my ear as he

simulated kissing me and running his hands over my body, "as for the timing . . . the initial marriage act is not supposed to take very long, you know."

"Yes, I've noticed that," I replied, squirming, trying to keep my voice down so that only he could hear me. "Your brothers mostly had that down."

I caught the quick grin. "The idea is," he whispered, "we're so mad about each other we just can't wait to consummate the union and become one—"

"Yeah, I get it. And we're not inhibited in the least, though we're surrounded by our friends, relatives, and neighbors, who are happily judging our performance."

"Right. No performance problems at all. Just make it snappy."

We were smiling at each other now. "Bodes well for the crops," I said.

"There you have it. Virility equals fertility. Oh, and we gotta look like we're lovin' it."

"Well, how are we ever going to convince them of that?"

"Shouldn't be difficult."

"No, I suppose not. When Harry met Sally . . . "

"What?"

"Never mind."

"Oh," he said. "You mean that movie where the girl shows the guy how easily she can fake it?"

"Yeah."

"So is that what you've been doing?" he asked. "Have you been faking it, with me?"

"Faking what? This whole production is fake," I hissed.

He laid his fingers on my mouth to hush me. "Don't tell me you haven't liked what I've been doing to you," he whispered.

"Me? You're the one who—" I blushed.

"Yeah, well, it's obvious you've got *me* worked up, as I can hardly deny it, can I? But I can assure you, it is nothing more than a mechanical response to friction."

"I see." For some reason, his dispassionate words, uttered in the midst of this strange, sensual setting, stung me to the quick. "All right, then," I said. "Let's cut to the chase."

"So you are ready for the grand finale of this *production*?"

"Give the people what they want. Are we going to get a glimpse of the family jewels?"

He was already fumbling with his trousers as if to open them, but he shook his head in answer to my question. "No, baby. In keeping with the spirit of the occasion, I'm afraid you only get the understudy, not the star." He reached down below the mattress and came up with a large cucumber in his hand. He held it for me to see, low down, so it would not show up for the audience. "What do you think?"

"Wow. You have the most well-endowed pickle of all the men I have ever known."

We both had to smother giggles.

"Lay down," I commanded.

"What?" He looked surprised.

I had decided to turn the tables. I was the aggressor now, sliding up to my knees and pushing *him* back down on the mattress. I grinned at his startled expression.

I grasped one end of the cucumber and let it rise over Yeshi's groin so the crowd could see it in silhouette through the curtain.

A wave of applause followed the exposure of this awesome spectacle. I slid into place beside him and played with the cucumber, tickling the tip of it with my fingers.

Yeshi let out a big breath.

I bent over him and began to work the cucumber with my mouth and tongue. I glanced down at Yeshi to see him watching me with large, amazed eyes.

Though it wasn't his real cock I sucked and licked, he seemed to be responding as if it were. Of course, he was acting. He groaned as if in pain, and began to move his hips in rhythm to my efforts. I encircled the cucumber with my fingers and moved my hands up and down as I took it more deeply into my mouth. To keep it looking real, I had to hold it against his crotch, between his thighs and the generous pouch of his genitals, and I was happy to torture him with this necessary additional "friction." Through his trousers, which he had only pretended to open for the benefit of the crowd, I saw the incredible bulge of his real cock, looking nearly as impressive in length and girth as the cucumber, straining so hard against the leather I feared he must be in pain.

This was the first time I had performed fellatio for the benefit of the people of the village during one of these wedding ceremonies. Judging from the enthusiastic response, the audience approved.

And I seemed to be making Yeshi completely crazy. I reminded myself it was all an act. Finally he grabbed the cucumber and pulled it out of my grasp, holding it so it still looked like he was really attached to it, and he raised himself up and pushed me down on the bed. He mounted me then, the cucumber cock jutting out over me.

Grasping it in his fist, he began to nudge me with it, rubbing it against my thighs, pushing it deeper between my legs, using his knees at the same time to force my legs open. He leaned down as if to run kisses over my breasts, my neck, my cheeks—though never actually touching me with his lips. It was insane.

I couldn't help it—I opened my legs to him, and the cool tip of the cucumber ran almost imperceptibly over the slit of my cunt, which was protected only by the thin silk of my scant underclothing.

"You want it, don't you, baby?" he crooned at me, but loud enough for the crowd to hear.

The response from the audience was a resounding, "Yeah! Do it! Do it! Take her! *Fuck* her!" And they used other equally graphic terms, both in English and the local dialect. The words became part of the chant, which became part of the rhythm of our bodies and the way we were moving together.

Yeshi reached down between my legs and ripped my panties off. He stared down at my nakedness with a look of fascination.

He arched his beautiful body over mine and hesitated a moment. Then, with a mighty roar, he pretended to thrust himself deep inside of me, and I cried out with an obligatory sound of pleasure mixed with fear that was actually quite spontaneous and authentic.

He brought his head down as if kissing me as he pretended to ram his cock into me, and dropped his voice to a murmur. "So you haven't answered me, Diandra. *Do* you want it? *Do* you?"

He asked again, and I knew he was asking me if I wanted him to really fuck me with the mock penis. I hated him because, in that moment, I *did*. I wanted him to slam it into me as hard as he could and keep thrusting it until I came to a shattering orgasm. That's what I wanted. Only no—no, what I *really* wanted was for him to throw away the silly vegetable and fill me with his real, live, warm cock.

I wanted *real* kisses and caresses. *His* kisses and caresses. I wanted real sex. With him. I wanted actual orgasms, not faked. That's what I wanted. And here he was, practically threatening me, because he knew I was vulnerable, and I felt suddenly awful and like a captive, and tears began to fill my eyes, so many tears I couldn't hold them back, and they began to spill over onto my checks and wet my eyelashes.

He had closed his eyes and continued the fake fucking for a few more strokes. When he opened his eyes and glanced down at my face again and saw my crushed expression and my tears, he stopped immediately, and the faltering concern in his body translated just fine into the crowd's perception of what was happening in our mock mating. It must have appeared that he had suddenly come to orgasm, ejaculated, and the thrusting was finished. He slid off me but lay close beside me.

He did not ask me what was wrong. We lay there for a while, not saying anything more.

The chanting of the crowd had reached its crescendo with our climax, and now it was gradually ebbing away. We heard the people laughing and joking as they slowly filed out of the amphitheatre.

At last, we sat up, gathered up our things and dressed. The women were just outside, waiting to assist me when I was ready.

"They're going to take you to my suite for the night," Yeshi said quietly to me.

I nodded. I knew how it worked. I was *experienced*.

"Go ahead and make yourself at home," he said in a businesslike way. "I'll find some discreet quarters so you don't have to worry about me invading your space."

"Thank you," I said tightly. I supposed "discreet quarters" meant he would go to his lover. Not for the first time, I felt pierced by painful curiosity. *Who the hell* was *she?*

The feelings that sprang up in me when I allowed these kinds of thoughts were not feelings I enjoyed, so I tried to push them away.

"Good night, then," I said.

He suddenly reached up and thumbed away one remaining tear from the corner of my eyes.

"Sleep well, Diandra," he said softly.

Shani met me behind the stage. She slipped a veil around my shoulders.

"Well, then," she said like a concerned mother. "How did it go? Are you all right?"

"Yeah." In her ear I whispered, "Were we convincing?"

"Very much so," she murmured, looking at me speculatively. "You *did* keep to your plan?"

I hesitated. Technically, the truth could get me kicked out of the valley. But Shani wouldn't use the truth against me. She was on *my* side.

She was looked at me compassionately, her eyes full of concern.

I nodded. "Please don't tell anyone," I said.

Chapter 18

❧

Good! I thought savagely. *That's* over.

I lay in my bed before dawn the next morning. I could not stop thinking about my mock wedding night with Yeshi. All night long I dreamed of the way Yeshi's body had felt against mine. The way his hands and mouth had pretended to play all over me.

I assured myself I would be more than happy to get back to my other husbands, to pick up where we'd left off weeks ago, each brother taking turns with me for sex. I couldn't remember whose night it was or would be tonight, but I didn't care. Whichever one of them it was, *he* would satisfy this raging sensual hunger in me.

But when I actually thought about having sex with Gazer, or Hama, or Rafe, I couldn't drum up the anticipation I wanted or expected to feel. I just wanted to keep thinking of Yeshi. The look of him, always changeable, surprising me with his beauty, the lines of his body so appealing. The sound of his voice, the cadences of his speech. The scent of him, so subtle, something I caught only when I was very close to him. The moods he slipped through—his seriousness, his boyishness, his humor. I wanted more.

He fascinated me. And what we'd done together the night before had affected me even more deeply than I feared it might. My feelings for this man seemed to be expanding exponentially. I felt restless and uneasy, wondering what I would do with these emotions, knowing how set against me he was. Because of his well-expressed dislike, it annoyed me to be so attracted to him, and I knew I would have to work very hard not to let him know how drawn to him I really was.

The difficulty of this was put to the test at breakfast, when we had to sit side by side at the family table and endure the smiles and jokes of the other family members. The benches were crowded with Yeshi's brothers, as well as some other friends and relatives who had spent the night after the wedding feast.

I was so aware of Yeshi, I could hardly hold my spoon. We weren't expected to mind being crushed together as the men flanking us playfully pushed against us, forcing us to touch, and our bodies seemed to shudder involuntarily at the contact. Awkwardly, I tried commanding my muscles to relax, as my natural reaction was to tense up. I wished I could be anywhere but there.

And yet I loved the touch of him, the feel of his warmth. I simply basked in it a moment before reminding myself to keep my cool. He mustn't know he had any power over me.

I just needed to have sex with one of my other husbands,

I thought. As soon as possible! Anything to get my mind off Yeshi.

I looked up and saw Gazer staring at me across the table.

Yes, Gazer! He would do it for me. He would wipe Yeshi out of my mind. I hoped it would be Gazer tonight. Hell, Gazer wouldn't wait until nightfall.

Rafe strode into the hall then, and I realized I hadn't even registered the fact that he wasn't already there. Any of my other husbands might have been missing and I wouldn't have given it a thought—as long as Yeshi was there to hold my attention.

"Brothers and friends!" Rafe cried out, lifting his hand to still the chatter in the room. "We welcome the newly wedded Yeshi and Diandra, and we join together in wishing them long life and rich fecundity! And, judging from the performance last night, the latter should *not* be a problem."

This was greeted by an enthusiastic chorus of approval and applause from the room. Something burned in me as I sat beside Yeshi, feeling his stillness in response to the crowd's playful fun. I hoped our family members, friends, and neighbors would not notice that something wasn't quite right between the newly married couple. That we weren't quite as easy and friendly with each other as might be expected after such a passionate joining the night before.

Then Rafe went on to say something that took the focus off Yeshi and me entirely.

"And since I've got you all assembled here, I would like to make an announcement." His voice boomed out over the big room. "Riders have returned from the west. We have green grass in the high country!"

An excited murmuring broke out among the crowd. I almost didn't hear the rest of what Rafe had to say.

"So early this year!" someone said, amazed.

"No doubt we owe our thanks to the virility of the Rulan brothers and their nubile young bride," someone else cried out, and the tankards were lifted with cries of excitement.

"Drink up, eat, and get ready, then!" Rafe exclaimed. "We move out to meet the herds this afternoon."

As he walked past us on his way down to the end of the table, Rafe stopped briefly, rested his hands on Yeshi's shoulder and said to me, "So you'll have extra honeymoon time, looks like." Then he winked at his brother.

The wedding breakfast did not spin out slowly in the leisurely fashion of those other mornings after. The party broke up shortly after Rafe's announcement. Yeshi seemed glad to have an excuse to get away from me.

I had no idea what Rafe meant by his honeymoon comment. And I had only a vague notion of what his announcement of green grass in the high country meant, but the sudden excitement in the room afterward was palpable.

Though it was already high summer in the valley, in the mountains it was just turning spring. Apparently there was a half-wild creature—goat or antelope, I couldn't quite determine from what people told me—that appeared in the meadows of the high country each spring. The animals were nearly extinct and their fine soft wool was prized and fetched a princely sum in the outside world. This was the main source of income for the people of the valley. But the creature was elusive and skittish and difficult to manage. In between planting and harvest time in the valley, some of the people temporarily migrated to the high country in support of the effort required to procure the animals' fleece.

Soon the whole village was buzzing with the news of the "green grass." I began to understand that most of the men of the village—including my husbands—were to leave immediately for the high meadows and would not be back for days or even weeks.

I watched with dismay as my husbands quickly mobilized, put their packs together, and instructed the porters to load their horses. As always, the ritual surrounding the packing of the animals was arcane and careful. I still found it funny and intriguing, but I was beginning to realize the importance of packing the right equipment for their journeys, that it was a key to survival.

"I wish you didn't all have to run off," I grumbled to Hama as he was preparing his load. Gazer and Rafe had gone off to round up the horses scattered in the pasture behind the farm.

Hama stopped what he was doing for a moment and looked at me darkly. "If it were my day to provide my husbandly duties, Diandra, I would take a little time out from our preparations to renew the affections I have not been able to show you since . . . since my youngest brother came home from abroad."

He looked at me as if hoping I would to encourage him to walk on the wild side and urge him to break the rules. We both knew he was capable of it. But I simply gave him a hug and wished him well. For a moment he looked as though he was wrestling with something in himself. I thought he would try to press for a quickie. But he didn't have a chance. There was too much going on; someone called to him and he went off, distracted.

I saw Gazer in the courtyard with the horses they had just brought in. He was having trouble, and I wandered over to see if I could help. His horse was jumpy, as he hadn't ridden her in a while. He tied the mare to his packhorse and lashed them to a post, then motioned for me to follow him, which I did, my heart beating in my throat. He had my hand tight in his, and I had a feeling he was determined to fuck me before he was off. Hama wanted to, but Gazer really would. He had held off for so long, and now he had his chance. Because Yeshi and I were official.

We went around the corner of the building to find some privacy and stopped in a secluded corner. He was taking me into his arms hungrily, roughly, his face like a file, unshaven, his tongue pushing into my mouth. With one hand he squeezed my breasts while he smashed his groin between my thighs, pressing me against him with his other hand on my ass. I felt his fingers digging down between my legs, and then he had his cock out and he was trying to get into my cunt somehow but was too wildly eager and couldn't manage it through the layers of clothing.

His penis was raging hard, so stiff it that it was curved like a scimitar and so full of pumping blood it was almost purple. He was grasping it down by his balls, stroking the shaft a little as he tried to force it into me somehow, panting and determined.

He grabbed my hand, pulled it against his leg and closed my fingers around his cock. I felt the hard bone beneath the velvet glove.

"No, wait," he said hoarsely. "I will just come all over you in a second if you do that. And you don't want that to happen. You want this big prick, don't you? You want it shoved up inside you, don't you? You like me to fill you up with my meat. In your mouth, your cunt, your ass. You like me to ram it into you really hard, don't you, you sweet thing? You like to suck it too, don't you? And you like it when I suck *you*. When I suck your tits, your clit. Everything. Everything I suck, you like. You like my mouth on you everywhere, just sucking. And you like to have me fill you with everything I've got. My fingers, my cock, my tongue. You like me to fuck you in every hole. And I am happy to do it."

As he murmured these words of endearment, his lips wet against my ear, he was fumbling along with his fingers on each of the ties of my dress. He very nearly had them undone.

"I am very happy to do it," he repeated. "Because I am tired of fucking my own hand every night, thinking of you. Only thinking of you, ha ha. Ah, the sea of nectar I have spouted for you, sweet girl. But right now, right here, I'm doing it my favorite way. I am going to pour it into you and all over you, and lick it, taste it mixed it with my own sweat and your juices—"

A loud screaming neigh pierced the air.

"Shit," Gazer groaned. "That sorry horse. Damn. I gotta go." He stood next to me with his hand around his hard penis and began to rub it against the bit of my leg he had been able to expose.

I felt the blunt, insistent stump moving in a frantic rhythm against the smooth flesh of my inner thigh. Then he held it away from me a moment and briskly ran his hand up and down the shaft, his eyes half closed. It was as if he was in a hurry and just wanted to come. At that point he had no need of my body anymore. But when he was about to ejaculate, he poked his erection through my clothes and held it against my thigh, stroking my skin with the silky tip of his cock, and I felt the warm sticky liquid.

He finished off with a shudder, shoved himself back into his pants, and kissed me hard on the cheek.

"See you soon—I hope! As soon as I can, anyway. Goodbye!"

As he ran off to his horses, I stood there in the secluded corner of the building, feeling torn and ashamed and sticky wet on my thighs. I felt so foolish, and so confused. I felt like I had just betrayed the man I really cared for by lending my body to another.

And yet the man I really cared for wanted nothing to do with me.

I followed Gazer out into the courtyard and met Hama and Gaja walking toward the stable. My sister-in-law was dressed for travel, with her own pack. She allowed a porter to take it from her, and he began to ready her horse as she looked on.

"But if *she's* going—" I turned to Hama. "I thought it was only men who were going. Am I to go too?" I suddenly liked the idea very much.

"Of course not," Hama said severely. "Women remain home to tend the affairs here. Except for the eldest unmarried sister, who traditionally accompanies her brothers, to tend to *their* needs."

"Hmm, that's some arrangement," I murmured, scowling. "And I can't go? But what will I do? Am I to be left alone?"

"No, indeed." He laughed at my expression. "You will not be alone. By custom, the youngest brother must stay on with the wife; together you will take care of the farm and household. You will not be here by yourself. You will be with Yeshi."

Chapter 19

This was awful! I couldn't believe what was happening. I would be practically alone in this godforsaken place—alone with Yeshi!

In a matter of hours the entire village had been drained of most of its men and a good number of its women too. My husbands, the ones who truly cared for me, were gone. Our hired hands had gone with them. My best advocate in this strange Shangri-la, Shani, was also gone, for as the eldest unmarried sister in her family, she had accompanied her brothers.

I would even miss the companionship of Gaja, though it was true I sometimes felt like she spent too much time skulking around, giving me the evil eye. Even our maid Tara was gone. Her own family needed her on their farm because of the labor loss of her brothers and her older sister.

The place seemed very quiet in its newly acquired solitude. The wind ruffled the air, stirring the leaves. The first night after the exodus, I slept fitfully, having dozed off on the low divan by the fireplace in the common room. None of my husband's quarters seemed to fit me, and my own room was dark and hot. I woke several times in the night, agitated with conflicting, sensual dreams. Was it the sudden departure of my other husbands that bothered me, I began to wonder, or the fact that I had been left alone with Yeshi?

How would I endure this time alone with him?

It was clear that with only the two of us to attend the farm, there would be more to accomplish than we had hours in the day to do it. It was never more obvious that we had to put our differences aside for a common purpose. And between us now was the strange, ill-conceived marriage ritual we had staged, making everything even more awkward.

When I woke up the next day, it was indeed awkward, and for most of the morning we were more silent than usual. But soon enough our old patterns of relating came up. After letting slide a couple of opportunities to hit me with a cutting remark, he said something sarcastic about my fumbling hands when I dropped a bag of feed, spilling the precious grain over the floor of the barn.

Nothing new, I thought. Besides, I deserved it. And he was just joking. In another context, another emotional milieu, his remark might have been taken as playful. Any good friend could have said the same thing with impunity. But his teasing words cut deeper than usual. Instead of returning them with my own wicked backhand, I felt like crying.

But of course I didn't cry. I let one fly back at him as expected, feeling his subtle wince of response in my own body, and I was suddenly aware of a deep loneliness, familiar and bewildering.

And I felt the lack of him physically, imprinted as I had been on the night of our mock marriage with the hot, powerful presence of him, heavy and rhythmic, simulating sex.

"*Diandra?*" I heard his voice. It was past nightfall.

He poked his head into my room, looking for me. I was sitting in my favorite chair, a neat pile of mending at my feet. I was almost finished with my work.

"Ah, *there* you are." He sounded happy to have found me. "Are you hungry?" A lock of dark hair fell over his upturned eyes. There was no denying his beauty, with those catlike eyes and that curvaceous, sensual mouth; while at the same time he struck me as incredibly masculine, with his broad shoulders, powerful neck, and the obvious endowment between his thighs, so tantalizingly evident when he wore his faded denim jeans. The combination of his sexy, commanding masculinity and charming, youthful sweetness turned me inside out.

What was he asking me? *Are you hungry?* Oh yes.

"I warmed up that soup for you," I said. "It's on the hearth."

"Are you going to join me?"

"I'm okay," I said. "I'll eat in a bit."

I bent my head over my needle and thread and wouldn't look up at him again. I felt a long moment pass as he stood motionless in the doorway. Then I glanced up and he was gone.

I took a deep breath and let it out, frustrated. What was the matter with me? I didn't play pouting games with men. But even though I wanted nothing more than to follow him out to the common room, just to be near him, I stayed where I was.

I felt unhappy and vaguely guilty, and dirty.

So much at the mercy of my own body! So unclear about what I should be doing anymore. Things were feeling way more complicated than they should have been. I was no longer convinced that the life I was living could be justified by my goals and desires.

Chapter 20

With all the manpower of the farm suddenly gone, the work that fell to the two of us demanded our constant devotion from dawn past nightfall. Yeshi and I were in each other's company for hours every day, and I found many old notions of myself turned upside down.

When we worked together, I was necessarily subordinate to him because he generally knew what to do and I did not. So he would instruct me, as politely and kindly as he possibly could. I took the position that I was there to serve and so I jumped to carry out anything he asked of me. I realized I was trying, probably too hard, to impress him.

Maybe I ended up impressing myself a little. We did work hard. Much of what we did was quite physical, sometimes even dangerous. I made mistakes and screwed up. When I tried to apologize, he would say something like, "No, that's my fault. I didn't explain it well enough."

He could be sarcastic and cutting, but he was also quick to appreciate and praise. He was open to my suggestions and questions, and I felt myself glowing when he admired an idea I might offer.

It seemed the animosity between us was gone, or at least put on some back burner.

After that first day we spent on the farm alone, no more spiteful comments passed between us. Respect and deference replaced the bitterness. Ever since the night of our mock marriage, we could no longer maintain the fierce denial of attraction between us. We both knew better.

But while *I* would have been happy to move into a new closeness with Yeshi, he seemed doubly determined to maintain the distance between us. And this new kindness with which he treated me was more a barrier to the passion simmering beneath the surface than the antagonism had been before. At least *then* he had taken the opportunity to touch me whenever he could. I began to think wistfully of the days when he dug his fingers into my flesh while clenching as his teeth in barely controlled anger.

*O*ne afternoon we rode out together into the hills to keep the ponies in condition. I loved the feel of the rounded body of the horse beneath me, spreading my legs, requiring my thighs to grip the moving, breathing being. I loved the wind against my cheeks, blowing through my hair.

Most of all I loved being with Yeshi. I liked the way he saw the world, the things he commented on, his humor. He questioned the things I said to him, responded in ways that made me know he was listening to me. I adored his childlike expressions, and was moved by his fierce male strength. I loved his lean, muscular body with its long torso and full thighs. I loved the compact muscles of his broad, strong shoulders, and I loved the sheer plane of his stomach. I loved his body. But even more, I loved the way he moved in that body. He had a muscular, prancing energy, like the spirited horse he rode, and with the wind whipping his dark straight hair around his animated face, he looked like an illustration in a book for some beautiful young deity.

He was riding his horse bareback that day, effortlessly clinging to his mount with leather-clad legs. The horses were excited, hard to restrain, and soon we were cantering together along the ridge above the farm. The exhilaration I felt was like a drug in my blood. As we reached the mesa and let the horses run full-out, I leaned forward and hung on tight. I wanted that plain to go on and on forever.

If I couldn't have Yeshi in the flesh, I thought, then let this moment never end—flying along together, side by side—

He surprised me when he suddenly turned away from the broad, open expanse of land where we'd been riding and moved into a grove of trees near a jumble of boulders just to the east. I followed, and we threaded our way into the woods on the bank of a stream and came to an outcropping of stone where a small waterfall fell into a tiny, luminous pool. There, we jumped down from our horses and let them drink.

"By the end of the dry season, this pond will completely disappear," Yeshi said. "When we come back here then, you'll be able to see the stone formations that are now hidden beneath the surface of the water." He tossed a pebble into the pool and we watched the ripples race across the surface of the water.

When we come back here then . . . So he was thinking of us being together . . . in the future? Until that moment, he had always talked as if he assumed I should soon be leaving the valley—because everyone knew I didn't belong there.

He took the canteen from his pack, slipped the cup from its top and scooped up some of the fresh water. He held it out for me to drink.

I was touched by the sweetness of the gesture. The water tasted sweet and cold.

I handed the cup back when I'd had enough. He took a drink himself, smiled at me, and brushed a drop of water off my lip with his thumb.

Why was the slightest touch enough to send me into uncontrollable shivers?

Probably because he almost *never* touched me anymore. And it had been weeks now since I'd had a man. Any man. Not counting my wedding night display with Yeshi, or the strange fumbling moments when Gazer masturbated against me before he left for the high country.

I was just sex-starved. It was only sex that I needed. Having gotten used to having so much of it, it seemed I was going through withdrawal.

Ha, quit lying to yourself!

I knew damned well what was going on here. It wasn't just sex, it was Yeshi.

I loved his touch, meager or otherwise. I loved feeling that current zap between us, because zap it did. I loved hearing his voice, just the sound of it when he laughed at my appreciation of the water. I loved . . .

I loved . . .

Okay, I thought. *Shit*. Why not just admit it?

I loved *him*.

I loved Yeshi.

$\mathscr{I}$ don't know how it happened, but one moment we were standing quietly by the side of the pool, and the next we were shoving at each other, laughing, joking about pushing each other in.

"Be careful," I said. "I'll really do it."

"Like hell you will."

I gave him a good, serious push. He teetered, with a look of surprise and then a huge grin on his face. But he recovered nimbly, regained his balance on the rock, and suddenly swooped down on me, picked me up, and tossed *me* into the drink.

The water was shockingly cold. I gasped when I popped up through the surface and tried to swear at him. "I don't know how to swim!" I cried dramatically instead, when I caught my breath, and sank, blowing bubbles.

I heard the splash and felt the waves in the pond as he dove in, and then he was beside me in the water, and I was aware of the strength in his arms as he pulled me close, his face close to mine, his silky hair dripping. He lifted me up out of the water a little, and I was laughing.

"Just kidding," I said. "I really do know how to swim."

"I knew that."

He was standing on a rock beneath the water, and I was floating in his arms. To avoid looking at him, I tucked my head into the crook of his neck and shoulder, my lips braising his wet skin, hoping he didn't notice. I felt ripped. Torn between the impulse to lean into him, pull him against me, and the impulse to swim away with a flick of my tail like a bashful mermaid.

The mermaid won out. I arched my back and brushed myself against his body as I slipped from his embrace and swam away from him. My wet clothing dragged a little, but my body slid through the water, humming; his cock had felt as hard and unforgiving as the rock spires growing up out of the water—blunt stone.

Am I crazy? I wondered. He had been holding me in his arms! And somehow I eluded his grasp. Why? Why had I done that? Why would I run—or swim—from something I wanted so badly?

His face had been inches from mine, his lips so close . . . I sensed his weakening. His body had been trembling. It wasn't just my own body I had felt, so charged with energy I could hardly stand it. He was there with me. I knew it. I could have moved into position, and I could have *had* him. Checkmate.

Yeshi swam after me, pursuing me, but I was up and out of the water in a flash. Hurrying, dripping in my clothes, I walked back to the horses. I turned to see him rising out of the pond, his clothes wet and clinging to his skin. His hair was dark and wet against his well-formed head. That beautiful head, and his body, revealed by the drenched clothing he wore, sent me into shivers. Everything about him. Not just the sight of that enormous log-shaped bulge that lay beneath his wet trousers alongside one of his thighs.

He was staring at me, and was enjoying the same enhanced sight of *my* body too, I think, my thin summer cottons clinging to my belly, to my thighs and my breasts, my cold nipples erect and prominently displayed.

He walked toward me, not attempting to hide the enormity of his arousal. And I was torn between the impulse to cover myself with my arms, to hide myself from his hungry gaze, and the equally strong impulse I felt to peel off my wet clothes, slowly, sensually, just to let him feast his eyes on my bare body. Feast his eyes . . . and simply *feast* . . .

I turned away as he came closer and tried to mount my horse, but here in the woods there was no block for me to step up on and I had trouble getting up on the horse's high back. I felt Yeshi behind me, felt his hands warm on my hips, the strength of his arms easily lifting me. And I felt something hesitant in his touch as I settled onto the horse's back, as if he might be debating whether to drag me down instead of helping me up. His hands lingered on me before falling away.

We rode home silently, and I knew we must make love. We must. It was all I could think about.

So why had I run from him?

Chapter 21

"Diandra, can you help me?"

He appeared the next afternoon in the open doorway to my room, his warm skin shining with sweat as if he'd been running, locks of his long dark hair starting to come out of the patterned head scarf he'd tied on to keep his hair out of his face.

"Sure," I said. "What's up?"

"You might want to put on your jeans and boots. The grain silo needs shoring up. It's kind of a dirty job and I wouldn't ask you, ordinarily, but there's no one else here to ask."

"No problem."

I quickly dressed and soon we were walking together up the road to the cluster of farm buildings beyond the domestic compound.

Where the path narrowed, our shoulders brushed and bumped. I was mortified when he shrank away from me like a sea anemone dabbed with a stick. Already the sultry encounter in the pool yesterday seemed remote, something out of the past. A sort of aberration.

"See, there was some erosion from the last rains and the footing has come loose," he told me when we reached the silo. He pointed out the problem and showed me what had to be done. He had already put up a temporary support.

"Wow," I said. "If we'd let this go any longer we might have lost the whole thing."

"Yeah. That's why I try to inspect things regularly. I should have caught this before now."

"Well, but you were away. Rafe should have been on top of it. Or Gazer—"

"We are all responsible for the farm. And except for Gazer, we have all been abroad at one time or another."

"Bu you've been gone quite a while, haven't you?"

"Two years, this time."

"Oxford, right? History. Gaja mentioned it—"

"No. Not this time. More recently I was at UC Berkeley, studying engineering."

"Berkeley. That's almost *my* neck of the woods."

"Right. You were across the bay. At Stanford."

"Yeah. That's where I got all my silo-repair training."

He laughed. "I thought I could expect some Ivy League work from you."

"All right," I said. "What do we do?"

We went to work, Yeshi explaining the process each step of the way.

I was always surprised and impressed by the skills he possessed. I loved that he was a scholar, an educated man, but I was even more impressed by the workman in him, the practical, hardworking mountain man. The carpenter and the mason. He seemed young to have such an assuredness in abilities that could have only come from experience.

Even without the unrequited lust about to boil over, there would have been something gritty and animalistic about the two of us that afternoon, working hard in tandem, our skin slicked over with perspiration, sweat dampening our hair, our bodies revved up and hot. I could hear it in both of us, the breathing coming harder. It radiated, the sheer joy of being alive and charged with energy. As he lifted a thick length of lumber or hoisted heavy stones for the foundation of the silo, I would thrill to hear his occasional passionate groan, his deep grunt of exertion.

Like the sounds of sex, I thought.

I reminded myself to keep my eyes on the task at hand, but my gaze kept wandering over to the man beside me, who had stripped off his coat and was down to his jeans and a cambric work shirt. The worn blue fabric draped from his broad, slender shoulders down over the long, lean line of his torso to his narrow childish hips. His arms were a deep cinnamon-stick brown, the boxy, slender muscles full and flexed and graceful. His thighs and calves were well-muscled and filled out the faded jeans that jammed up into the tops of his big, high boots.

I felt his eyes on me too, on the clothing I wore that was so similar to his—jeans and a button-down shirt, work boots—but fitting me so differently than his clothes fit him. I could practically feel it physically when his attention moved over me, his gaze dropping from my eyes to my lips, moving down over my throat, lingering on and caressing the rounded swell of my breasts as if his hands were actually roaming over the thin, damp fabric of my shirt. But he didn't need to touch me to tease up my nipples—he could do it with only a lick of his gaze.

My own attention moved all over him too, my eyes flickering down over his belt, drawn inexorably to the heavy pouch between his legs, so tantalizingly full, the shape of his fire-hose column of cock just visible beneath the rough denim.

But it was our eyes that met most.

As he slowly walked past me, he turned his head to keep looking at me.

It was getting dark, and we were almost finished with our work. I glanced up and our eyes clashed. He was staring at me, looking into me deeply. He paused, and it seemed we both suddenly forgot what we were doing.

"Watch that—" I cried out a warning, and he turned to see that he'd almost run a beam into his eye.

"Damn." He swore and laughed at himself. "I'm fucking bewitched!"

Turning away, I had to catch my breath. Why did he look at me that way?

He feels the same way I do, I thought. He must.

Forget it, I told myself. *You're imagining things.*

If he truly wanted me, he would say so. He would do something about it.

So are you glad to be back from your travels?" I asked him.

We sat together beneath a tree, gazing at the silo, which was now sporting a new underpinning. We were sitting so close our legs brushed when one of us moved. I was always astonished at how Yeshi stirred me. I longed to lean into him, to feel him gather me into his arms. And yet the thought that he might withdraw from me, to avoid touching me, filled me with humiliation.

"Am I glad to be back *here*, in the valley?" He considered the question, nodded. "Sure. It's my home. I always like coming back. I love seeing my sister and my brothers. But I like California. A lot. Especially northern California, the Bay area."

"Yeah . . . it's beautiful there."

"Do you miss it?" he asked me.

My turn to consider the question. "Sometimes. I do miss having the ocean nearby."

He seemed to be pondering something. "That whole area is gorgeous," he said. "Fantastic culture. The weather is great." He looked at me, his expression veiled now. "Did you know that here, during certain times of the year, you can't leave the valley? For months at a time? Because the pass gets snowed in. The route becomes impassable."

I shifted uncomfortably. Actually, *I hadn't* known that. But it was his tone that startled me. Suddenly so hostile. Sneering, almost.

"What are you saying, Yeshi?" I asked him.

"What am I *saying*?" A short, bitter laugh. "I'm not saying anything you're not hearing, Diandra."

"And nothing I haven't heard before, from you. You don't think I should be here at all."

He seemed to need a moment, then, to catch his breath. "Well, you know," he said, "I do have to wonder just what the hell it is you're doing here. In this godforsaken place. Where you don't belong."

"I know you think I don't even have a *chance* of making it here. So I don't know why you're even worried about it."

"I'm not worried about it. Some of us have a wager going, you know, as to when you're gonna bail. I've already lost."

I cast about for some sharp, witty comeback. But all I could think about was that he still wanted me to go. Once upon a time I had felt defiant when he said things like this to me. I had felt like, *Fuck you.* As long as the others wanted me to stay, I would stay. Now, I was surprised to find I just wanted to give up and run away.

Maybe he was right. Maybe this had never been a good idea.

And you know what? The thought suddenly came to me. *I should go. I* would. *I would leave.* It was time.

I didn't belong there.

Even if, at times, I felt I might never want to leave.

Even if sometimes I felt like I could be perfectly content, happily ever after, just living in that valley, in that strange Shangri-la.

I could be perfectly happy. If *he* lived there with me.

If Yeshi were mine.

But that's not what *he* wanted. So how could I be happy?

I swallowed back the emotion, the urge to cry. "So how long have I got?" I asked in a quiet voice, staring down at the ground.

"What?" His voice was sharp. I didn't look up at him.

"When does the pass get snowed in?" I asked.

"Why?" His tone had changed yet again. An attempt at light-heartedness. "You're not actually suddenly planning on *leaving*," he said drolly.

I felt his hand on my cheek.

"Are you?"

With his fingers on my chin, he turned my face so I had to look at him. He seemed astonished and bewildered to see the tears.

"*Are* you, Diandra?" he demanded.

"Well, that's what you've wanted all along, right?" I demanded, easing away from his touch. "Isn't that what you want? For me to go? And I'm suddenly thinking, yes, maybe I should. I'm not sure I can handle all this so well anymore."

"Hey, look," he said, "I'm sorry about the hard labor stuff, Diandra. If I'd had anyone else to ask for help—"

"I'm not talking about the *work*, Yeshi!" I snapped at him. "I don't mind the work. I *like* the work."

"Then why are you crying?" he asked wonderingly, thumbing a tear off my cheek. His slightest touch felt like a brand, and I expected the tears to sizzle on my skin.

"Because . . . because I don't *want* to leave," I said. "But I'm beginning to think I *have* to . . . "

"Hey. Come on. Don't do that."

His hands fumbled awkwardly as he brought me against him, his arms suddenly warm around me. He seemed to be offering a protective, brotherly affection. But the sensation of solid muscle beneath his shirt when my hands made contact with his belly had me letting out a sound that was almost embarrassing. I felt overpowered by the sensual phenomenon of him—the combination of the sound of his voice, the sight of his body in motion, how it was always changing. The touch of his hands, how they were sometimes rough on me, sometimes so terribly gentle. The warmth of his arms, the delicious male scent of him. I wanted to lick his skin, to drink him in, to quench my thirst and assuage my hunger for him. I could hear him, I could see him, I could smell him, and at times I could even touch him, however fleetingly. I wanted to *taste* him too.

God help me, I'm so greedy.

I was just way too vulnerable.

The moment passed. A sense of self-preservation kicked in like a timed-release drug, the wild emotions he aroused in me taking on a desperation that I could only perceive as fear.

Fight or flight, I thought. And there was no way I could fight this.

I pulled away from him, jumped up and began running through the orchard, half fearing, half hoping I would hear his footsteps behind me.

I did.

Chapter 22

❧

He gained on me with ridiculous ease. I heard him closing the distance between us with a few easy strides, felt his hands on me, hauling me back from my head-on flight. Together we tumbled into a patch of long, thick grasses, his arms encircling me like a snare around a frightened rabbit.

I was tumbling into space, and he caught me, but he brought me down.

I wasn't hurt, only startled. I was on my back. He was on top of me.

He had me pinned to the ground. We were both panting.

He held me captive with his entire weight settling down on me. I felt him grinding himself deeper between my thighs, making me feel the hardness of him there, sending me into shivers of ecstasy when he pushed his stone hard cock against me, both of us fully clothed but feeling what it might be like if we weren't. I gasped again, arching and lifting my breasts to him almost involuntarily, offering my neck like a sacrifice. And like a wild animal bringing down prey, he claimed my throat. I felt his teeth teasing over the tender skin, and I felt the heat of his breath and the indescribable feather bliss of his lips. I shuddered and whimpered and writhed against him, rubbing myself against the hot column pushing between my legs as the touch of his mouth on my neck became a lingering, erotic kiss.

Kiss my mouth, I thought. *Oh, kiss me and then I'll know if you love me.* Love me. *Love.* The word kept going through my head, but not just in English. I was hearing in my mind a particular phrase the people of the valley sometimes used for love, in their dialect. Romantic love. Head over heels till death do us part kind of love. So different in character from the love of family or friends. In his language the word meant a deep heart connection infused with a powerful sexual connection. From the way I had heard people using the word, it was a kind of love that was revered but also suspect. That sort of love didn't happen often, and it was probably better that way. That sort of love was dangerous.

Love? Why was I thinking that word? In any language? I felt afraid and wildly happy at the same time. Were we to be lovers, finally? Was he throwing aside the vow he had made never to touch me in that way, never to make love with me? Never to be my husband?

My fourth husband. Dear God.

I think he was. He seemed to have lost control. I wanted his love but I had won him with sex. He sank his teeth into my neck, tempering the pain with his hot tongue and his lips sucking on the bruise. His hands were moving all over my body, his powerful thighs squeezing me possessively. The sensation of his mouth on my neck did something crazy inside me, opening me wider and yet spurring me on to resist him as if I feared for my life. Maybe I did. He had yet to kiss me on the lips.

Maybe if he didn't kiss me on the lips, on my mouth, we could pretend this had never happened.

As if reading my mind, he moved his mouth up over my throat and chin and cheek, and lingered there. His arms tightened around me, gently but inexorably. I felt the warmth of his breath on my skin. But still he didn't kiss my mouth.

"Let me go, Yeshi," I breathed. "Please."

He gave his head a shake, and his black hair moved like strands of silk curtaining his topaz eyes, which were keenly fixed on mine. He held me tighter and I squirmed, trying to get out of his grip. His sex surged against mine and I shuddered and cried out at the sublimity of the sensation.

My struggling seemed to make him even wilder, stronger, and more determined to possess me. Because now he was holding my arms so I could not resist him, and he was bringing his lips to meet mine, whether I liked it or not. Of course I liked it, but on some level I was still trying to escape the inevitable. I thrashed and shook my head from side to side. I knew if we kissed I would drown. I would be lost to him. And he would hate me for making him do this. This thing he had vowed he would never do.

But the pressure of his cock pushing up between my thighs was heating me up and melting me from the inside out. And melting flesh has no strength. I could not help but respond to him and welcome him even as I struggled against him.

My arms grew limp, no longer flexing, trying to push him away. My head lolled back and I gazed up at him. He gently cupped the back of my head with one hand, his fingers threaded through my hair, and gave me a searing look, agonized and wondering. He moved closer. Then our lips touched.

I felt his mouth, so light, sweeping and feathery, exploring my lips. Kissing my cheeks, my chin, my neck, and then my mouth again.

That's all, that's all, that's all, I told myself. *We can still end this.*

But I didn't want to.

Lips parting slightly; a touch of tongue. Tongues tentative, testing. I felt his body deepening into mine, all up and down the length of me.

My body was trembling, and I felt the tremors move through him too, the hunger of the kiss increasing. His tongue, delving deeper into my mouth. His body moving rhythmically against mine, moving in time with our heartbeats, our hands clasping, fingers entwining, hands squeezing, breaking apart to roam over each other's bodies. And this never-ending kiss.

I felt so in love it was like stars shooting off in my brain and body, stars shooting off into space. *This endless, endless kiss. Our first kiss. Our first* real *kiss . . .*

And perhaps our *only* real kiss, if he realized what he was doing and came to his senses, I thought. Or came out of his senses. It wouldn't be me who stopped this madness. I couldn't and I wouldn't and I didn't want to. But I knew that *he* didn't want to be doing this with me. He'd been dead set against it, and now he was doing it and I didn't know what would become of us.

And as I feared, I was drowning, drowning in a kiss that was eternal, blissful and deep and ravenous, sexual and penetrating

and violent with the male thrusts of his tongue into the dark softness of my mouth.

"Yeshi, please . . . " I tried to speak but my voice was a useless
whimper against the onslaught of his mouth on mine.

"What?" He was breathing hard. He didn't stop kissing me.
I felt his hands on my breasts now, silky and sensual, as he held
the weight of them, his fingers feeling for the nipples beneath the
cotton of my shirt. The touch of his hands on my breasts was like
nothing I had ever felt before, as if he had flipped a switch and
flooded my circuits with pulsing currents of bliss.

Deftly and sensuously he slipped his hand down the partially
unbuttoned front of my shirt and I felt the warmth of his fingers
on my bare skin, the pinch of his fingers gently closing on the
swollen nipple as he sucked my tongue.

My cunt was throbbing and the motion of his cock rubbing
against me through our clothing had me very close to orgasm. My
whole body moved in rhythm to the beat of his body and my own
deep, fast breathing.

"Hey-o!"

We both heard the voice at the same time and froze together,
a motionless lover's tableau. Our mouths slowly parted. Reluctantly.

"Yeshi! Is that you? Are you there?"

It was the voice of a man, coming from beyond the trees.
Someone looking for Yeshi, obviously.

And very close to stumbling upon the two of us, laying there
in the grass, fiendishly disheveled, if not quite completely naked.
Not that it would be so terrible, to be discovered this way. After
all, we were a married couple, right?

No, not a married *couple*, exactly—

I pushed that thought aside.

And not exactly married. Because technically we weren't, yet. In order for me to be legally and spiritually married to Yeshi, according to the laws and customs of this land, the union would have to be consummated. Which it hadn't been up until now. And apparently it wasn't going to be *now* either.

Agonizingly, I felt the sudden lack of his warmth and his weight as Yeshi slowly, unwillingly, with one last lingering grind, lifted himself off me just in time to greet the stranger who was striding along at a brisk pace, coming at us through the trees.

Lopsang was Yeshi's cousin, a merchant importer and a great bear of a man, vigorous, handsome, and friendly. Though he lived nearby and was invited to the wedding feasts of his cousins, he had been away on business and so, to his regret, missed them all.

"I *am* sorry I missed your wedding night," he said to Yeshi and me in English for the second or third time, after congratulating us once again very wholeheartedly. In the dialect of the valley, he added slyly to Yeshi, "*Doubly* sorry, now that I've seen the bride."

I pretended I didn't understand what he had just said. Even Yeshi did not realize that I understood more and more of his language, because my attempts to speak it with the people were so inept they would interrupt me with laughter. In any case, though I knew facility with language came about best through practice, I also knew, from my experiences in other unfamiliar lands, that I might learn something unusual about the culture I was studying when the people assumed I was ignorant of what they were saying to one another.

I couldn't decide whether I was grateful for Lopsang's appearance or aggrieved by his sudden intrusion. His presence had definitely and decidedly put an end to what surely would have happened between Yeshi and me. I had wanted it to happen so badly, but at the same time, if Yeshi were to regret becoming intimate with me and be resentful of me, *I* would regret it too. So Lopsang's appearance, I decided, had been a good thing.

If only the aching need I felt would cease as well.

*O*ver ale by the fire that night, the men talked about some business deal Lopsang was involved with. He was clearly rehashing a long-standing discussion with various players and past episodes. I was only half paying attention, daydreaming about Yeshi. Trying not to stare at him. Remembering, reliving, reimagining in my mind the moments that were like a slice of eternity when he was kissing me.

Lopsang was relating the most recent installment of his tale of business woe when the discussion suddenly turned to what constituted "honor" and "integrity" in personal and professional dealings. I found it rather charming, these two big guys earnestly discussing the concept of Honor as if they had been dubbed Knights of the Round Table.

"Mingma told me those shipments would be there in December." The room boomed with the hearty sound of Lopsang's passionate voice. "I said, 'Is that a promise?' And he said, 'Sure, it's a promise. It's right there in black and white and a handshake!'"

He reached out and touched Yeshi's knee for emphasis. "If a man gives his word—makes a promise, takes a vow—then damn it, I say he's not a man if he breaks his word! His promise! Or his vow! I am right?"

Yeshi was silent, staring into the fire.

"I say a man has got to live up to his word!" Lopsang exclaimed.

The subject of the conversation was beginning to make me uncomfortable. I wished Lopsang would just shut up about all this "man's word" stuff. It was almost like he knew Yeshi had vowed not to touch me and had been about to break that vow.

Yeshi had solemnly promised he would never make love to me—*ever*! It was like Lopsang was rubbing it in.

"I agree," Yeshi said absently.

I glanced at him uneasily. He looked so distant, so lost in thought. I knew these people of the valley had a very significant code of honor. Now that we had kissed, would Yeshi come to regret knowing me even more bitterly than before? Was he regretting it already?

Was he grateful we had been interrupted?

Or was he aching with need for me, like I was for him?

I wished Yeshi's cousin would leave, go away and leave Yeshi and me alone. But judging by the lateness of the hour and the amount of ale he was drinking, I knew Lopsang would be spending the night.

Chapter 23

The more deeply I became involved with this culture, the stranger it seemed to me. And yet at the same time the less strange it seemed. This contradiction confused me. And where, I asked myself, was my place in this odd world?

It came to me again that I had to get out of there.

The night after Lopsang paid us a visit, I stayed up even later than usual, writing in my field journal. I wrote painstakingly, struggling to translate my very personal experiences into professional-sounding text I could share with my academic colleagues. I didn't know how to present the facts of it without divulging more of my own participation than I felt comfortable sharing.

So absorbed was I in my musings and the attempt to put them down in coherent fashion, I had no idea Yeshi was standing behind me or for how long, looking over my shoulder at the pages of my journal.

"What the hell is this?" His voice was soft.

He startled me, and I nearly jumped straight up out of my seat and hit him in the chin. He reached around me and for a moment I thought he was going to take me in his arms but instead he seized my journal.

"Hey—" I tried to grab it out of his hand but he was too fast for me. "Put that down," I said. "That's no business of yours."

"Like hell it isn't."

I jumped to my feet, outraged, crossing the lapels of my dressing gown and cinching the belt tightly. "Give that back. Right now."

He ignored me, turning away, thumbing through the journal. "What a bunch of crap," he said, shaking his head. "Turning our lives into a fucking academic dissertation."

"Give me back my field notes," I said.

"Fuck your field notes." He flung my journal across the room. I watched it arc through the air; it smacked against the wall and landed on my bed.

"How dare you, Yeshi!" I cried. I felt incredibly violated. I was seething with anger at him for calling my work "a bunch of crap." I had never been so angry with anyone in my life.

"How dare *you*," he countered. "Writing like that, about what we have here." We faced one another like two rams about to charge.

"Get the hell out of my room!" I yelled, pushing at his chest with my open hands. Against his rocklike body, my efforts meant little. He closed his fingers around my wrists.

"Is that all we are to you?" He yanked me closer against his body. "Some experiment you're studying for your Ph.D.?"

With a shock of pleasure, I felt our bodies collide, and I let out a breath. He released my wrists and slid his arms around me, holding me tight, so tight I could hardly move, and I felt his breath hot on my ear. "Is that what I am to you? Some kind of lab rat?"

He held me close, but not like a lover. I wondered what he would do with me. But I wasn't waiting around to find out. As soon as my hands were freed I tried push against him and wiggle to escape his hold, but his grip on me only tightened and for a moment I couldn't move at all.

His breath came raggedly now, close to my ear again, as he quoted from my notes. " 'But the fourth brother shows marked antisocial behavior as evidenced by his continued refusal to consummate the marriage his eldest brother has sanctioned.' " Abruptly, he opened his arms and freed me.

"Get out of my room!" I shouted, like a sparrow chirping at a wolf.

"Your room!" He scoffed at me. "*Your* room. You have nothing here."

I felt the tears stinging my eyes and fought furiously to contain them. I would not cry in front of him. "Women in this society have equal property rights in marriage," I retorted. "This is my space. Now get out."

"Women have rights in marriage," he said. "But *you* are not married."

I caught my breath.

So. He was hammering it home to me once again. He had said he would not have me. That he would always refuse to make love to me, refuse to consummate the marriage as my fourth and final husband. And until he did, the marriage agreement was null and void.

And technically, by law, I was not even supposed to *be* there.

He had insulted me enough. If he was not going to get out of my room, I would have to get out of there myself, just to get away from *him*. I walked over to my bed and picked up my journal, squared my shoulders and tried to keep a regal bearing as I passed him on my way to the door.

"Diandra—"

I did not look at him or make any effort to stop.

"Diandra. Stop and talk to me."

I didn't answer. I was nearly through the door.

"Stop and talk to me. You owe me that."

I whirled around. "I owe you nothing, Yeshi Rulan. As you say yourself, I am not your wife. You are not my husband. We will not consummate any kind of union. There will be no marriage. That was *your* choice, in the beginning. Now, it is mine as well. And I will pack my bags—*myself!* And I will be gone from the valley before your brothers come home."

I marched out of there holding my head up high. When I was alone in the common room, I let out a huge, sobbing breath. I felt incredibly sad. Beaten emotionally. And a little battered. But I also felt a huge sense of relief, having decided.

I had to leave the valley.

Yeshi had made it impossible for me to stay there any longer.

I slipped the journal beneath a jacket and hat I'd tossed down on a chair earlier. Trying to clear my head enough to think about what I had to do. I felt uneasy, wondering how much of the journal Yeshi had seen. Though I was heartily angry at his treatment of my professional efforts, I had to admit that if the situation were reversed and he was writing about *me* in that way, I wouldn't like it either.

Distractedly, I began walking around the room, picking up things that belonged to me. A pen. A hair tie. A small carving of Kwan Yin that I had bought from an old man in the village.

Thinking of that day when I bought the carving, all the reasons it would be hard to leave this place came rushing at me furiously. I remembered how lovely the warm breezy air had felt on my skin as I walked through the open air market. Gaja was there too. Yeshi was with us. He was making comments about the things we were seeing, always sharp and funny, and I was laughing, so happy. Something about him made me happy. This was during our let's-be-mean-to-each-other phase, and yet as hard as we tried to be nasty and cruel, we just couldn't help liking each other and enjoying each other's company.

I had stopped to chat with an old man who had a few wood carvings set out for sale, but what caught my eye was a small golden bell under glass. I asked if I could see it, so he carefully removed it from the case and handed it to me. Before he released it into my hand, he looked me straight in the eye, summing me up, it seemed, as if he wanted to make sure I was worthy to hold this precious object.

I accepted it and held it a moment, feeling a strange peace settle over me. I then lifted it by its handle and shook it. The bell made the most beautiful soft pealing sound I could have imagined, shimmering and bright.

"What a beautiful sound," I said. "It's as if the ringing had color. Like shining gold."

I looked up to see Yeshi nearby, observing my interactions with the old man. He was suspicious of the market vendors, concerned they might take advantage of me. I felt him hovering close, just watching me, protective, letting the old man know I was not unaccompanied.

I was enthralled with the little bell and knew I had to buy it. But when I asked the price, the answer was a sum so ridiculously high, even this "wealthy American" could only shake her head. I thought at first it might be just an exaggerated version of the usual and expected an invitation to barter, but the old man shook his head at any mention of a deal. His price was firm.

Instead of the bell, I bought the little Kwan Yin carving at a price that was a mere token. I think the vendor had sensed my disappointment and wanted to offer the statue as a gift.

I walked away with Yeshi, pleased with my Kwan Yin but strangely regretful about the bell.

"Obviously he didn't want to sell it," I said to Yeshi. "And I don't blame him. I can't explain it. It wasn't so much the bell itself—it was the *sound* it made. It was like a ring of gold. That's the only way I can describe it. A ring of gold."

Now, I picked up the Kwan Yin and set her on the chair with my jacket. I knew it would take me several days to arrange porters. Maybe longer, given the shortage of labor in the village. But I could get started packing right away. I picked a couple of books off the shelf and added them to the pile on the chair.

I looked up, startled to see Yeshi in the doorway, watching me intently.

"What are you doing?" he asked in a low voice.

"I'm gathering up my things," I said, haughty. "The few things here that *do* belong to me. You're right. There isn't much. So it won't take me long."

"Diandra—" I could hear the contrition in his voice. I knew he was at heart a sensitive, caring man, and he was well aware that he had pushed some mighty important buttons in me. Of course, he would be gracious enough to offer an apology.

But damned if I was going to give him the satisfaction of uttering it!

"Forget it, Yeshi," I snapped. "I'm just tired of this whole situation."

"I know. I've made it really hard for you." He walked up to me and reached for my hand, taking it in a tentative, brotherly fashion. "Please forgive me."

I looked at him, frowning, wary. The sincerity and concern in his expression was so acute my heart began to soften at once, but I reminded myself that *brotherly* just didn't cut it for me. He was supposed to be my husband. I withdrew my hand from his and turned away from him. I was shaking and trying not to show it. I busied myself awkwardly, looking hard at every object in the room to ascertain whether it belonged to me and me alone.

"Please," he repeated softly.

"Oh, Yeshi," I said with a sigh, blowing dust from the cover of a book I had plucked from the shelf. I remembered buying the book in a bazaar with Gazer. Did he pay for it, I wondered, or had I?

Did I really give a shit?

I turned and looked at Yeshi. He was so beautiful, a lock of dark silky hair falling over one of his topaz eyes, his black brows drawn up with an anxious expression. Just looking at him broke me up.

"You know, Yeshi," I said in a soft voice, "I never blamed you for not wanting to . . . to be with me. In a way I respected you more, that you were being true to yourself. And I'm sorry your brother betrayed you with the marriage in the first place. And I'm just sorry for how it all went down in general. I guess I *was* hoping it would work out between us somehow, but it didn't, and that's just the way it is." I shrugged. "That's really all more my fault than it is yours."

"But you're still very angry with me."

I nodded, gave him a weak smile. "You called my work crap."

He smiled. "Not your *work*, but . . . "

"You insulted me."

"No."

"And you felt I insulted you. Made you my lab rat. You think I'm exposing the secrets of your culture."

"The secrets of my culture!" He let out a bitter laugh. "I don't give a damn about that. That's not what hurts."

Hurt? Had I *hurt* him? Angered him, I knew that, yes, but *hurt*? "Then what—"

"You seem to look at things so *objectively*, Diandra," he said in a dull voice. "So coldly. So cold and calculating. It's like I'm a cipher to you. Just one of the many things you need to *figure out* to get what you want."

Though his expression was extremely serious, what he was saying was almost laughable to me, given the looming, all-important place he occupied in my psyche.

"What?" he asked sternly, noting my attempt to suppress a smile.

"My God, Yeshi." I shook my head. "You have no idea how wrong you are."

"Yeah?" He slowly closed the distance between us. "How wrong am I?"

I moved away from him uneasily, crossing the room, flopping down on the divan, drawing up my knees to my chest, hugging my legs.

"How am I wrong?" He followed me and stood above me, looking down on me. "I read enough of what you wrote to know how you're thinking."

"No," I said. "You don't know what I'm thinking at all. Not from *that*."

"Are you admitting you are less than honest in your writings, then?" he asked. He sat down beside me on the divan and looked at me, waiting for my answer.

"Yes," I said, trembling at his closeness.

"How? How are you being dishonest?"

"I have tried to keep my personal feelings about the situation out of my field notes. And judging from your reaction, it seems I must have done a pretty good job of that. But the truth is, my personal feelings are completely overwhelming me."

"So what *are* your personal feelings, Diandra?"

"It doesn't matter. It's over now, anyway." I sighed, weary. "And I've got work to do, to get ready." I unfolded my legs and was about to get up from the divan, but he reached out and held my arm.

"Don't go," he said.

I slowly sank back into the cushions. I tried to shrug his hand off my arm, but he wouldn't allow it. He moved close beside me and reached his arms around me, taking me against him. He said again, in a whisper, "Don't go, baby." And he was seeking out my mouth with his. I turned my head away, overcome. I felt his fingers gently tilting my face so he could kiss my lips. I pushed against him halfheartedly but sensed something new in his body, in his arms, in the way he was touching me. A different kind of determination this time. Subtle but unmistakable. I might try to push him away, but I would never succeed.

"I want you to be my wife, Diandra," Yeshi said. "I want it more than I've ever wanted anything. There, there . . . why are you crying?"

"But you made a vow," I said. "You swore you would never . . ."

"I am breaking that vow," he declared softly. "And I am making a new one. To be your man. Right now."

This was strange and wonderful and alarming to me. For all the deliberations and weighing of rights and wrongs in deciding to marry Hama and his brothers, I had never been faced with a moment like this. If Yeshi and I mated, it would change everything. *Everything.* It would make the marriage—all the marriages—legal. Binding. But I was okay with that, right? Always had been. Nothing would actually change. Theoretically it would only get better. I'd have four men to fuck.

But here was the thing. I knew that consummating my marriage with Yeshi would mean something way beyond any of that. Something deeper. And I was only just beginning to fathom how deep. How far beyond what I knew. And that made everything else dangerous.

I heard the warning voices in my head. There was still time to turn back. To escape.

But if you do this, there will be no going back.

I felt so overwhelmed with emotions, I had to get up. I slipped out of his hold, rose from the divan and moved away from him. He was up and after me in an instant. I felt his hands on me, on my arms, sliding over my hips. Turning me to face him. His hands were so strong, his arms pulling me hard against him. He forced me to kiss him. His mouth on my mouth tasted hot. He kissed me hard and sensually, holding me tight, rubbing himself against me, between my legs, and I ached at the feeling of him, all through my body but especially there, wanting him so badly I could hardly think. My arms and my hands refused to do my bidding and I could only hold onto him tightly too. I ran my hands over his body, trailed my fingers over his bare skin where I could get to it. I threw my head back, bathing in the rain of kisses he was pouring over my face and throat and down my neck. Then he was holding my breasts and kissing them through my blouse.

Suddenly, he scooped me up as if I weighed no more than a bundle of fine wool and carried me toward his room.

He paused in the doorway. "I'm carrying you over the threshold, see?" He smiled. "I want this union to be sanctified where you come from too."

He set me down, gently but resolutely, onto his bed. He undressed me deliberately, as if he was trying to move slowly but couldn't quite restrain his eagerness. There was no way I could get away from him, even if I wanted to get away from him.

I reached up and opened his belt.

"Wait a minute," he said. "I have something I want to give you." He jumped up and opened a chest in the corner of the room, returning in a flash with a little cloth bag. "I give you this golden ring, as a token of my troth."

"I didn't think you observed that custom here," I murmured, remembering Hama's words.

He put the bag into my hand. In it was a small, heavy object. Too heavy to be a ring, I thought. I opened the drawstring and turned the bag upside down. Out slid the small golden bell I had fallen in love with in the bazaar. I lifted it reverently and heard the sound.

"My golden ring!" I said with a wondering laugh. "But how did you—"

"Magic," he said.

Being naked with Yeshi was like coming home. The most wonderful sensation imaginable, the feel of skin against skin, the weight of his body on mine.

I felt famished and unfamiliar with the physical act of lovemaking, and awkward, as if I had not had a man in a long time. This was so new, in its way. I reminded myself I was sexually experienced. I had almost always found sex to be thrilling and pleasurable and sometimes even deeply emotional. But only with Yeshi had I ever felt this strange mixture of yearning, tenderness, and terror. This feeling that I should run for my life combined with the certainty that I was powerless to do anything but stay. I had to submit to these caresses.

His body was smooth, a sculpted landscape, his skin dark and shining, the hard muscles close to the surface, and I reveled in the curving planes of him beneath my hands. I felt his stomach, like rippling stone. I ran my hands up the curve of the small of his back, opening my fingers over the muscles as they broadened over his shoulders, and my hands curved over them and moved down over his arms, squeezing his beautiful biceps. I ran my lips over his neck, tasting his salty sweet sweat. Taking in his textures. The rough whiskers on his jaw, the silkiness of his hair, the satiny skin of his throat. I kissed and sucked my way down his body, parting his shirt, until I was sucking one of his nipples and listening to him moan.

He seemed to love everything I did to him. He seemed to love it that I could no longer hold myself away from him—that I had given myself up completely to my hunger for him. And he was growing impatient to feed his own hunger and devour *me*.

I had to hold him off so I could taste him. I slipped down on his body, nestling between his legs, trailing my tongue over his belly and then moving even farther down, finally reaching and nuzzling my face into the dark warmth between his legs, breathing in the scent of him, pressing my lips against the soft, bulging sack with its tight balls resting between the hard thighs, the enormous erection towering from a scant tangle of dark hair.

Smelling him, his male musk, tasting him, salty and delicious, I thought I would go crazy. The muscles of his powerful thighs were constricting and tightening around my body as I began mouthing his balls and running my lips up the long, smooth shaft. I reached under him and found his little ass and held his muscular cheeks in my hands, pulling him tighter against me as I licked him. He moved against me, dancing his cock against my tongue. My mouth watered and opened wider to take him in. I cushioned my teeth and encouraged him to slip his erection between my lips, teasing him to fuck my mouth.

He was trembling as he slid it into me, deep into the wet dark, sliding it against my lips, slipping it back and forth, groaning and grasping handfuls of my hair with shaking hands as I began to suck him in earnest.

He was pumping my mouth now, and I tried to take in as much of his length as I could, still squeezing his tight little ass in my hands. The motion of his body, the insistence of his movements, the smell of his sweat and the sound of his passionate moaning, all of it turned me to jelly. Still fucking my mouth, he moved himself around into position beside me and pushed his head between my legs. He pulled me up on top of him, and I opened with no resistance at all. He surged into me, an ocean of pleasure drowning my senses as his tongue and lips met my soft warmth, parting the lips between my thighs with teasing fingers.

I sucked his cock while he licked and nibbled my clit and filled me with his tongue. I rolled over into orgasm without meaning to, whimpering pitifully and thrusting myself against his mouth, my mouth on him, sucking him voraciously; and I became aware of the taste of him changing, a sudden salty nectar dripping from the tip of his cock. I sucked it out greedily, bringing my hands up to hold the bone-hard shaft and balls, fondling them delicately with my fingers. I knew he was going to come soon and I was eager to taste his cream and feel it hot in my mouth.

Chapter 24

B ut Yeshi had other ideas.

He pulled his cock out of my mouth, lifted me, pushed me down on my back and mounted me so he was looking down into my eyes, and I felt him press his enormous cock between my thighs, and suddenly he was shoving it into my tight wet cunt. Hard. Deep.

I gasped out loud as he penetrated me.

My breath came hard and ragged. As did his. Our faces were inches apart.

Oh my God. He's fucking me. He's fucking me. I couldn't believe it. I wrapped my legs around him and pulled him in deeper.

He dipped his head to suck on my nipples and then gently scraped his teeth up my neck. Then we were kissing again, tongues tangled and sucking, his eyes flicking open to meet mine with something like surprise at this amazing connection. And all the while, he was inside me, huge, filling me, hammering himself even deeper and more insistently inside me, like he couldn't get in deeply enough.

The thrusting strength of his haunches as he pumped himself into me, the knife edge sensation of his teeth on my skin, the squeezing caresses of his hands, almost rough on me now, and the look of intensity in his smoky topaz eyes, brought strange, throaty cries from me. I hardly recognized the sound of my own voice. Or the things I was saying, crying out. I was literally begging him to fuck me. And he responded with even crazier passion.

"Oh, God, Diandra," he panted. "I'm torn between wanting to spend all night doing the Kama Sutra with you and holding off coming in you as long as I can—or just letting myself go crazy and fucking the hell out of you right this moment and just—just *spilling* it, just filling you with my come as I have been dying to do for so fucking long—" He spoke against my ear, softly and harshly, with ragged breath and emotion.

"Yeshi—"

"I'm sorry—" he cried out, his voice strangled. These words had me suddenly alarmed, until he explained roughly: "I have to come in you. *Now.*"

"I *want* you to," I breathed, pulling him in deeper with my hands on him.

For a moment he was still and I was aware of him inside me, filling me completely, and my heart and soul seemed to swell and become the entire universe; then I felt him pulsing like a heartbeat, his body jerking and slamming into mine as he let out a lionish roar, and I felt the heat inside me, the hot explosion, the liquid prana. The syrup spread down over my thighs and licked between my ass cheeks, a hot trickle.

He was kissing my mouth and I began to cry.

He held me for a long time.

He did not seem to need to know why I shed those tears, or more accurately, he seemed to understand me without needing me to explain. I remembered how I had cried after our mock sexual union on stage before the entire village. I hoped I wasn't always going to be crying after sex with this man.

There was something epic in our togetherness, as if we were both acutely aware that this singular thing we had found together was by its nature doomed. It was in the way the morning light illuminated the windowpanes in his room. It was in the way we couldn't let go of each other, how we had to be touching, even if it was just a hand resting on a hand. But most of all it was in his eyes, in the way he drank in the sight of me. Gazing at me with a dazzled expression as if I were the most beautiful thing he had ever seen.

I wanted to soak in the glow of our lovemaking, but I was troubled by the antagonism that had so recently passed between us. His resistance against this union. The vow he had broken, the vow he had made when he said he would never be my lover. My mate. My husband.

But he said he had broken that vow and made a new one. To be my man.

Still, if he had broken one vow, I worried, might he not break another?

* * *

"Was she so important to you?" The question had haunted me since the day I first met him. "Do you love her that much?"

It was in the lull after our third—or was it our fourth?—bout of lovemaking that night, and the mystical light of dawn in the room was like a manifestation of something we had created together, Yeshi and me, just the two of us.

My voice, with its flat tone, was like some blunt thing crashing into the room and shattering an enchanted mirror. Immediately I regretted my words, but it was too late.

"What?" He spoke drowsily, his voice dreamy. I think he was almost asleep.

I took a deep breath and plunged in. "The girl you wanted to marry. Your lover."

He propped himself up on one elbow and regarded me with a quizzical frown. "What the hell are you talking about?"

"It's because of her that you didn't want *me*."

"Didn't *want* you? Not wanting you has never been the problem, my girl."

"But you vowed—"

"I was determined that I wouldn't make it easy for Hama. That's all. He betrayed my trust. I wanted to punish him." He sounded slightly ashamed at his admission.

"Yes, I know he violated that trust," I said. "He told me only later . . . I didn't know, Yeshi. I didn't understand until it was too late."

"I knew that, Diandra, but . . . I could see how badly he wanted to be with you. Hell, I could understand that. And it got me to thinking. He couldn't be with you . . . until *I* had you. So I resolved to stay away from you."

"I thought you hated me."

"I hated how hard it was for me to stay away from you!"

"But there *was* someone . . . else. For you, I mean."

He didn't answer me. He simply looked at me with a bemused expression.

"There *is* someone else," I tried again, tremulously—courageously, I felt—changing my statement to the present tense.

He rolled on top of me and began pelting me with kisses, holding me tighter as I tried to struggle against him.

"Listen to you," he whispered. "*I'm* the one who has to think of *you* . . . with all my brothers. But you know what? Right now, right here, you're *mine*. And only mine."

We had been in that bed together for hours, with very little sleep. We had run through a healthy chunk of the Kama Sutra indeed, fucking in every imaginable position. Though our first time together had been crazy and wild and a headlong rush to completion, Yeshi subsequently proved himself a master of extended foreplay. He seemed to have a voracious hunger for eating cunt and an unquenchable thirst for sucking tit—not to mention toes, fingers, earlobes . . . Usually by the time he got around to filling me with his cock, I was begging for it.

But this time he dispensed with all that and was suddenly and roughly entering me, shoving me hard against the mattress with his brutal force. His muscular thighs and ass flexed as he drove himself into me, harder and deeper, until I was moaning and he was crying out, clinging to me and pouring himself out into me, and I wondered how he had anything left to give.

Chapter 25

We spent every spare moment in bed. Or in the long meadow grasses beyond the orchard. Or pressed up against the wall in the barn. I couldn't get enough of being filled with him. With his fingers and his tongue and his cock.

Yeshi was too disciplined to let his work suffer, but he somehow completed his tasks with record-breaking speed. He seemed as eager to get back into me as I was to have him. And after we had exhausted ourselves physically, we would spend hours penetrating each other's minds, talking about everything imaginable. About sex and politics and culture and the meaning of life. But he never volunteered any information about his sexual past. Or about any women he had loved.

I knew that some of the rumors around him were false. But I had the feeling he was keeping something of himself from me. And I was afraid that it was his love for another woman.

When I was with him, I forgot my uneasiness. But when we

were apart, I obsessed on *her*. Yeshi's mystery love. I realized that since the moment I heard about her, I had never stopped wondering and worrying: Who was she? Was he really in love with her? To what lengths would he go to for her? It had long been a slow simmer in the back of my brain, but the recent transformation of our intimacy brought my curiosity to a boil.

Logically there was no reason for me to fear this apparition, whoever she was. Yeshi's expressions and his touch told me he only had eyes—and hands, and heart—and *everything!*—for me. Only for me.

But still I worried.

One night, I found him outside, scanning the sky, staring up intently at the stars.

"Hey," I said, coming to stand beside him. "What's going on? You look like you're waiting for a sign from God."

He turned, his face in the darkness set and grim; I could see it even in the darkness. "My brothers return tomorrow," he said.

"Hmm," I replied, and turned away. I didn't want him to see how shaken I was to hear this news.

He grabbed my hand and turned me back to face him. No words were spoken as we exchanged glances. I think we were each wondering what the other was thinking and didn't want to ask.

Suddenly, he started kissing me ferociously and was pulling me down to the ground. He was on top of me, lifting my skirts, thrusting my legs apart, and I felt his huge cock pushing against the softness my sex, and then he pushed it deep inside me. I let out a cry as he forced it into me before I was ready for him. Strangely, at the moment of pain I felt at his insistent violation, the arousal I felt whenever he touched me kicked in, and then I was thrashing against him, pulling him deeper into me, mad for him.

He fucked me for what seemed like hours, the stars wheeling above us.

Afterward, as I lay against his chest, fingering the dark hair that swirled around his nipples, I asked him, "How do you know they're coming home tomorrow?"

"I'm sorry," he blurted out. "I was so rough."

I nodded. "I guess I wouldn't want a steady diet of that, but I have to admit—I liked it."

"Yeah. You seemed to like it."

"So how can you tell?"

"That you liked it?"

"Well, *that's* obvious. No, how can you tell they're coming home tomorrow? Did you receive a message?"

He shook his head. "I can tell by the scent of the air and the position of the stars. Just as I knew, two days before it happened, they would be leaving for the high country."

"So you knew your brothers would be leaving right after we had our wedding night?"

He nodded.

"It's almost like you deliberately set our marriage ritual for that time."

"I did."

This surprised me. "Why?" I asked.

"To keep you from my brothers as long as possible."

"You mean Hama, right?"

"No, by then I wanted to keep you from *all* my brothers."

This struck me as absurdly funny and sweet. I burst into

laughter, but let it die away as I could see he did not find it funny. I asked gently, "It doesn't *really* bother you, does it? I mean, sharing a wife? That's just the way it's done here. Right?"

He shrugged, frowning. Then we just held each other, saying nothing more.

Chapter 26

Just as Yeshi predicted, the travelers began arriving back in the village the next afternoon. A huge banquet was prepared, with tables set up in the square so the entire community could participate in the welcoming celebrations. It was good to see Shani again. I was even pleased to see Gaja, and I was shocked when she gave me a grudging hug in greeting. Soon I was surrounded by all my other husbands, who were smiling and laughing and happy to be home, telling tales of their travels. They were pleased with the yield of wool they had brought back on the packhorses. It would be a very prosperous year.

They looked good, all three of them, with their deeply tanned skin and lean bodies. I felt their eyes on me, and their hands. I wondered idly which one of them was meant to have his turn with me that night. I had forgotten the order.

It wasn't long before Gazer came to me and slipped his hand into mine, murmuring some endearments against my ear—how he had missed me—and hinting that we ought to slip away from the crowd and get "caught up."

So it was to be Gazer, I thought. But it didn't matter to me which one was first. Gazer, Hama, Rafe. To me they were all alike—merely men. Lovely, sweet, sexy men. And I *did* care for them, all of them, which made the situation even more difficult. Because difficult it was proving to be, when I thought of making love to anyone but Yeshi.

With his hand still grasping mine, Gazer pulled me away from the throng of people.

"In the barn behind the general store," he said, "I know of a nice dark stall with a bed of straw, where I will lay you down and strip you, and feast on you for an hour, until they start to miss us . . . "

"Not so fast." Hama loomed up in the darkness of the passageway between the store and the barn. "Let us not forget precedence. I do believe this lady is *mine* tonight."

I felt Hama's hands slide over my hips.

Gazer sputtered a little. "But—I'm pretty sure it was *my* day, the day we left, and I didn't—" He hesitated, looking up into his older brother's determined face. "Okay," he grumbled. "You may have her, if you please. And then *I* shall!" He placed my hand in Hama's slightly sweaty palm and walked away.

Hama pulled me into his arms. "God, I've missed you," he said, his voice hoarse with passion. He rubbed his clothed cock against my belly and cupped one of my breasts in his hand, pinching the nipple through my blouse. I felt strangely numb.

"My little brother had the right idea, though, didn't he?" he whispered. "Such an intelligent lad. I think you and I are going to get reacquainted right now, right here." He tried to usher me into the barn, but I slid out of his embrace.

"I'm sorry, Hama, but I don't feel very good."

"Oh really?" He seemed torn between skepticism and solicitude for my health. But I think he wanted to believe in me. "Well, it is true, you *have* seemed a little under the weather since we got back this afternoon. What is it? Your stomach?"

"Yeah." I nodded. "My stomach, and my head." *My heart.*

"Well, let's get you home, then."

We turned away from the barn, but he kept one arm around me possessively. I wondered where Yeshi was.

"I had hoped you would be as happy to see me as I was to see you, Diandra," he said.

"I *am* happy—" I stopped. I hated lying to him. I just wanted to be let alone. Alone with Yeshi.

At least I wasn't lying when I said I felt sick. By the time I said my good-byes at the feast and returned to the farm, I was feeling quite ill.

I came to myself hours—or was it days?—later.

I felt diminished and weak, with vague memories of a feverish dream. Lying naked in the soft bed, I stared up at the ceiling and wondered how much of it had been real, how much of it fantasy. I wondered if I had actually been undressed by those gentle male hands I remembered, and if those hands, those sensual hands, had actually rubbed ointment on my body—several pairs of male hands gliding over my body. I was unable to do anything but lay there in a trance while men massaged me and rubbed me and lusted—I could feel it—over my body.

Somehow I knew it was supposed to be healing therapy they offered, not sensual pleasure. But I had felt fingers lingering over my nipples, subtly teasing them until they tightened and became erect. Deep inside me a heat flamed, but I could not move in response.

And I remembered hands massaging my thighs. Moving closer and closer to the softness between my legs. Fingers like soft snakes licking and coiling and undulating over the soft furred mound. Pushing tentatively between the lips, touching the core, the peak, the essence. In my torpor I cried out, but it must have sounded like a muffled whimper to *them*. The fingers withdrew from my sex and moved on down over my thighs.

I was aware that some of my husbands were at my side. Gazer and Hama, if I remember correctly.

And Yeshi. Yeshi was there. He looked as bad as I had ever seen him, dirty and unkempt. Very unlike his usual appearance.

The other brothers took turns at my side, but Yeshi never left.

They called it the Bewitching Sickness. I never learned its equivalent in English. All I knew was that because of my illness and the apparent seriousness of the affliction, I was granted a reprieve from my wifely duties.

Several weeks, I learned, was not an uncommon recuperation period, and during that time I wasn't expected to have sex with my husbands. But the strange lassitude that filled me, and from which I was only slowly recovering, did not dampen my sexual response in the least. And because the treatment for what ailed me was apparently nothing but constant sensual touch administered by a team of hot men, I was kept perennially aroused. And yet I felt too weak to move my body in response.

I began to register the fact that Yeshi touched me least, though under his watchful eye the others massaged me daily and anointed me with the healing oils.

Now that I was recovering, I was fully awake and aware during these sensuous ministrations, but I still felt very weak. Though my nipples tightened and my pulse quickened when Gazer or Hama or Rafe ran his hands over my body, I let no other sign of my arousal show. Though my body was willing enough, my heart wanted only Yeshi. *Let them think I'm not up to it!* I said to myself, only too glad to have this time without pressure, putting off the day I would take up the role of wife again.

But the very sensuality of the treatment seemed to take its toll on me, on my body. After a while I was feverish again, tossing and turning on the bed.

It was a sultry night and Yeshi and I were alone in the room. How seldom we were alone together these days!

He rose from his chair by my bedside and leaned over me. He placed his hands on my forehead and looked deeply into my eyes. He lifted the sheet and began to apply the medicinal ointment, slowly stroking my naked body with the fragrant oils.

"You are very hot tonight, my love," he said. "You sizzle to the touch."

"I'm only hot for you," I whispered. "For *you*, Yeshi. If you don't make love to me, I'll die."

He let out a long, labored breath. "My God," he sighed. "Don't do this to me, Diandra. Please."

"I'll die," I moaned.

He swung himself up on my bed, threw his leg over me and mounted me. He let his body down on mine, seeking out my lips with his. I purred with happiness. He dipped his tongue inside my mouth, but I remained deliciously passive, as if heavily drugged. I couldn't help it. He lowered the sheet and took my breasts in his mouth.

He sucked on my breasts as if expecting sustenance from them. The insistent dance of his tongue and the suction of his lips on my nipples combusted like a fire on the launch pad, and I was getting ready to blast off.

He slid himself down over my belly, pulling down the sheet as he went, exposing my nakedness, kissing and licking, licking all the way down to the soft cleft between my thighs. Seeking out the slick slit. Licking and probing. His hands were running up and down my hot, shivering body. Curving over my breasts and belly, reaching down to press my thighs wider apart. He began to finger me as he licked me.

"Come inside me," I whispered. "Please. Just come inside me." I needed so badly to be fucked.

With a groan, he reared up over me, releasing his cock from his trousers. He grabbed it in his hand, huge and engorged with blood, pressed it against my tight hole and pushed it deep inside me. He was fully clothed but for his naked cock as I lay there nude beneath him, the sheet cast aside. He sucked on my neck and kissed me and tongued my ears, nursed my tits, and rammed me hard. It was exactly what I needed, and I wanted to cry out with relief. He did it so long and he did it so well, pulling up against my clit until I felt the shaft race along the edge of my pleasure and pushing me over the edge. I was falling, falling, and my lifeless body began to tremble.

I lay there quivering in a strange pleasure limbo as he continued fucking orgasms out of me.

I wasn't sure whether he'd had *his* release, because when he seemed certain I had achieved my satisfaction, he quickly pulled out of me, stuffed himself, still enormous, back into his pants, and jumped off the bed.

He stood at my bedside and looked down on me, his face as slick and sweaty as mine now, his dark hair lank over his forehead, curtaining his jewel-like eyes. He grabbed the edge of the sheet and pulled it up to cover me, but for a moment he held it high, gazing down over my still-heaving nude body as if reluctant to shroud it from view.

The door opened and Hama entered the room.

Yeshi dropped the sheet quickly, making a show of tucking it around my body. Hama immediately looked suspicious. I suppose the heat in the room was palpable.

"She's feverish again?" Hama asked.

"Yes."

"We must bring her temperature down. I know the best way."

Together they lay me down on a bed of rose petals on the tile floor in the bathhouse and poured clear, cool water on me.

I could feel the tension between the two men, both of whom had enormous bulges between their thighs, which they tried to conceal from each other as they bathed me. But the water felt wonderful and refreshing, a reviving tonic, washing away the sweat and the oils on my skin and the sticky cream between my legs.

Later that evening I sat up in bed on my own for the first time in days.

I was reluctant to demonstrate my rapidly returning health, because I was pleased to have a reason not to let my first three husbands fuck me. Especially if I could have my fourth husband, Yeshi, on the sly.

But if Hama had walked into my sickroom a minute earlier and discovered me shuddering with orgasms while Yeshi pumped his cock into me, I would have had no excuse but to entertain Hama as well.

But I didn't want Hama.

I didn't want Hama. I didn't want Gazer. I didn't want Rafe. I didn't want a yak driver, a sexy pair of twins, or anybody else. I wasn't sorry I'd had any of them—I had enjoyed them all immensely. But things were different now.

Now I only wanted Yeshi.

Chapter 27

My husbands were patient with me, but I knew they were eager for me to recuperate completely so we might resume carnal relations. When enough time had passed, I began to feel the pressure to get back to our "normal" married life. Whatever the hell *that* was! It brought to mind the weeks before Yeshi and I had staged our mock union.

I too wanted to end the deadlock, but only because Yeshi had withdrawn from me completely and I knew it was because he was torn about having me when his brothers were not. I desperately wanted his hands on me again, and for that I would have done almost anything. But since I'd fallen in love with him, I dreaded the thought of any man making love to me but him.

One afternoon Gaja and I were out in the courtyard together, washing the family's clothes in the stone basin, and I brought up something I had been wondering about for a long time.

"Gaja," I said to her, "is there ever a situation . . . that is, when brothers marry the same woman, does it ever happen that the woman falls for *one* of the brothers . . . more than the others, I mean?" I tried to keep my voice casual.

She eyed me shrewdly, scrubbing fabric against stone. "Why do you ask, Diandra?"

I had a feeling she already knew the answer.

"I was just wondering," I said lamely. "Since I came to the valley, I have seen that for the families I've encountered, it works fairly smoothly, the system of polyandry . . . you know, all the brothers in a family marrying the same woman."

"Yes, I know what the word 'polyandry' means," she said. "And yes, in general the system does work well for us."

"But what if . . . what if it *didn't* work so well?"

She scrubbed hard at the wet cloth, and after a while I thought she wasn't going to answer me.

Finally she set the shirt aside with a brusque motion and looked at me hard.

"Of course, it happens," she said. "We are only human. Sometimes people start playing favorites. But we would hope, with a little maturity, to move beyond this way of thinking only of ourselves. And we learn to attend to duty. Because if the people involved *can't* work it out, can't live with the situation as it's got to be, then somebody has to leave. It *has* happened, yes. It tears families apart, but it happens."

With that, she swiped up a pair of dirty trousers and dunked them in the water. I dared not ask any more questions.

*W*e hung the laundry to dry, and Gaja glared at the clouds that had suddenly blocked the sun and brought a chill to the air.

It was mid-afternoon and the house was silent. I went into my room and changed out of my work clothes. I put on a pretty, sexy dress, thinking of Yeshi. I wanted him to see me in it. But I was too cold wearing only the light, breezy dress, so I put on my jacket, a little embroidered thing I loved. It was handmade by Gaja, who had decided that her sister-in-law ought to be better dressed. Fortunately, it suited me. It was also quite warm and had nice deep pockets.

I paced my room, wondering what to do next to keep myself occupied. The men were all out in the fields and would take their siesta there. It was hard for me to rest in the middle of the day, especially when my mind was preoccupied, as it was now. My conversation with Gaja had left me feeling even more unsettled.

My gaze fell on the golden bell sitting by my bed. Just the sight of it brought up a welling of love for Yeshi. I picked it up, just to hear its chime.

My golden ring. My wedding ring, I thought. *Because I'm wedded to Yeshi.* I let the tone peal out, holding the bell in my hand as I studied its delicate curves, felt its delicious weight.

I heard Hama's smart, quick footsteps outside my room. I closed my fingers around the bell to mute the sound, slipping it into the pocket of my jacket just as he appeared in the doorway.

He came in without an invitation.

"Diandra," he said. "I need to speak with you."

I had come to dread that tone. Patronizing, patient, and plodding.

"What is it, Hama?" I asked, a little too uppity.

He walked up to me and took me in his gentle embrace. "Come. It is time. Let me take you to my room."

I did not answer. I did not move as he leaned forward and began kissing me on the cheeks and nose and forehead, kissing my chin and then my mouth. His arms enclosed me and I felt a sensation like suffocation. When he rubbed his penis against me through the thin fabric of my dress, I felt like someone was poking the mouth of a shotgun against my thigh.

It enraged me that he could not feel my stiff nonresponse to his caresses, but he didn't seem to notice that I wasn't encouraging him or returning his affections. I hated myself for just standing there and letting him touch me.

"No, Hama," I finally breathed out the words. "I am not ready."

"So you are still feeling unwell, then?"

I sort of nodded and shook my head at the same time. I wanted to give him a better explanation. But I didn't know what to say.

"Will it be soon?" he asked. The plaintive questioning note in his voice annoyed the hell out of me. It was worse than when he sounded bossy and stiff.

"Yeah, maybe," I said.

I slipped out of the house and headed briskly toward the woods, where I liked to walk when I needed to clear my head.

I needed to make a major decision.

I can't go on like this.

And it was all because of Yeshi.

I needed to tell him.

I found him sitting alone on a pile of boulders near the edge of the woods. The land rose sharply into the mountains on one side and abruptly dropped on the other into a canyon carved by a small tributary of the river that wound through the valley. It was twilight, and the sky was immense and silver above the purple rim of the valley.

He had regained his full-blown health and beauty since his long vigil at my bedside. His raven hair was sleek and winged away from the clear eyes that shone like gemstones from the perfectly imperfect setting of his face.

He jumped to his feet when he saw me, and I wished he would relax and let me sit down beside him. To just *be* with him. He was so skittish lately, always running from me, it seemed, anytime I got too close.

"I only wanted to sit next to you," I said softly, as if I were talking to a wild animal. Slowly, I approached him. I knelt and settled down close to where he had been resting a moment earlier, but he did not join me. He remained standing, pacing back and forth over the wide tops of the boulders.

I felt flushed and heated, from the walking, and from seeing him. Shrugging off my jacket, I tossed it down on a rock. I wanted him to notice my bare arms, my partially uncovered breasts in the thin, low-cut dress.

"I've missed you," I said, gazing off at the forests on the lower ridges of the mountain.

"Diandra," he said. His voice was dark and deep. "I can't do this."

His pacing ceased. He waited until I looked up at him.

"I can't share you with my brothers."

I was startled and shocked by his words. I had suspected he wasn't very happy about the situation either, but I figured that for him, cultural conditioning would trump personal preference. I'd been so wrapped up in my own preoccupations, my own inability to give myself to Yeshi's brothers, I had no idea he was feeling so strongly about it himself.

A mingling of happiness and dread was rising in my heart. "Do you know," I said to him, "the other day I asked your sister what might happen if . . . if something like this ever came to pass. She told me that unless we could work it out . . . somebody would have to leave."

Yeshi nodded. "Yeah. That's about how it goes."

I sighed heavily. I stood up, turned and fixed him with a long, considering look.

I saw him warring with himself, trying not to touch me, but he was pulled by some inescapable gravity. He moved to me, and I moved to him, and we were together, our bodies, arms, and legs entwined, then our lips and tongues.

God, it was a relief to be touching him again.

And I was relieved too that it had come to this. I wasn't sure what would happen next. For all I knew, this meant good-bye. In fact, I couldn't see any other way around it. But at least we were facing it now, the two of us. I was scared, because I knew there was no way we could "work it out." Not if working it out meant I would be sleeping with four different men on four different nights. Because ever since the day Yeshi rode into my life on his white stallion, I had been unable to give myself to anybody else.

I was about to explain that to him when we heard the thunder rumbling down from the mountain. I turned away from Yeshi to an astonishing sight.

Chapter 28

They emerged from a cloud of mist on the hills, nine warriors on horseback, all armed—with spears and lances and crossbows. One of them had a rifle strapped to his back. The largest and strongest-looking had nothing but a knife on his belt.

The horses were all white, like Yeshi's, and were draped in elaborate decorative trappings, swags and tassels and bells, their long flowing manes and tails laced with colorful ribbons. The men were all dressed alike, in thick embroidered trousers, high leather boots, and multicolored capes over tan, naked torsos. Their heads were shaved but for the topknot, which was worn long down their backs and braided, festooned with tassels and ribbons. Geometric tattoos encircled their powerful arms, and heavy silver and gold gem-studded rings stacked up on their wrists and around their necks.

As they rode closer, I saw the trousers they wore were actually split up the sides so that the long, taut muscles of their golden brown thighs could be seen all the way up to the groin.

I stood motionless, staring at this striking procession as they approached at full gallop.

"Diandra, take my hand," I heard Yeshi call as if from a distance. Vaguely, I noted something strange in his voice. In its timbre was a high-pitched, panicked note I did not associate with his usual composed, deep tones.

I hesitated, not paying attention to him, too full of the sight of the virile riders, overwhelmed with the pounding of the hooves and the strange white mist that swirled with them over the hill as they bore down on us.

"Diandra, look at me!"

Again there was something in his voice that should ordinarily have commanded my attention, but I was more concerned then with these men who had just come down from the mountain.

Diandra, wake up!

I snapped myself back to consciousness, turned and glanced at Yeshi in time to see his face, contorted with fear, his hand reaching out for me, desperately straining as the rocks beneath his feet gave way. And then he was sliding down the hillside, losing his footing, falling along with the rain of rock and gravel down the slope.

It seemed the heavy vibrations of the mounted warriors had caused an unstable slab of ground to shift and fall, but for some reason I sensed that although it had been brought about by the men on horseback, this sudden cataclysmic landslide was the result of a subtler though no less powerful form of vibration they were emitting. Whatever it was, it tore Yeshi from my side. I flung my hand out for his but was too late. I knew instinctively that it was my hesitation when he'd called out for me that cost me our connection.

By then the riders were upon me.

"Yeshi!" I screamed as one of the warriors reached down and pulled me up onto his horse.

I found myself in a strange violent dream, riding high on the withers of the horse against the rider's spread legs and naked chest. I leaned out and looked behind us, and I saw, with an overwhelming rush of relief, Yeshi pulling himself up the edge of the broken hillside.

I screamed out his name again. He gained his footing and began running after us, yelling almost hysterically. The rider who had taken me rode on, unconcerned, while a couple of the other warriors wheeled their mounts and loped back toward Yeshi.

"No! Leave him alone," I cried, but couldn't see anything more as we were all swallowed up in the white mist.

The horse was moving so fast up the narrow, steep trail into the canyon, I was terrified that I would be flung to my death into the abyss, so instead of fighting to escape, I clung tightly to the man who had abducted me, just trying to stay on the horse with him. His body was solid as stone and his naked chest smooth-skinned beneath my grasping hands. He held me before him on the horse, with one hand on the reins and the other on me. Wearing nothing but the thin, low-cut, sleeveless dress, I felt bare and vulnerable against him.

The horse was well-trained and responded impeccably to signals from the grip of the man's thighs. I noticed the big knife on his belt. The handle was set with large round turquoises. And close enough for me to reach out and pull from its sheath, if I could let go for a moment without risking a fall from the fast moving horse.

When I finally made a play for it, the man stopped me without even look down, his hand clamped firmly around my wrist.

For an hour, maybe longer, the movement of the horse brought me against his groin, rhythmically and without relief. I felt the lay of his cock rubbing against the back of my left thigh, while the pommel of the saddle relentlessly rubbed against the mound between my legs. I was very aware of the warrior's hand, warm through the sheer cloth of my dress, spread over my belly and under my breasts, holding me steady me as we rode.

Abruptly, the horse came to a halt and all was silence. We were alone on a rise above the valley. I could see the shapes of the familiar buildings of the village below us, in unfamiliar geometry from that height. The view was permeated with the strange white mist. The other riders had completely vanished.

"Do not be afraid," the man whispered softly in my ear in English. "If you do not struggle, you will not be hurt."

"Of course I will struggle," I snapped, feeling goose bumps run up my spine from the touch of his lips near my neck and his hands on the silk of my dress, sliding up higher beneath my breasts, his thumbs a breath away from stroking the nipples. "I won't meekly consent to being kidnapped. And I'm sure you're not foolish enough to think I will."

"Kidnapped?" He sounded surprised by the word. His voice was rich, melodic.

"Yeah, kidnapped. What would you call it?"

With his fingers on my jaw, he gently turned my face so we were looking into each other's eyes. He gazed at me with such a pure, sweet expression, I thought he must be insane. "But you begged for this," he said. "Have you forgotten? This is your dharma. There is no reason for you to be frightened."

He was murmuring these words and massaging the back of my neck. I suddenly felt incredibly sleepy and longed to simply close my eyes and rest against his body, even as I realized how incongruous that was, given the nature of my plight.

"Be calm," he said. "You will soon be at your destination."

Riding with the persistent white mist made it difficult to judge direction or the topography of the land, and somehow it even made it difficult to judge time.

As we climbed the mountain through the mist, I thought I saw a white palace emerge from the clouds on a distant mountainside, but in the next instant it disappeared. We rode on; the trail grew steeper and narrower until I was certain we would not be able to continue on horseback. But we did not stop, not even when the sky turned so white and opaque I could no longer see the horse's ears in front of me.

All at once the mist cleared and we came to a halt. I looked around. We were standing in the marble courtyard of a magnificent palace. I knew this place was the distant mirage I had caught a glimpse of through the clouds. I had seen other examples of this sort of strange mythical architecture when I had traveled to the Lost Valley. But nothing like this. Nothing with this grandeur and beauty. Soaring towers and lofty pointed arches of incredible proportions, graceful and glowing, as if every column, every architrave, had been carved by hand from the most translucent stone imaginable.

I still wasn't convinced it was real.

The warrior had jumped from the horse and lifted his arms to help me down. I felt his hands around my waist, felt his hard warm body against mine as I slid to the ground, felt him prolong the contact before letting me go. I bit my lip, struggling to stay cool, thinking of Yeshi. I was furious that another man was taking these liberties, touching me in such a sensual fashion, on top of everything else.

Then the other warriors entered the courtyard with the clatter of hooves on tile. I glanced at up them anxiously, but there was no sign of Yeshi. He was not with them.

From within the palace a dozen men in white robes and shaved heads appeared. They moved silently and swiftly to tend to the horses. I could not help but notice that they seemed keenly interested in me, stealing quick glances, though apparently trying hard not to stare at me.

As the warriors began to leave the courtyard through an arched doorway in the wall, one of the monks came to my side and bowed to me.

"Welcome. We have been preparing for your arrival, Kama Kami," he said in stilted English.

"Where is Yeshi?" I demanded. "What's happened to him?"

The monk bowed his head, unperturbed by my wild and belligerent manner. "Please. Find yourself at peace. I bring you to the high lama now. He will answer your questions."

The warrior who had held me stepped back. I was given into the custody of this monk and told to accompany him. They did not try to restrain me, confident that I would not try to bolt. From this eagle's aerie of a castle in the clouds, it was easy to see we were surrounded by steeply pointed, snow-covered mountain peaks. What good would it do me to escape? Where would I go?

Nevertheless, of course I would have to try.

Chapter 29

We entered the palace and I was taken into a domed room where I met the high lama. He was an elderly man with clear eyes of the palest blue—so alluring and strange with his Asian features—and his manner was so calm, serene, and benevolent that I had to remind myself he was my enemy.

"Welcome to Shahalah-kam," he said. "The fulfillment of desire."

"*Whose* desire?" I asked sarcastically.

"Yours."

I laughed bitterly, looking around. In spite of my anger and fear, I couldn't help but notice I was in one of the most beautiful places I had ever seen.

The room was a lofty, light-filled dome of sparkling white marble. Slender columns held up arched openings leading to out-door terraces overlooking a luminous blue vision of mountains and sky, earthly and unreal, like something out of a nineteenth century romanticist painting. The floor was mosaic tile in cobalt, turquoise, and gold. In the center of the room, richly uphol- stered cushions were piled on a thick rug, and a silver samovar sat steaming on a low table. A wonderful smell of spice and fresh baked cakes filled the air. In spite of my best efforts, I wanted to eat, I wanted to drink, and I wanted lay down on those cushions and rest.

I felt disoriented. How had I come to be in this place? We had been riding several hours, to be sure, but on horseback, and the distance we'd traveled would not have been considered excessive in this part of the world. If a place like this existed so close to the valley, why hadn't I heard of it?

"Where is Yeshi?" I demanded. "What have you done with him?"

"Yeshi. He is your man?"

"Yes. He is my husband."

There was a crinkling at the far corners of the startling blue eyes, a faint suggestion of a smile. "A valiant one, indeed. They tell me he tried very hard to save you."

"What did they do to him?"

"He was merely left behind, that is all."

"He is not hurt?"

"No."

"But he'll try to find me. He'll follow me and he'll find me."

"He will try to find you, yes, but he will not find you."

"But of course he will. The canyon is narrow, and he knows which way we went."

The lama continued to gaze at me with his serene, blue-eyed countenance.

"Why did you bring me here?" I asked.

"Do you not know?"

"No," I said, exasperated. "I don't know. I have no idea."

"It was your own desire that brought you here."

"What the hell are you talking about?"

Now the monk looked truly baffled. "Has it not long been your desire to reach this place?" he asked.

"This place? *This* place? Where *are* we, exactly? Look, I don't even know what *this* place *is*."

"But that did not stop you from wanting to find the Lost Valley. You wanted it desperately, and you had no idea what it was you were wanting."

For a moment I pondered what he was saying. How did he know how keenly I had wanted to get into the Lost Valley? I rubbed down the shivers on my arms, then reminded myself that it was never any big secret. I had let lots of people know. But it proved one thing. These guys knew who I was. They had kidnapped me for a specific purpose.

"Yeah, I wanted to go to the Lost Valley," I said. "And I did. I went there. I reached it. So what?"

He nodded. "But you see, the place you reached was only the entrance to the place you truly desired."

"No. It was the place itself," I said stubbornly. This is ridiculous, I thought. Why was I arguing with this crazy old man? I just needed to figure out how get out of there.

"So, it was the place itself," the lama said, repeating my words and frowning. "It was merely a *place* you desired to find?"

I was about to answer, *Yes, it was just a place*. But that wasn't true. It was the *people* I had wanted to find. The people I would find in a "lost valley." I was, after all, an anthropologist, not a geologist. I was interested in culture.

"And you found the achievement of all your desires there? When you reached that place?"

"Well . . . no," I said, annoyed at the question. Then I thought of Yeshi. I had found *him* there.

But had I found him only to lose him?

"The point is, I don't want to be *here*, in *this* place, that's for sure. You are holding me here against my will."

The old man tilted his head and looked at me innocently. "You are free," he said simply. "Do you not understand this?"

"This is not what I call 'free.'"

The monk's voice sounded sad. "How often we achieve something we have tried so hard to bring into being, only to reject it once we have realized it. You are here to fulfill your dharma. Do you not feel this yourself?"

"Just tell me what it is you want with me," I said.

"What I want is to see you writhing in ecstasy with a man's lingham penetrating your yoni, and another man's lingham in your mouth, the life energy pulsing through your body as you slip into samadhi, nirvana . . . "

He spoke the words in a matter-of-fact, pleasant voice, without a hint of lechery in his tone.

I tried not to show any emotional response to what he had just said. I was shocked, but not frightened, as I reasoned I bloody well should have been. In fact my fear had receded, and something else had taken its place. An avid curiosity, an alert fascination to the situation at hand. It was what I thought of as my professional anthropologist mode, and it was always piqued whenever I encountered humans in what others would ordinarily call "strange" circumstances.

"Just what sort of monastery *is* this, anyway?" I asked, surprised and rather proud of my own calm tone.

"I will answer all your questions in time. But I imagine you are quite tired from your journey and would like to rest before beginning your Vision."

"Beginning my what?"

"Your Vision. It is the reason pilgrims come to us, here. To find fulfillment of desire. To do so, you will undertake your Vision."

I wanted to protest that I did not come here for a *vision* or for any other purpose of my own choosing, but I found myself hesitating. I was curious about this place. I wanted to know what these odd people were doing here in this spectacular palace on a remote Himalayan mountaintop.

"Okay," I said with a sigh, and in my mind I saw myself swan diving over a cliff. "Whatever. Bring it on."

"Good. I am not surprised by your courage. I will meet with you tonight at supper. Now, Cedric will show you around."

Cedric looked to be in his late twenties, with light sunburned skin and a decidedly red cast to his topknot, which was coming loose in a frizz and was not as long as that of the other monks.

"Okay," he said. "I think I'll show you the pilgrim's dormitory first, then the workrooms. Or—let's just start with the workrooms. That's what everybody wants to see, right?" He chuckled nervously. "Oh, God, did you notice that? I almost knocked that statue over with my robes. I am such a cow."

"So what *is* this place, anyway?" I asked him. "Pretty strange for a monastery."

"This place? What is *this* place? Hey, this is *the* lamasery to be at, honey," Cedric replied. "Seriously."

"Are you from southern California?" I asked, startled by his familiar accent.

"Not anymore."

"Wow. We're practically neighbors," I told him. "I'm from the Bay area. But I lived in Ventura growing up."

"No way." He sounded let-down. "They said you were a *goddess*. You seem totally mortal. *Ventura*." He wrinkled his nose.

"Who said I was a goddess?"

"I don't know. Everybody. They made it sound like you were, you know. From another realm."

"Well, if you're talking about California, it kinda *is*."

"True that."

"So how did *you* end up here?"

"Oh. It's a whole soap opera. But I was like, this *huge* fan of the movie *Lost Horizon* when I was a kid. Then when I nineteen, I met this strange old Tibetan guy who told me there was this place in the Himalayas that really existed, this remote, out-there in more ways than one sort of lamasery, where the devotees develop incredible powers, only it wasn't about walking on coals or sleeping on a bed of nails, it was about, *you* know. Wink wink."

"No, I *don't* know," I said with annoyance. "Why don't you just spell it out for me?"

"You want me to spell it out? Okay. It's spelled S-E-X."

"You mean like tantric yoga or something?"

"Sort of. It's actually even older than tantra. Our tradition goes back thousands of years. Anyway, so when I found out about Shahalah-kam, I'm like, lost worlds and sex? I'm *there*."

"Did they kidnap *you* too?"

"Yes. Wasn't that just the hottest thing you've ever experienced?"

"No!" I said indignantly. "It is *not* erotic to be taken against your will on the back of a horse by some half-dressed, muscle-bound warrior—"

He raised one very expressive reddish brow. "Listen, honey, relax. You don't have to do anything you don't want to do while you're here. I promise."

"But what I *want* is to get back to where I came from. Before I was abducted and brought here. Against my will."

"Against your will?" He looked skeptical.

"Yes." I said it forcefully: "Against my fucking will."

"Okay, shhh. Will you just chill? We're going into the work-room area now. We're not supposed to make any noise. Come on. You can see here what the novices are studying. Just to get an idea."

I followed him into a wing of the palace that housed various small rooms, all equipped with comfortable couches and carpets piled with cushions.

I gave a start when I peered through the arched doorway of the first "workroom" and realized what it was I was seeing. A naked man sat in the full lotus position, and in his mouth was the penis of another man who was upside down with the first man's penis in *his* mouth, his legs wrapped around the sitting man's head.

I shrank back, instinctively hiding myself, but my guide didn't seem worried about being seen. He was more concerned about maintaining silence. He spoke in a whisper. "They've been in that position for three days."

"Holy shit," I whispered.

In the next room two monks sat in the full lotus position, facing each other, naked, silent, each with an erection that stood up from his body. Looking into each other's eyes, they seemed to be concentrating on nothing more than keeping their penises erect without touching them. I wondered how long they had been doing *that*.

In each "workroom" we found monks involved in various sexual practices, most of them conjoined in some type of intercourse. There were no doors on the rooms, only open archways with perhaps a thin muslin curtain draped to one side.

But when we reached the doorway at the end of the hall, Cedric had to lift the curtain, which had been deliberately closed, so we could see what was going on in the room.

A man was kneeling on the floor as another man humped him from behind. A third man fucked *him* in the ass, and yet another man pumped that one from behind, and so on. I think there were seven of them. The room was full of grunting and the smell of sweat. They glanced up at us with wide, animal eyes.

Cedric leaned over and said in a low voice, close to my ear, "I think that's extracurricular activity. Not on the syllabus. Exchanging chi with multiple partners isn't covered in class until after novice training is complete. But experimentation in the meantime is not discouraged."

"Extra credit, huh?" I murmured.

"Wanna join 'em?" Cedric's eyes were gleaming. "They would welcome us. You could be on the bottom."

"Yeah, right. Maybe later."

He blew out a sigh of disappointment and dropped the curtain. We moved on. I began to relax a little. Maybe I *did* have *some* free will here.

"Is it all guys?" I asked.

"What?" He frowned at the question.

"The monks. They're all men."

"Yes, all men, though sometimes we are visited by the nuns from the forest."

"The nuns from the forest!"

"Yes, the ladies of Shahalah-kam. They're too wild to live within the walls of a palace, so they stay in the forests below the snows except for certain times of the year when they come to the men. Other times the men go to them."

Curiouser and curiouser. I knew then that I was licked. I wasn't even thinking about escaping anymore.

I would return to Yeshi one day soon. Of this I had no doubt. But I wasn't going anywhere just yet. I had to stick around and find out more about this place.

Chapter 30

Cedric brought me to the high lama before dinner, and the old man escorted me to the dining hall himself. I had hoped to use this opportunity ask more questions, but the meal proved to be a quiet time, with all of the monks sitting on individual cushions, their rice bowls on their laps, concentrating on nothing but the food.

After dinner I was given my own room, a small cell with a slit of a window looking out over dozens of mountain peaks. The room seemed austere for an establishment devoted to sexual practices. There was a single candle in a bracket on the wall, and a pallet on the floor with one pillow and one blanket. But I slept well that night—and I slept alone.

I had been scared I'd be visited by some monk looking for a study partner, but nothing like that happened.

* * *

I woke up thinking of Yeshi, wondering if he was okay.

If he was okay, I was sure he'd be worried about me. So he wouldn't be okay.

I found the high lama after meditation, as he was going into the dining hall. "Can I get a message to my husband?" I asked him. "I know he's worried about me. It would be good if I could just let him know I'm all right here. And that I'll be back *soon*. Right?"

He looked at me, smiling. "We *have* let him know that, already, of course. Still, it's doubtful he will understand, or trust."

I bit my lip. He was right about that. And I didn't feel good about it. "He'll come find me," I said. "If he thinks I'm in trouble."

"Then I suggest you get right to it."

"Get right to—it?"

"The reason you have come here. Your Vision."

"My vision . . . you mean, like a vision quest?"

"If by 'vision quest' you mean an *erotic* exploration, then yes."

"Why does it have to be erotic?"

"It doesn't have to be. There are many paths. But this is the one you have chosen, and the one we offer."

"Will you stop saying I *chose* this!"

"You will live out, in trance, your most alluring fantasies. You will experience things you have wondered about and wanted, but only in your dreams. Every lover you have ever desired, every setting you have imagined to be the most sensual, every position and every act imaginable, is here for you. It will be as *you* wish in every way."

"But I'm married!" I said. "I can't do that."

"You have agreed to be faithful in marriage?"

"Yes." I sputtered a little on the word.

"And do you ever have fantasies?" he asked.

I hesitated before answering, resenting his personal questions. "Sure."

"Sensual dreams that do not include your husbands? Do you allow yourself these?"

"I guess."

"What you will experience here will be like a vivid, sensual dream—it will feel completely real to you while you are *in* it, but it will be like a waking fantasy, in that you can direct the action to your liking."

"Huh." What a concept, I thought with mistrust. Wasn't there an old *Star Trek* episode like this?

"The only thing you cannot control," he said, "is that it must be a *sexual* fantasy. Because that is the energy of the catalyst."

"So what *is* the catalyst?" I asked. "Some kind of psychotropic mushroom or plant?"

"This *place* is the catalyst," he said. "You have found your way here. You are already in your fantasy."

I was startled and unnerved by his words. Already in my fantasy? Hey, come *on*, I thought. Abduction by a virile, half-naked warrior on horseback was one thing—but a bunch of partially shaved guys in long gowns? It wasn't working for me.

And then suddenly—and I could practically hear the dramatic music swelling in crescendo around me—a man appeared. He was walking toward us, the sexiest guy I had ever laid eyes on, tall and lean and—*so cute*. Like a composite character made of the best aspects of all the men I had ever found attractive.

Oh my God, I thought.

He was looking directly at me with that incredible, once-in-a-lifetime spark of recognition. The look that said both, *I need to spend the rest of my life getting to know you because this thing has so much depth and I'm already in too deep,* as well as, *I'm so hot to fuck you I can hardly wait to bring you down.*

"So . . . " This paragon of manhood spoke softly as we joined up outside the dining hall. "You're obviously the goddess everyone is talking about."

His voice resonated through me, massaging me, from the surface of my skin down deep into my guts, and the very vibration of it was immensely pleasurable, let alone what was going on in my head at the sight of him, the lanky body, the big, broad shoulders, narrow hips, succulent thighs. Dressed just the way I like, in faded jeans and work boots, a white oxford shirt, and a dark wool sport coat. His hair was chestnut brown and he brushed it out of his eyes to get a better look at me. His eyes were heavily lashed, their expression dark and sincere.

"Goddess, right, that's what I am," I murmured. "It says so right on my passport."

Okay, so if he was my dream man, he would laugh at my joke, however feeble it might be.

And laugh he did. He looked down, suddenly shy, his mouth still in a smile. God, but he was charming.

The words of the high lama hit me with force. *You are already in your fantasy.*

I turned to ask him about it, but he had disappeared.

I looked back at my dream guy, who was waiting for me to go through the door. "After you," he said.

Sigh. A gentleman.

I found my seat on the floor, and of course I somehow ended up sitting next to fantasy man.

He leaned close to me and said in a low voice, "Where's a big, upholstered recliner when you need one?"

I had to clap my hand over my mouth to stop the laughter, and I nodded in agreement. Sitting on the floor gets old fast.

Oh dear God, I've only known of his existence for thirty seconds and already he's made me laugh!

And he smelled incredible. Wearing some familiar guy-cologne that had done it for me since I was a young girl.

I was a goner. He looked good. He smelled good. He had a great voice. And he was funny. All my weaknesses.

He *must* be a fantasy, I thought. Nobody is *that* perfect for me. Then again, I hardly knew him. He could be an asshole, for all that.

But if he was just a fantasy, why would he be an asshole?

I could hardly eat, I was so aware of this man sitting next to me. Strange, how much like Yeshi he was, in a weird way. But he wasn't Yeshi.

And thinking of Yeshi made me want Yeshi terribly.

I need to get away from this place, I thought. This was not good for me.

I caught up with the high lama after the meal and pulled him aside so I could speak with him privately.

"So," I said.

"You have become aware of the state you are in?" he asked.

"Do you expect me to believe he's not—real?" I said. "He's *too* real!"

The high lama smiled at me.

"You know who I am talking about, don't you?"

The high lama did not answer.

"If he's all in my mind, how do you know who I'm talking about? How do I know you didn't just hire that guy to play a part?" I asked.

"Who would I have hired?" he said. "How would I know what *your* fantasy is?"

"Is this just a way to get me to disregard my marriage vows? Convince me I'm living in a fantasy world? What about you?" I demanded. "Are *you* real?"

"You will find that the difference between what you call 'real' and your Vision is quite easy to discern, once you know how to play with the energies," he said. "Remember, you can *instantly* control your fantasies. Once you get the knack of it, you will understand."

He turned and walked away down the corridor. I wanted him to stop and turn back, to talk to me some more, to reassure me. But he was like a busy father figure who had no time for foolish trivialities.

Well, I thought, I guess *he's* real enough, because I was certainly not controlling him. But what about my guy? Mr. Perfect-for-me. According to the high lama, if he was a fantasy, I should have been able to make him do whatever I pleased.

Now I was stumped. What *did* I please? A few moments ago I had fled from the dining room, wanting only to get away from him. He freaked me out, to be honest. I was having some powerful feelings in his presence. Feelings I didn't want to be having for anyone but Yeshi.

But I was too curious not to experiment. What *would* I want to do, I wondered, if that hot guy was a mere mirage and anything I did with him was harmless and happening only in a dream? What would I want to make happen?

Well, for starters, I thought flippantly, I'd have him appear at that moment and start rubbing my shoulders! What the hell! How about a complete, full-body massage?

I waited a moment. Nothing happened. *Okay.*

He had to be real, like the high lama. Not a fantasy at all.

But then I felt a warm, gentle squeeze. On my shoulder. It lasted a moment; I turned and he was standing there.

"Hey," he said.

"Hey."

"The high lama told me to come get you. They're doing a prana-exchange class in the dome, and he thought you might be interested."

"Oh, yeah, okay, thanks." *Prana-exchange?* What was that?

"Do you know the way?" he asked.

"Well, sort of. This place is like a—what do you call it?"

"A labyrinth."

"Yeah, that's what I was going to say. Only it's not really like a labyrinth, is it?"

"Well, it's definitely a maze. It took me a while to get used to the layout. Come on, I'm going that way. I'll take you there."

I didn't even know his name yet.

What would my guy's name be? I wondered. "Michael," I thought. Like the angel.

"What?" he said.

I hadn't realized I had said it out loud.

"Is your name Michael?"

"Ryan Michael Phillips," he replied. "You can call me Michael."

"I'm Diandra," I told him, offering my hand.

"God, that's a beautiful name," he said, pressing my hand.

Only the shy way he suddenly let go of me and looked away saved him from being too much of a very good thing.

"Have you been here long?" I asked him as we walked together along a vaulted corridor.

"About a year."

"But you aren't dressed like the other monks."

"I'm not a monk yet. I'm not even a postulant."

"Then what are you doing here?"

"I'm studying. Hoping they let me become one of them."

"When will you know?"

"It's hard to tell. Could be months. Could be years. Sometimes people stay the rest of their lives without ever receiving the training or being asked to join the community."

"What do you have to do, to prove you're worthy to join the community?"

"It's not what you have to do. It's what you *can't* do. You can't have an orgasm."

"You're kidding."

"No."

"No orgasms? Of any kind?"

"Nope. Except for wet dreams. Wet dreams don't count. That takes the pressure off. A little."

"So . . . you are celibate?"

"Yes. Since the day I arrived."

Hmm, I thought. Intriguing. If he was a phantom, he was an awfully realistic one. He even had a backstory. But would my fantasy guy really be a celibate aspirant to a strange order of sex monks in the Himalayas?

It was true that I was always fascinated by the man I couldn't have.

Like Yeshi.

Chapter 31

We entered the lofty marble room and joined a number of monks who were waiting for class to begin. The teacher, an older, bald monk, started the class right after we came in, as if he had been waiting for us. He told the class to pair off. I did so, naturally, with my fantasy guy.

The next thing I knew, I was reclining on a low divan with Michael massaging my shoulders. And there was nothing unreal about his touch.

Slowly, sensually, he worked his hands all over my body. Touching me everywhere I wanted to be touched even as I thought of it.

Okay, I thought, so this was a pretty weird coincidence if I wasn't manufacturing the scene from my own imagination. One minute I was idly imagining this guy giving me a full body rub, five minutes later he's doing it. Incredible! *Fantastic.*

And yet indescribably real. I felt something so real, so true, so much like love, coursing through my body, stimulated by the touch of these warm hands on my skin.

I tried to focus on my feelings for Yeshi.

And I realized I felt for this man the same way I felt for Yeshi. And then I thought: He *is* Yeshi. And he was. He was Yeshi in the guise of a California white boy, the sort of guy I had always fantasized about. He was just like Yeshi, or Yeshi was just like Michael. Only he wasn't. They had the same lanky, slender sexiness, the same expressions, the same *essence* . . . and yet . . .

"Have we met before?" I asked him suddenly.

"I don't think so."

"Are you *sure*?"

"Yeah. I would have remembered you. Trust me."

I wouldn't have thought my fantasies included clichéd dialogue, but I found I didn't mind.

From then on I forgot to think about Yeshi. It was as if he did not exist. I didn't have to yearn for him, or pine for him, or feel conflicted feelings when Michael touched me, because Michael was Yeshi. And the only Yeshi I knew was Michael. It was like a dream in which all the rules of reality have been suspended.

"So," I said. We were walking together on the terrace outside the dome after class. "Giving a massage like that isn't breaking your vow of celibacy?"

He blushed.

Really, it had been a perfectly innocent massage. Except for the log roll in his pants, which he had tried hard to keep from brushing against my ass as he straddled me.

"Actually, I never took a vow of celibacy."

"But you said—"

"I said I was celibate. And I *have* been celibate, for two years. But that's just to make it easier. Easier not to orgasm."

"Oh. So—it's *orgasm* you're forbidden. Not sex per se."

"Well, technically it's not even orgasm that's forbidden, it's ejaculation," he explained earnestly, as if I had asked him about the workings of the internal combustion engine. "But for me, I'm afraid they'd be one and the same. They tell me you can orgasm without ejaculating, but I've never been able to do it. And I've never been able to have sex without an orgasm . . . hence the celibacy."

If this is a lucid dream, I thought, I can get him to risk it. He wouldn't be able to help it.

And suddenly he was pushing me against the wall, whispering in my ear. "You *are* a goddess, aren't you? You're a witch. You've completely bewitched me."

Where had I heard these words before? It was like déjà vu.

He started kissing me, gently ravenous. His erection jutted out like a hook on a wall, and I was practically hanging off it. He was pressing it against me so precisely and so iron-pole hard that when he cupped my breasts in his hands and dipped his head down to suck the nipples through the cloth of my blouse, I nearly exploded. But just before I was about to come, he pulled away.

"I'm sorry," he panted. We were both chuffing like steam trains. "I'm gonna go crazy."

"That's not fair."

"No. It's not. Let me come to your room tonight and make it up to you. I want to taste you."

"But you'll just stop me," I moaned.

"Not if you just let me pleasure you," he said. "I can do that. Please."

I shook my head, overwhelmed with lust, unable to think clearly. "I have to go," I said.

I left him alone on the terrace and hurried away into the palace, found my own cell and closed myself in, being careful to bar the door.

I moved rhythmically against my own fingers, pinching my nipples as I lay naked on my pallet. I was beside myself. I wanted him so badly. He was offering his tongue in my cunt, which would be lovely, but I wanted his cock, too. Because he had denied me his come, it was what I wanted most.

I was waiting for him, thinking that if this was truly my fantasy, he wouldn't let the locked door come between us.

The night was silent but for the wind.

And then a door opened in the wall, a door I had not noticed before, and he was standing there with a candle in his hand.

He was naked but for a loincloth, and his physique was breathtaking in the candlelight. Holding the candle high, he took in the sight of my naked, aroused body. Then he lit the candle in the bracket on the wall, blew his own candle out and set it down. He knelt and climbed onto my pallet with me, mounting me quickly, finding my mouth and kissing me. I opened my thighs to cradle his body, feeling the marvelous shock of his full, hot pouch sliding over the lips of my cunt. The loincloth was made of the thinnest silk, and it felt like he wore nothing. As he kissed me, he fondled my breasts and continued sliding his cloth-swaddled erection over the spreading folds of my sex. I felt the hard cock enclosed in silk, probing between the moist slit, dipping down to press into my tight opening. He sucked my nipples, pushing himself in farther and deeper, as though he would try to fuck me clothed.

I reached down and pulled on the loincloth, which unwound from his hips in one long ribbon. I pushed him off me and went down on him. His cock was long and thick but I had no trouble sliding the whole thing into my mouth.

He swore and cried out and with his fingers in my hair held my head steady as I sucked him.

This was my fantasy, so what was I doing pleasuring him, instead of him pleasuring me? Well, frankly, I love to suck cock, so that *was* part of my ideal encounter. But there was also something else I recognized—as if I were looking at myself in a mirror: the element of going after the impossible attainment. To get a man to change his mind. To get Michael so worked up he would be willing to spill it. Even though he had vowed he would not.

Something in this line of thinking tripped me up. I stopped sucking, felt the trembling of his massive member against my tongue.

"I don't want to go too far," I said. "You can't ejaculate, remember?"

He rolled up to a sitting position and climbed over me, pushing me down flat on my back. "I don't care anymore," he said. "Fuck the monastery. I want *you.*"

Fine. That was what I'd wanted to hear.

What the hell? The part of me witnessing all this was astounded. Here I was, apparently in the middle of what could be my wildest fantasy with the hottest guy imaginable, and I was living out all my old issues.

I had a vivid memory then—a dream within the dream— of the first boy I ever French-kissed, who, the day after kissing me, pretended nothing had happened between us. I had taken that as a challenge. For weeks or maybe months afterward, I dressed in my most casually provocative clothes and made sure I crossed his path in the school hallways at least once a day. I went through some major changes that year, my fifteenth, morphing from a chubby, insecure bumpkin to a voluptuous, witty girl who was at ease in social situations. My crush finally deigned to have another encounter with me and we somehow ended up "going together" for a few weeks, until I realized that having to scheme and manipulate to get a guy made the guy not worth having.

But if I realized that truth even then, I had not internalized the knowledge very well, and it played out again and again in the encounters I had with men.

During my living fantasy in the monastery, I became not so much aware of these dynamics, which I already understood, but rather, that I was able to *transcend* them.

The sex with my composite dream guy was awesome. After hours of fantastic foreplay and countless orgasms, I was satisfied. He shattered his vows for my sake and ejaculated like a geyser.

Afterward, Michael gave me some sweet cuddling, and he would have waited for me to fall asleep before he did if I had wanted him to. But I found myself getting bored with him and wishing he would go away and let me have the little bed to myself. On the other hand, I didn't like the idea of him ditching me.

A knock came at my door. The monastery secretary was look- ing for Michael.

He kissed me and reluctantly said good-bye. Perfect! I thought. He was gone but didn't *want* to leave me. So it was okay.

Alone on my pallet, I lay there in contented bliss, counting orgasms instead of sheep. Yes, I thought, dozing off to sleep. This business of living out fantasies certainly has its charms.

But thinking about the experience the next morning, I realized I was disappointed in myself. There had been a decided lack of imagination in my fantasy.

If I had a chance to do it again, I would definitely come up with something more exciting.

Chapter 32

"So how long does this last?" I asked the high lama after break-fast.

"How long does what last?"

"This vision quest thing I'm doing. Living my sexual fanta-sies."

"It lasts as long as you desire."

Good. It wasn't too late. What I needed, I decided, was some help brainstorming. Wouldn't it be nice if I could get together with the Shahalah-kam monastery ladies and compare notes?

No sooner did I have this thought than one of the monks ran down the corridor, excitedly informing those he passed that the nuns of the forest were making their way up the mountain and would be joining us later that day.

In honor of the women's visit, a feast was prepared and tables were set up outside beneath a canopy of trees, which should not have been growing at that altitude. The monks were clearly excited to be in the company of women, and I gathered that many of them were heterosexually oriented, despite the homoerotic curriculum of the monastery. Cedric had told me that man-on-woman training did not commence until the third year of instruction.

In a twinkling, there I was, sitting beneath the trees with a group of beautiful, vivacious women who began talking about their own Visions, comparing notes, just as I had imagined. Clearly this was all still part of my own fantasy.

"I do love coming to visit this lovely palace," said one woman, a curly-haired redhead with enormous black eyes. "I have such good memories. Memories of a mere fantasy, but delightful memories all the same!"

"I need some ideas, if you care to share," I said. "Any of you . . ."

"It's funny, at first it's hard to think of things!" another woman said. "It took me several weeks into my quest to come up with the really good stuff."

"Several weeks!" I exclaimed. "Does it really go on that long?"

"It all depends. I know of one girl who had men licking her pussy for three months straight," said the redhead.

Someone else chimed in, "Yeah, and she had a different guy doing it every day."

"Remember Vera? She had men of every race. One after the other. We used to ask her which one was best kisser, which one had the biggest cock, who had the most staying power. She loved giving us the details. And there was that American girl who wanted to be chained to a locker and fucked by an entire professional football team."

"Second and third string, too!" laughed one of the women.

"I just wanted breasts," said one little dark-haired sprite. "Big, full, round, rosy breasts with dark nipples. I wanted to suck them while a man was fucking me. It's weird because I usually don't even do women."

Another said, "I had a famous movie star, who shall remain nameless, rub his cock on my pussy, and then ejaculate on my breasts, then suck up the come like it was oozing out of my nipples."

"I tried to get the high lama to fuck my tits during *my* fantasy," said one woman in a low voice. "But it didn't work. He wouldn't do it."

"It didn't work because you were just trying to see if he *would* do it," said her friend. "You were trying to manipulate him. Having him fuck your tits wasn't really your fantasy."

"I suppose that's true."

One of the nuns, a tiny, frail-looking thing, said, "My favorite fantasy was when these soldiers used a battering ram to force their way into my castle. A wonderful metaphor, don't you think? And then they each took turns doing the same thing to my body, using their battering ram to get in!"

"Oh, I just wanted to be gently massaged by an angel," said another girl.

The monks caught wind of what we were chatting about and began to gather around, listening avidly, as if to get ideas. I wouldn't have been surprised to see some of them taking notes.

It was a diverse mix of people, sitting close together, or standing around us, laughing, listening intently, young people mostly, but not all of them; people from the local countries, mostly—India, Nepal, Tibet, Bhutan—but there was a decidedly international flavor to the group.

After a while the men began to chime in with some of their fantasies, too. I was amazed at the diversity of the human imagination.

I was so intrigued by this institution of "higher learning" that I lost track of time. I had tried to immerse myself, getting into it as much as I could, in order to get the most out of it. And at first I had wanted to do it quickly. I wasn't even sure why; I just knew there was something else I had to get to, something that was more important . . .

But as time passed, I began to feel so dreamy and content, I forgot to be in a hurry. I was just happy to be there, in that wild, beautiful, sensual place. And I took advantage of my surroundings. I learned to fantasize like a pro. I tried everything, every appealing erotic scenario I could think of. I made love to a devastatingly beautiful sheik on a flying carpet over Istanbul. I had ships' captains and fighter pilots. Firemen and astronauts. I was courted by the sexiest men in the world, celebrities and men of history, living, dead, or in my imagination. They all came alive for me. I had sex in submarines, skyscrapers, and backstage at rock concerts. I had every man I had ever wanted. In every sexy setting I could imagine.

Acting out fantasies in a very real setting challenged me to consider what I truly did want to experience. It is one thing to *fantasize* about being raped by soldiers, quite another to actually experience it in the flesh.

But the more adept I became in creating my fantasy world, the more rich and varied the scenes. I had complete control.

I still had a lot of questions about how I came to be in that place, questions that were never fully answered. Cedric told me it was my "karma" to be admitted there, according to the fulfillment of my desires.

I protested, "But I don't remember ever saying, 'Gee, I wish I could get kidnapped by sex monks and be taken prisoner in an orgy palace!'"

"But on some level you *must* have intended it, Kama Kami," Cedric insisted.

Kama Kami. The high lama had translated the name for me as "one who desires to fulfill desires."

"You must have determined you would find training like this," Cedric said. "Your karma was developed to the point that you were able to manifest your desire."

"Training in *sex*? I didn't have to travel so far for *that*," I said, cynical.

"Not sex. Training in kundalini rising, using the energies of desire. Tapping into the life force. Learning to master it for manifestation. That's what we're here for."

One night we had a fantasy party at the monastery. We all came together in the palace, all the monks and nuns and visitors like myself, mingling men and women, just for fun, and everybody brought their fantasies. Michael was there; I saw him looking as gorgeous as ever, waving at me eagerly from across the big domed room. He hurried to my side and greeted me with a sensual hug, but I wasn't interested in him anymore, and he faded away.

I wondered what had happened to him after he broke his vows and had all those orgasms with me. But then I realized that since he was a fantasy, and *just* a fantasy, *nothing* had happened to him. It didn't really matter.

The party was like a giant, incredible costume ball. In every room of the palace you could find a different era or scene. Incredible people, props, costumes. Except they weren't props or costumes. It was all *real*.

Real within the fantasy, that is.

There was a Roman toga party in one room and a Japanese tea house staffed with gorgeous geishas in another. Medieval knights jousted in a torch-lit stadium behind the palace. I saw half-naked Tahitian fire eaters, 1920s flappers with long cigarette holders, and gangsters in wide-shouldered suits; witches in tight black crepe, virile young wizards, and here and there, the random naked person, oiled-up gay bodybuilders, and women in stiletto heels. We had strippers, ballet dancers, and belly dancers—of both sexes. Flirty French maids and distinguished schoolmasters. We had rock stars and movie stars, any celebrity you could name. There was a pirate ship moored in the moat.

And the settings matched the players. You could create your own world or explore someone else's. Say "Open sesame" at a doorway and enter a chamber of treasures, find three gorgeous naked blond girls in a dimly lit cave, covered with piles of gold coins. Or imagine yourself in a seraglio, a harem, only the concubines were all virile young men and they all belonged to you, their absolute master. And everything was real, down to the blue-tiled walls and the eunuchs brandishing whips to keep the men in line.

It was astonishing and fascinating. And what a strange interplay between the various fantasies! This party was definitely the culmination of my experience in Shahalah-kam. As a professional observer, I was finally fulfilled. Not exactly what I'd had in mind when I became an anthropologist, but definitely provocative and possibly groundbreaking. Carlos Castaneda goes behind the green door.

But down in the basement there were other, darker fantasies being played out. These were the scenarios I avoided. The things I didn't want to see. In Shahlah-kam there were no limits. You could hurt somebody, in your fantasy. If that's what got you off.

And you wouldn't actually be hurting anybody.

"What's the matter, doll?" Cedric found me sitting alone near the entrance to the dome room, watching people go by.

"Nothing. Just observing."

"So I see. This is it, you know. Your big chance to jump on any merry-go-round you choose. Don't sit it out."

I nodded, blowing out a sigh. "Listen. Do you hear that?"

The air was full of music, laughter. And the faint, high-pitched strands of someone screaming. It was coming from down in the basement.

"So?" Cedric shrugged. "You just don't go down there if that's not your scene."

"I know. But I feel like I should *help* them. I can hear them crying out for help."

It didn't seem to matter that they weren't *real*. I couldn't get past it.

"Come on," Cedric said, taking my hand. "Let's go dance."

* * *

*I*t was just what I needed. Cedric took control and he was a great dancer. But after a while I noticed that he was acting very sexy with me, undulating against me, kissing my shoulders.

"Cedric," I said, "you *are* gay, aren't you?"

"Yes, of course."

"Then why the dirty dancing?"

"Do you like my freak? Well . . . it's always been my fantasy to get it straight, with a girl. Just once. And I *like* you."

I burst out laughing. "Let's just dance, okay?"

Chapter 33

I didn't feel like having sex with anyone that night. So I found a secluded niche in a tower with a window looking out to the stars, and I sat there for hours, just thinking. I felt empty and lonely, homesick for a place I could vaguely remember.

The tower was suddenly filled with noisy laughter. Revelers looking for novel places to make love. I made my way down the marble steps, passing Robin Hood, Maid Marion, and Alexander the Great, with his handsome face, strong shoulders, and bare thighs flashing beneath his short tunic.

I stole out into the gardens surrounding the palace. The night was strangely warm, and I wandered into the woods, away from the music and light.

I was filled with the disquieting thought that I was almost empty of desire. There was only one thing I wanted now. I just wanted to go home. And home was . . .

Yeshi.

Home was Yeshi. With a jolt, I thought of him. Maybe for the first time in weeks. It was like suddenly remembering a vivid dream from the night before.

I remember . . .

"There you are," he said.

His voice was so mellow, calm and vibrant. He came out of the darkness, and I felt him, warm and real, taking me against him, wrapping his arms around me.

"You found me!" I exclaimed in his language. "How did you find me?"

"I never let you go," he said.

"Are you just a fantasy?" I murmured, playing with a lock of silky black hair that had fallen over his smoky topaz eyes. "Or are you real?"

He smiled. "Can't you tell?"

"Sometimes with you I feel like I'm in a dream and I'm going to wake up."

"If I *am* a dream, please don't wake up."

We found a soft and secluded spot beneath a sheltering tree. We undressed each other and began making love. I sat on his lap, resting my face in the crook of his neck, impaled on him for what seemed like hours.

All my fantasies had come back to him.

We fell asleep together, and when I woke, the sun was shining and I was still in his arms, and he was looking down on me, and we were both naked under his cloak.

Above us spread the lacy leafed branches of the ancient tree. I sat up a little and noticed, in the distance, smoke coming from the chimney of the bathhouse. We were in the woods at the edge of Yeshi's farm.

Still half in a dream, I wondered, bewildered, how we had come to be in this spot without making the journey back.

Yeshi didn't seem to think it was strange at all. Wordlessly, he began to kiss me, moving against me.

"Yeshi," I whispered. "What happened last night?"

"I don't know. I feel really wiped out. Like I was hit over the head. But in a good way. All I remember is making love with you, and it was like we were stars, exploding in space. It knocked me out. But it wasn't like I was unconscious, it was more like I was *super*conscious."

I felt his mouth on my mouth.

"And I wanna do it again," he murmured.

He was tender and selfish at the same time, always considerate of me but immersed in the pleasure of his own body and how his pleasure rose from mine. I loved how aroused he would get at the sight and touch and taste of me, and how appreciative he was of everything I did to make him feel good. How he sometimes couldn't help himself and would rush to enter me.

And God, I loved having him inside me.

He drew himself up higher with long, deep strokes. My head fell back and I let out a loud sigh of bliss.

We were like that when Hama found us together.

He just stood there, staring down at us as we fucked, waiting for us to notice him. I don't know how long he watched as

Yeshi pounded me, his haunches strong and tireless, kissing my mouth and dipping down to kiss and suck on my breasts. I was crying and moaning with the ravaging bliss of Yeshi's body, but when I opened my eyes and saw Hama above us, I let out a shriek.

If I had found that having others watching me during sex could be a turn-on, I now found that it could have the opposite effect.

I was grateful for Yeshi's big cloak and his large body, shielding me from Hama's chill stare. The icy temperature of Hama's expression could have frozen me solid.

Yeshi pulled out and rose above me. He seemed intent on protecting me. He made sure I was wrapped up in the cloak and then stood to face his brother. I thought he was at a disadvantage, being stark naked.

But what was I worried about? We were doing nothing wrong.

"I see wifey is back to her full strength," Hama said. His tone was as cold as the look in his eyes. "Which is weird, because just yesterday afternoon when I asked her about it, in my admittedly indirect fashion, she said she wasn't 'ready.' Just yesterday afternoon. She wasn't up to it yet. Unlike she obviously is this morning. With you."

I kept hearing one thing. *Yesterday*. Surely that conversation I'd had with Hama had taken place not *yesterday*, but days, weeks ago.

I shook my head, trying to think. What the hell happened?

I remembered that day, leaving Hama, looking for Yeshi, finding him out on the edge of the woods. He had told me he could no longer share me with his brothers . . . and then we were in each other's arms, and then—the warriors came down out of the mountain—

And I had been kidnapped and held in a sex monastery for weeks.

Until Yeshi arrived and became the embodiment of all my desires. And we finally made love again and . . .

And then I woke up.

No, I thought. It was *not* just a dream.

And yet . . . *was* it? Only a dream?

I had spent the night with Yeshi beneath a tree in the woods behind the farm. Was that all? I could not believe it. I felt like I had lived through a great, transforming experience.

I scrambled to my feet, clutching the cloak tightly around me, trying to ignore the weird spectacle of Yeshi standing there naked, facing his glowering brother. I glanced about, looking for my clothes. But they were nowhere to be seen. And neither were Yeshi's.

Of course, I thought. We had left them behind.

It was only a dream, I told myself yet again. But I still could not believe it.

I really *didn't* believe it until I went back to the house with Yeshi and nobody made reference to the fact that I had been gone so long. There was some teasing about Yeshi and me spending the entire night outside in the woods, however.

Later that morning Yeshi took off on his horse without saying anything to anyone. I walked back up to the site, just looking around, wondering. I stared up the road where the warriors had appeared.

Okay, I thought. The whole thing was just an hallucination. Probably something to do with stress and altitude.

So then what had happened to our clothes?

Did Hama take them? No, he would not have taken our clothing. Indeed he seemed most anxious to have us dressed immediately after he found us.

Rafe? Hardly likely. Gaja? Inconceivable. Gazer, being a practical joker? Possibly. But he would have taken credit for the prank by now.

I never did find our clothing. Except for one thing—the embroidered jacket I wore when I ran after Yeshi the afternoon I was abducted.

I found it just down the hill from where we had been together, by a large boulder that had become dislodged and fallen down the ravine. Besides the boulder, there was no evidence of a landslide. I saw the crumpled bit of woolen cloth and climbed down the hill to retrieve it. I was glad to get it back, as it was a jacket I liked and a beautiful example of local handiwork.

But when I picked it up, it nearly fell apart as I pulled it from the rocks where it was wedged. The fabric was weathered and faded as if it had been left outside, exposed to the elements, for weeks.

This can't be my jacket, I thought, disappointed.

But as I examined it, I was puzzled by how much like my

jacket it was. It was exactly the same, only sun-bleached and battered.

I slipped my hand into the pocket and heard the soft chime as I pulled out my bell.

Chapter 34

꩜

Gaja had told me a storm was coming. The skies were still bright and sunny, but the winds down from the mountains were picking up, and I finally abandoned my search for the clothes.

As I walked back up to the house, carrying the bell and what was left of my jacket, I was just in time to say good-bye to Rafe and Gazer, who were off on a two-day trip to deliver grain they had sold to some farmers in the northern reaches of the valley. Yeshi was nowhere around.

I went into the house with Gaja after the men had gone and asked her if she'd seen Yeshi.

"No, I haven't seen him since you two came in this morning," she said. "He's not in the fields or near the woods? Or in the gardens?"

I shook my head.

She looked at me solemnly. Her dark hair was pulled back

from her face, giving her a sinister appearance, her dark eyes sunken into the delicate skull on the slender stem of her neck. "You know, from his behavior yesterday, I thought he might be getting ready to leave us again."

"What do you mean?" I demanded, my voice unnecessarily sharp. "Why do you say so?"

"Oh, I don't know. Nothing so unusual, really. But he was making sure all his belongings were clean and organized, and that the affairs of the farm were in order. Yeshi's the kind of person who, when he decides to go, he's *gone*. I was thinking he might even be gone by nightfall, though he hadn't said anything. When he didn't come in last night, I was almost sure of it. Not like him to just leave without saying good-bye, but I thought perhaps he had his reasons." She looked at me pointedly. "Then we realized *you* had turned up missing too. Gazer thought you had run away with Yeshi. I too thought it was possible. But Hama could not accept this, so he went out to see if he could find you both. And it seems he did."

Yeshi, gone?

It was the only thing I clearly heard her say.

Would he really leave without saying good-bye to his family? To me?

"I did not tell you this to upset you, Diandra," Gaja said. "And anyway, you see I was mistaken, yesterday. I'm sure there is nothing to worry about."

Shani arrived then and Gaja and I stopped talking. We could see her from the kitchen window and hear the chickens cackling in the courtyard as she made her way in.

"All right," she said with a mild reproach when she saw us.

She seemed out of breath, her plump breasts heaving. "What's got you two looking all grim and sober?"

"It's Yeshi," I said. "I don't know where he is. Gaja thinks he might have left . . ."

"But without saying good-bye?" Shani cried, incredulous. "Would he just go off like that?"

"I don't know."

"Well, so what if he did. What do *you* care? I thought you were going to stay away from him, and he from you . . ."

"Yeah."

Shani studied me carefully. "Something has happened," she said in a soft voice. Her dark eyes were gleaming. "You've . . . become lovers."

I nodded.

"Husband and wife."

"Well actually," I said, " we never signed the papers." I gave a bitter laugh. I didn't tell her the point was moot. I didn't need the papers anymore, because I was leaving.

"If he wants you, then why should he leave you?" Shani asked.

"He didn't, I'm sure," Gaja said crossly. "I don't know why we're even talking this way. He's probably just gone for a ride."

Shani and Gaja went off to gather herbs in large, flat baskets. They had invited me to come along, but I was too agitated. I wanted to stay near the house until Yeshi appeared. I needed to talk with him. We had started something, and we needed to figure out how to end it.

*   *   *

I was in the pantry, clearing space so the women would have a cool, dry place to hang the herbs, when I heard the footsteps. Brisk. Militaristic.

Hama's footsteps, I thought with disappointment. I kept hoping Yeshi would show up. My heart kicked up as I thought of Hama's cold expression when he found me unclothed and entangled with Yeshi. There was no way I could go on pretending I wasn't healthy enough to engage in sexual relations.

Hama blocked the doorway of the little room. I tried to pass by him but he kept his well-toned bulk in place, staring down at me hard until I looked up at him.

"Diandra, I think it is time," he said.

"Okay. It's time," I replied stonily, looking away.

"I've had enough of this. I demand that you take up your duties."

"My *duties*."

"Your duties, yes. You understand what they are. We had a very *clear* understanding."

"Yes, you have always made it clear just exactly what it was you wanted me to understand, every step of the way," I said in a voice poisonous with sarcasm.

He closed the door behind him and locked it.

My heart was pounding hard. "What are you doing, Hama?"

"What am I *doing*? I think you know *exactly* what I am doing, my dear wife."

He stepped toward me. His posture was erect and purposeful, his shoulders squared. He was like a lion tamer with his whip, and I was the cowering, captive beast. There was no space in the little room to maneuver.

Hama went through a strange transformation. It was as if he became the beast himself, a mighty, powerful lion. And then the lion pounced. In a second he had his arms around me. I turned away from him but he still held me fast in his arms. I felt his lips on the back of my neck, on my shoulders, sucking hard. His teeth, sinking into the flesh. He obviously intended to leave his mark on me. His arms tightened, constricted, around me as his hands grabbed at my flesh, whatever he could squeeze. He found one of my breasts and fondled it brutally.

"I think it's about time I did what I wanted to do the first night I got back from the highlands," he said. There was no tenderness in his tone.

"Hama, let me go!" I wanted my words to sound playful, but they came out sounding shaken.

He whirled me around to face him and pushed his mouth against my face, pressing his lips hard against mine. He jammed his hot tongue against my tight lips, forcing them apart. With one hand he held me locked against him as he ripped my blouse open, his fingers rough on my breasts. I cried out in pain, but his mouth covered mine and the sound emerged as a shrill whimper. His plundering hand moved down over my body, yanking up my gown to expose me.

When he thrust his hand between my legs, I screamed, but he cut off the sound with another hot, forceful kiss.

"What's wrong, baby?" he crooned when he pulled back. "Aren't you ready for me? All that attention you're giving Yeshi, what? There's nothing left for big brother?"

"Hama, stop—" I gasped, struggling against this invasion.

In response, he grabbed a fistful of my hair and pulled my

head down, pushed me roughly to the floor. I let out a shriek as I fought and struggled against him with everything in me. But he was so much larger and stronger, I was virtually powerless against his determination. He clamped one hand over my mouth to shut me up, sat on me and forced me all the way down onto the floor. Now he had me flat on my back, and with one effortless thrust of his knee he pried my thighs apart.

He lay down on top of me and our mouths were almost touching. I could smell him, acrid and sweaty, and wondered how I could ever have desired this man. He was heavy, humping me frantically, struggling to enter me, but I wasn't making it easy for him with my writhing and struggling. He lifted his hand from my mouth to hold my body still, and I began yelling again, but again he stifled my cries with his hot lips, his tongue raping my mouth. Our bodies were slick with sweat as he worked his hips between my legs. He got me into a death grip and I could not move.

The door burst open, literally kicked off its hinges, and over Hama's shoulder I saw Yeshi like an avenging angel, shrouded by a pale, mystical light, framed by the doorway. He was naked to the waist.

"Help me!" I screamed.

"Get the hell off her." Yeshi's voice boomed in the little space. *"Now."*

Hama just laughed. "Fuck off, little brother," he panted. "You have no business here."

Suddenly, Hama was flying backward. With one motion, Yeshi had thrown him across the room like a bag of fertilizer. I was free. I scrambled to my feet and pulled my gown tightly closed.

Yeshi stood over Hama, who had landed in a heap against the

wall. I ran past them both and dashed to my room, where I shed my ripped clothes and quickly threw on a clean dress. I began to hear voices from the common room. Raised voices.

"Don't you dare walk away from me, asshole," I heard Hama bellowing. "Turn around and face me when I talk to you."

I came out of my room to see Hama and Yeshi by the fireplace. The room was lit only by brass oil lamps, and the men's shadows struck the smooth walls, shrinking and elongating in a macabre dance. Hama was getting into Yeshi's face, screaming as he shoved him. Yeshi's hands knocked Hama's away, then Hama took a swing at him, a maneuver Yeshi easily blocked.

"Guys, come on," I said, my voice quavering. "Cut it out."

They ignored me.

Hama was trying to provoke Yeshi into fighting him, and Yeshi was resisting the challenge. So far. He stood there without retreating but made no move on Hama.

"Fucking coward." Hama spat at his brother. A moment passed, and Yeshi still did not move. This seemed to infuriate Hama, who utterly lost control. He launched himself into the air with a kick, aiming at Yeshi's jaw. Yeshi crouched, catching Hama in mid-flight. Hama tumbled to the ground, then rolled and sprang up into a deadly crouch, facing Yeshi and clearly just warming up to brawl.

Once Yeshi had made the decision to fight, he was like a terrible panther. The struggle was blistering and brutal. And as they fought, I stood on the sidelines with a look of horror on my face, like the leading lady in an old action thriller. I cast about for some way to assist Yeshi, but they were like two snarling rabid dogs, and I knew that interfering might make things even worse.

This seemed to be no ordinary male-bonding, establishing-the-pecking-order sort of battle. There was something eerie and violent about the way these two were going at it. Dark and strangely beautiful, and I was struck by the athletic movements of their bodies locked in hand-to-hand combat, the slick dark skin over the powerful muscles, straining and flexing, white teeth bared, the desperate groans vibrating through the room as the two well-matched combatants struggled.

I felt helpless to do anything but watch as the two powerful male animals fought to the death.

To the death.

I shuddered as this thought whipped through my brain. *It couldn't be.* They were brothers. *Family.* They loved each other. Young men fight all the time, I reasoned. Especially brothers. They wouldn't really *hurt* each other.

They knocked each other to the floor and rolled around, wrestling like enraged wildcats. Then they were up on their feet again, dancing and charging. When Hama jumped on Yeshi and shoved him to the floor, he seemed to have the upper hand, but he was struggling to keep his younger brother pinned down.

I saw my chance then, with Hama on top of Yeshi. Grabbing a heavy brass oil lamp from the table, I hoisted it over my shoulder, ready to slam it down on Hama's head. But their bodies were so closely entwined and they were writhing so violently, rolling back and forth on the floor, I was scared I would hit Yeshi instead of Hama.

With a graceful roll, Yeshi was up again and on top of Hama, his body lithe and muscular, Hama collapsed beneath him.

A moment passed, then another. Yeshi had his brother into a lock he could not get out of.

Hama lay nearly lifeless but for the heaving of his chest and shoulders as he gasped for air, his face crushed in defeat. The struggle was over. I took a deep breath in the moment of stillness.

Yeshi waited a beat to make certain his brother was no longer fighting him, then relaxed his hold.

Thank God, I thought. Yeshi wasn't hurt. Thank God he'd come in time. We were all okay.

But the moment of calm was shattered as Hama reared up with a terrible cry. He scrambled to his feet, looking around madly with glazed eyes and his nose running with blood. In a surrealistic nightmare haze I saw him reach up and watched in horror as he grabbed the ancestor's sword from its niche over the fireplace mantel. With one long motion he closed his fist around the hilt, raised the sword in the air and swung it down with a vicious expression, the long, sharp blade slicing through the space where Yeshi had been standing only a split second earlier.

Only Yeshi's nimble grace had saved him. I heard myself screaming as Hama, crazed with rage, swung the sword at Yeshi again, and again. Yeshi dodged the blade, his silky dark hair flying, his face running with sweat. His quick reflexes and agility served him well, but he was unarmed and Hama had him cornered. Yeshi didn't stand a chance in such an unfair fight.

I lifted the glowing oil lamp I was holding and rushed forward without thinking. With a dull thud, I brought the heavy brass lamp down as hard as I could, aiming for the top of Hama's head.

He was so intent upon hurting Yeshi, he had no idea I had stepped up behind him, But he was thrashing about so wildly, swinging the sword back and forth, I didn't get a proper fix on him and my blow proved a glancing one.

Hama screamed in pain as the heavy lamp smashed against his shoulder and hot oil spilled down his bare chest and over his back, and yet my attack only aggravated his fury. He was still determined to prevail, and with the sword in hand had the advantage on Yeshi.

But Yeshi used his brother's brief loss of focus. Leaping forward, he tripped Hama and brought him down to the floor in a heap.

Gripping the handle of the weapon, Hama lifted the sword, which wobbled uncertainly in the air from his prone position. "Fucking bastard!" he screamed. "You die—"

Yeshi kicked him in the mouth then, ending the struggle. With a swift, feline lunge, he grabbed the fallen sword.

Half naked and bronzed in the dim light, the sword clasped in his hand, Yeshi stood above Hama, who lay subdued beneath his boot, the gleaming silver blade at his throat. It was only a breath of movement from slicing Hama's jugular.

I could almost see the debate going on in Yeshi's head. *Show mercy? Or finish the fight?*

"Enough," I whispered.

I don't think Yeshi heard me, but it appeared that he felt the same way. Hama lay groaning on the floor, his face badly beaten, his mouth gaping open, bloody and toothless. His eyes were swollen and blind. Clearly, he was no threat to Yeshi now, and no threat to me. And yet, the decision to spare his brother seemed difficult for Yeshi, and he only withdrew the sword reluctantly.

He started to turn away, then abruptly leaned down, grabbed up a handful of Hama's thick black hair, and with one deft flick of the blade sheared off a lock just at the scalp. With a gesture of contempt, he threw it over his brother's sweating, panting body. Stray black hairs fluttered down around Hama like raven feathers.

Yeshi did not look at me.

Gaja and Shani had appeared in time to see the end of the fight and were now standing just inside the doorway, clinging to one another with horrified expressions.

Yeshi, who was pretty beat up himself, did not look at any of us. As he passed by his sister, he barked, "See that his wounds are dressed."

He was there, and then he was gone. He had taken the sword with him.

Much later I learned that he'd gone down to deepest part of the river, heaved it out into the air over the depths and watched the ancient family heirloom disappear beneath the churning black water.

Chapter 35

✗

That night I paced uneasily, wondering where Yeshi had gone.

It was nearly midnight. The house was silent. Hama was sleeping fitfully in his room, and Gaja had dozed off in a chair at his side. Shani was there earlier, but I had not seen her in a while, so I assumed she went home after making sure everything was settled down with us.

I was alone in my room and unable to contain my emotions. I went outside and used the path between the kitchen garden and the dairy to let off some energy. Walking briskly. Back and forth.

"Oh, Diandra," came the soft voice. "Let me help you."

The shadow of Shani's curvy form fell like a cartoonishly distorted version of the woman herself on the moonlit walkway. And then she was beside me and I felt her warm, sisterly hands on me, stroking my arms and my back. I leaned into the comfort of her soft, sensual body, and she held me gently, kissing my hair.

"Shani," I said, and the urgency in my voice surprised me. "You *can* help me. Please help me."

"Of course I will, Diandra. Anything."

"I have to get out of here. I need to leave the valley. As soon as possible. I know it will take time to arrange the porters, but if you could—"

"You can leave tonight."

I stopped in my headlong rush of words when she interrupted me with those four words of her own.

You can leave tonight.

"Tonight," I breathed. *Yes. Tonight. Escape.* "Are you serious? Is it really possible?"

"Quite possible." She added, with a hint of apology: "If you have the right kind of money, that is."

"Of course. Cash. Local currency and American dollars. All that I have left."

I named the amount and she hesitated. "All right. That should be enough. Give me an hour. Get ready. Tell no one. You must pack your own belongings." Again, an apologetic tone.

"No problem," I said with a short laugh. "Thank you, Shani." We fell into another embrace, one she prolonged, clinging to me, pressing her soft breasts against mine. She reached up and smoothed my hair. Kissed me softly on the cheek.

"Are you sure you want to leave, Diandra?" she murmured, and I felt her breath hot and moist in my ear. "It could be dangerous to travel now, you know, with autumn coming . . ."

I had the strangest feeling she wanted to kiss me on the mouth. I eased my way out of her embrace. She seemed reluctant to let go of me.

"I have to do this, Shani," I said. "I don't *want* to. I *have* to."

"Very well, then," she said. "If you are quite determined. One hour."

"Thank you. Thank you, Shani. I'll never forget this."

"You'll need some time to get away, but I can buy that for you with a good story," she said.

I had done as Shani told me, and was back with her one hour later. She was waiting for me with a horse. I hoisted my pack and fastened it to the saddle.

"When do I get started?" I asked.

"Right now."

We were standing in the darkness behind the barn. Dawn would be breaking soon. I wanted to be away. I wanted to leave before Yeshi returned from wherever he had gone. I hated the thought of simply disappearing, not even saying good-bye, but I didn't trust myself to be strong enough to do what I needed to do if I were to see him again.

Shani gave me my instructions. "Under the cover of darkness, you will leave the farm and go through the village. Ride until you reach the upper river. Do you remember the way?"

"If I stay on the road through the village—"

"Yes. If you keep to the road, you'll be fine. But let no one see you. It should be easy enough, given it's so early, to hide from anybody passing by."

I wondered why it was important for me not to be seen. I wasn't doing anything *wrong* by leaving the valley, was I?

But Shani was speaking quickly, and I tried to focus on what she was telling me. "You will cross the river. Pay the ferryman to cross." She handed me a small purse. "If asked where you're going, say this: 'I'm going to Boksuara, to visit the aunt of my husbands.'"

"I am going to . . . Boksuara? To visit the aunt of my husbands," I said, repeating her words.

"Right. The ferryman might even warn you against riding toward the south, and you will agree with the folly of such an action. Thank him for his trouble. Ride to the crossroads," she continued. "And then turn south. I see you've packed light, which is good."

She looked around, as if afraid someone might be watching, then reached up and unbuckled the straps, removing the thick blanket and winter coat I had strapped to my pack.

"To avoid suspicion," she said, "you shouldn't have a lot of supplies at this point, like blankets and heavy winter gear and such."

"But won't I need them while traveling over the pass?"

"Of course. But the porters will have everything you need. After turning at the crossroads, you must ride for some distance on your own," she said, "but the porters will be waiting to escort you over the pass and out of the valley. Until you meet up with them, simply stay to the right of the gorge, and keep to the trail."

"How long will I ride before I meet up with them?" I asked.

"It is difficult to say precisely. Depending on the weather, and the presence of wolves."

"Wolves?" I said, surprised and a little alarmed.

"Not real wolves, though *they* could be out there too. But it is the human wolves you have to watch out for—the soldiers who prowl the mountains this time of year, when the pass is forbidden. Looking for people traveling without good papers. And I happen to know your papers are not so good."

"Oh. I see." My marriage papers, confirming my right to be there. They had never been signed. "What happens if I am found without the proper papers?"

"The worst possibility? Well, sometimes when somebody stumbles into the void between where they should be and where they don't belong . . . unscrupulous officials will take advantage of the situation. Extortion, robbery. And if they make you disappear afterward, there's no trace of you. Because your papers were never filed."

"Ah," I said faintly.

"Not that *you* have anything to worry about. As an American, most likely you would just be escorted out to civilization. The problem is, at best, you're going to be held back, stuck with red tape. You know how it is."

Yes. I knew how it was.

"But it won't be a problem if you do exactly what I tell you," she said breezily. "That's why you must be discreet, and also why it will cost you, you see. One must pay to avoid difficulties."

"Shani," I said, "I really appreciate you doing this for me, putting all this together. How were you able to set everything up so quickly?"

"I have connections." She smiled winsomely. "But doing it this way is much more costly than the usual, of course."

"Of course." I slipped her a large bundle of cash; it was most of what I had left.

She accepted the money with a sigh of regret. "I wish I could refuse to accept this," she said. "But it will go to cover what I have put in these purses I have prepared for you. And if my brothers were to discover I have taken money from the household—"

"I understand. Forget it, please. What's next?"

"Okay. Now, if you are going to do this, you must waste no more time."

Wordlessly we came together for one final embrace. Her manner was cool. Unlike her seductive touch an hour earlier, she now seemed eager for me to be gone. I checked my pack, which held my notebooks, a change of clothing, my passport and visa, and my bell, the "golden ring" Yeshi had given me. Then I mounted the horse.

"Good-bye," I said. "And thank you."

She let out a sharp, disparaging laugh. "Don't thank me!" she replied, sounding almost angry.

I wanted to ask her to say something to Yeshi for me, but seeing the tight, cold look on her face, I held my tongue. I had decided not to leave a note for Yeshi; it would have felt so trite. He knew damn well why I had to leave; I didn't need to explain it. And I assumed he also knew how it would rip me apart to leave him. I didn't have to tell him that either.

And the rest of the family would understand as well. The marriage papers were incomplete, so there was no marriage to dissolve. Nothing more anybody had to do, or say, anymore.

And yet I was already regretting my decision not to say good-bye. It was stupid, I thought. And mean. Not to say *something* to these people. These people I had come to care about. These people who had become my family. I should have said something. Even if just on paper. Suddenly I was seized with a terrible feeling, as if I were doing something wrong.

But now it was too late.

I set off down the road. At the gate, I turned and saw Shani standing in silhouette on the porch as if she were now the mistress of the house. She slowly lifted her hand.

A chill passed through me, and as I turned to head out into the darkness, I called out softly, "Please say good-bye for me."

Chapter 36

❧

I followed Shani's instructions, making my way quickly down to the village, keeping to the shadows, avoiding the few people who were out and about so early.

Once I was beyond the village, I thought I would breathe easier, but a strange anxiety had gripped me and I wasn't able to leave it behind, however brisk my pace.

I came to the river and paid the ferryman. He was an older gentleman, squinty-eyed, friendly and garrulous.

"Wonderful morning to be out and about," he said in dialect. "Smell the air. The smell o' dawn. Sun'll be rising soon."

Indeed the sky was pearling with light over the peaks to the east, and the air was fresh and potent with the perfume of the surrounding woods, the river adding its scent and sounds, mineral tones and rushing whispers.

"Still," he said, "you won't want to be too long on the road today. Weather's turning."

"I am just going to visit my husbands' aunt, in Boksuara," I said, a little awkwardly.

"I expect you have plenty of time for that." His expression was philosophical. He steadied the barge with his pole.

By the time we reached the distant shore, I was even more agitated than before.

"I see you are traveling with a day pack only," the man said. "You will arrive at your destination before nightfall?"

"Yes. I'm on my way to Boksuara," I repeated.

"Just make sure you turn right at the crossroads on your way out of town, or you'll end up as food of the mountain gods." He grinned at me and led my horse down off the boat.

"Remember, north at the crossroads," he called after me.

*T*here had been something kind and protective about the man, and I almost felt guilty when I disobeyed him and turned left at the crossroads.

There! I thought. I was riding a strong horse and making good time. I had negotiated the required hurdles and was on the right road. All I had to do now was ride. Ride until I met up with the porters who would act as my escorts. Up through the pass and down into civilization again.

Maybe my delicious yak herder would be one of the group.

Maybe.

Flirting with him would be such a nice way to pass the long, weary days of the journey to come. And when night fell, he would appear in my tent. He would be surprised to find I knew his language now, more than just the dirty words. We could spend every night together, all the long journey back.

Maybe.

I tried to feel the thrill of anticipation for such a possibility, but nothing came up. I knew it would be a long time before I could let a man who wasn't Yeshi touch me like that again.

I also tried to muster up some excitement about getting back home. I remembered how eager I had once felt, thinking that someday I would return from my travels with an incredible anthropological study. "My Sojourn in the Lost Valley of the Himalaya." How my colleagues would marvel at what I had seen and experienced. Back then, when it all started, my ego had hardly been able to contain my expectations for the future. Now I wondered if I would ever tell anybody about what had happened to me in the Lost Valley.

I was a little uneasy about getting lost, but once I was on the trail, I realized there were really only two options—forward and back. The trail grew steeper and impossibly narrow as it wound along the canyon walls. I leaned against the steadily strengthening winds and hugged the wall to keep from plummeting deep into the abyss below. When the horse's unshod hoof slipped on the slick rock, I clung to his back, terrified, as my world lurched a thousand feet below me.

There was not another living thing in sight, animal or vegetable, only mineral, these immense rock walls, and the screaming winds racing down the canyon.

I wasn't riding particularly fast, given the difficulty of the terrain and the beating of the wind, but hours had passed and I began to wonder how many miles I'd gone. A vague gray darkness swallowed the sunlight, and suddenly it seemed nightfall couldn't be far away. The temperature was dropping rapidly.

Where are the porters? I wondered, growing uneasy. I rued my acceptance of Shani's sketchy answer to my question of when I should meet up with them. I was tired, lacking a night's sleep, and cold. I wanted to find my contacts and set up camp for the night.

But it wasn't that late, I reminded myself. It was just a cloud blocking the sun. And it was a cloud that I was riding through now. Visibility had shrunk to nothing before me, and the horse picked his way along blindly. The wind brought something new, stinging and fresh. I felt the first chilled shots of icy rain slicing against my cheeks.

The frozen rain blasted me and my poor horse, who bent his slender neck against the wind and the onslaught of the punishing frozen sky.

The winds had rapidly gained such power and ferocity that we could hardly move against them. The air was full of thick white stars shooting sideways like bullets. Visibility was less than a few inches in front of my blinking, freezing eyeballs. I slipped down from the horse's back and tried to get a feel for where I was, and realized we had left the narrow canyon trail and were standing on a high and unprotected outcropping of rock. I had no idea what lay beyond.

The driving snow and winds obscured any trace of where I had come from or where I might reasonably proceed. I was afraid I might slip and fall into the swallowing mouth of the gorge with one false step. But if I managed to avoid that fate, dying of exposure was a likely possibility. No, make that a certainty. My inadequate clothing was already allowing the cold to seep through my body in a very big way.

I was in trouble.

Chapter 37

I found a ledge to huddle beneath for some meager illusion of protection. I hauled on the horse's bridle until at last he sank to his knees, probably more exhausted and cold than I was. I tried to bury myself beneath his big, warm body, half hoping he would not roll over and crush me. Half hoping he would. Maybe death would take me quicker that way. But then, death would be taking me soon enough, it seemed.

How long would it take? I wondered.

No. Must fight. I just couldn't let go so easily. Some part of me was insisting upon this.

But another quite reasonable part of me was beginning to think that, yes, perhaps just dozing off for a while would be best after all . . .

Really. Why fight it? I was feeling more and more comfortable, oddly, the colder I became.

After all, I thought, suddenly delirious with happiness—

happiness that coursed through me like warm gold—I had known a great love.

How many people were blessed with that kind of love, at least once in their lives? Deep and sweet and passionate and soul-piercing?

I didn't know the answer to that, but I did know one thing.

I had been so blessed.

And it was enough.

It had to be.

"*W*ake up. *Wake up*. Now. Do you hear me? Wake up."

I responded instantly to the command in his voice. I tried to open my eyes but my eyelids were frozen shut. As they slowly pulled apart, I fancied I heard them crackling. I listened to the odd sound, fascinated.

"Wake up, Diandra. *Please*." Yeshi's voice. No longer commanding. Pleading.

He must have discovered me within moments after I decided it would be all right if I were to slip away. I was jolted into consciousness so abruptly, so rudely. And I was still alive!

It hurt.

Yeshi poured some strong liquor into my mouth. He forced me to stand, and I think we were both relieved that I could still use my limbs, though not at all skillfully. He lifted me onto his horse's back, then mounted the horse behind me. He wrapped furs around us both to keep the warmth in, and I felt our bodies warm together, painful pleasure, as the blood came back into my face and hands and legs and toes.

The horse carried me along, with Yeshi sitting behind me,

holding me, massaging me with his thighs and his hands, his body swaying to the rhythm of the horse's movements. The other horse stumbled along, following us.

I heard Yeshi hammering at my brain with his tender, insistent voice.

"Stay awake, Diandra. Stay awake, my love."

And I felt his hands on me, all over me, squeezing me, drawing the blood into my flesh, and it hurt, and I was never so grateful for anything, and nothing had ever felt so good.

The hut was small and warming up from the fire he had hastily built in the fire pit hollowed out of the wall. The little shelter seemed like a different place than on the night I shared it with Hama, Rafe, and Gazer. Yeshi brought me down into the bed, climbed into it with me and covered us both with furs. He rubbed his hands over my arms. The warmth of him infused my body and my being. He was so big and hot-blooded. He worked on me for hours, it seemed, getting the blood flowing back through me until it no longer hurt but felt like heaven on earth.

Yeshi's touch was businesslike. There was no passion in his ministrations, but there was heat.

Slowly, the life force began to move within me. Something began to stir. I smiled at him and stretched out my limbs. "Where did *you* come from?" I asked wonderingly.

"Your guardian angel sent me."

I laughed. "I think you are my guardian angel."

By the mellow golden lamplight, I watched his expression change from worried intensity to surprise, relief, and pleasure. I realized he had been quite worried about me.

"Thank you for saving me," I said.

"I am not finished yet," he replied in a low voice. He continued massaging me, slowly moving his fingers deeply and gently into my muscles. He wouldn't let me move. If I so much as squirmed, he commanded me to lie still.

He flipped me gently onto my belly and began running his hands slowly up and down over my back. I thawed out and warmed up and then began to melt. His hands gradually ventured farther over my body, gliding over my buttocks and along the sides of my breasts. Then a soft feathering touch accompanied the deep penetration of his massage; he was placing kisses all over me. He slid his hands beneath me and cupped my breasts, lightly pinching the nipples. I reared up a little to give him better access. He kissed me down the long valley of my spine, running his fingers along my belly until they swept into the hot crevasse between my legs. He gently spread my legs, and I felt the moist warmth of his tongue as he pressed his face hungrily against me from behind. I thought I would erupt. I opened my legs wider for him.

He tongued me and nibbled and sucked me hungrily, pushing farther into me with his tongue and his fingers until I thought I would die from the intensity of the sensation.

Then he withdrew a little, left me panting. I think he wanted to make sure I was up to this. I was.

He replaced his tongue with his cock and slowly pushed himself into me, deeper and deeper into the tight, dark warmth. He fucked me like a dog on a bitch, and I felt the finger-on-the-trigger sensation of his cock as it pulled up slick against my ass.

He pulled out and turned me over so we were face-to-face,

with him on top. He lay on me with most of his weight, rubbing himself against me, teasingly withholding himself. I loved the feeling of his cock just sliding across my clit.

But I ached to be filled with him again. I arched my back and spread my thighs, tilting and nudging him down deeper. With all the power in his muscular haunches, he pushed himself into me and started pumping me hard. He filled me with himself, with his cock, his fingers, his tongue, his seed—the intensity was such that I felt the boundaries of my body dissolving. For hours he made love to me, inflicting pleasure on me and yet holding himself back until it was nearly torture. He waited for his release until I was on the brink of mine.

"*Y*ou saved my life. You know you did, Yeshi." I could hardly manage the words. I was overcome. With spent physical expression, with love. With exhaustion. With sheer gratitude for being alive.

"Why did you leave?" he asked. "You didn't even say goodbye," he added reproachfully.

"*You* disappeared," I countered. "I couldn't find you all day. I thought maybe you had left for good. Gaja told me she thought you intended to leave. She saw you getting ready. Making preparations."

He was silent.

"Is it true?" I asked. "Were you leaving?"

"Yeah." He let out a bitter, short laugh. "As I tried to tell you. It wasn't working, the idea of sharing you with my brothers . . . so I *attempted* to leave. But I had trouble walking away from you."

"But I never got the chance to tell you it wasn't working for *me* either. The only man I want is you, Yeshi. I can't be married to your brothers anymore. I just can't handle it."

"Is that what was going on with Hama?" he asked. "You refused him?"

I nodded. "Thank God you came when you did," I murmured.

"When I walked into the house just before dawn this morning, Gaja told me you had gone. She told me Shani had sent you out into the storm."

"How did Gaja know? I thought she was fast asleep when I left."

"She was on her guard. She knew Shani was jealous of you. Gaja never liked Shani, never trusted her. When I returned from abroad, I remember thinking it was strange how they seemed to be spending a lot more time together than they used to. Gaja wanted to keep an eye on Shani. She didn't believe Shani had accepted the situation so gracefully."

"So it was Gaja . . . " My voice sounded far away, even to me. "I didn't think Gaja even *liked* me . . . "

"Maybe she didn't." Yeshi grinned. "Not at first. But you were the wife of her brothers, and she had to respect that."

"It was Shani all along, wasn't it?"

He frowned. "What do you mean?"

"When Shani told me about this secret love of yours, she was talking about herself."

He looked puzzled.

"Shani told me the day you arrived that you had another woman. A woman you were crazy about and wanted to bring into the home as wife to all your brothers."

"The only woman I've ever been *crazy* about is *you,* Dian-dra." He kissed me.

I understood now. Shani had been fine with me as long as she was convinced Yeshi was keeping me at a distance. But when she learned that was no longer the case . . . she had worked quickly to eliminate me.

"There was never anything between Shani and me," Yeshi said. "Ever."

"She loved you," I said. "Shani wanted what she thought I had."

"Which was what, exactly?"

"*You.* Your body. Your heart. She was afraid I would take them away from her."

"She never had them to take."

"Neither did I. But she thought I did."

"Well, you do now. And she was right about one thing, any-way. You've had my heart since the moment I laid eyes on you. And now you've got my body. You've got all of me. And I want *all of you.*"

Chapter 38

That night in the hut we came together again and again, snatching much needed sleep between interludes of passion. Deep in the darkness, Yeshi whispered that he loved me. I had never known such a melding of body and heart. What I felt for him was something new for me. And it was so life-altering, I knew I was changed forever.

As dawn approached, I moved even closer beneath the covers and slipped my arms around him. I held him and listened to him breathe. My heart, and all the rest of my body, felt like it would burst with love. I knew Yeshi was my real husband. And that I only had one.

It was killing me, this ridiculous situation. It was tearing the heart out of me, the heart I had only just discovered. The incredible sweetness of what I'd found, desire mixed with tenderness and gratitude . . . and the devastating knowledge that this was good-bye. I couldn't stand it any longer.

I left him sleeping and jumped out of the fragrant nest we had shared all night. I ran to the doorway, naked, and stepped out into the cold. The sky was beginning to lighten at the horizon, but it was still dark enough to see a few stars shining in the west.

What will I do, I asked myself, now that I've known Yeshi? What will I do without him?

Then he was behind me in the doorway, his warm naked body pressing against mine. He wrapped his arms around me, and it felt like his whole being was holding me, and he said softly in my ear, "Now don't run away . . . "

I looked away, not wanting him to see the tears that were beginning to sting my eyes.

"Hey," he murmured, not fooled. "Come here . . . Come *here*," he repeated, turning me around to face him, and it was funny, because I was already about as *there* as I could be, but he kept saying it. "*Come here. Stay with me.*"

Finally I said, "That's just the problem. I can't. I have to leave."

"I know."

The silence filled the vast landscape spread out before us. The rays of morning sun now struck gold on a distant mountain peak.

"I will miss you," I said. "More than I can . . . " I stumbled over the clichéd words that would not do justice to what I wanted to express.

"Diandra, what are you trying to tell me?"

"I don't *want* to go," I blurted. "I want to stay here with you, Yeshi."

"I know."

"But I *can't*."

"I know." A hint of a grin.

"God damn it!" I exploded. "Stop agreeing with me!" I began to cry for real.

He was laughing gently, kindly, trying to hold me, but now I wouldn't let him. And he said again, "Hey. Come here."

"I just wish *I* could be as easy about all this as *you* seem to be."

"Well, yeah," he said. "I *am* doing pretty well, aren't I, considering I am going to be living with an anthropologist who will be studying my behavior all the time. 'The transplanted specimen is showing significant signs of successful adaptation to a new environment in which the climate and socioeconomic factors are largely disparate from that which—'"

"What are you *talking* about?"

"Well, when we get back to California, I do plan to live with you, Diandra. You *are* my wife, after all. And I am your husband. I will be your unemployed husband, at first, but with my engineering degree and a work visa, I should do okay."

It took me a moment to understand his very simple words. He spoke so teasingly, I almost wondered if he was joking with me. But at the same time I knew, deep down, that he wasn't.

He was coming with me.

"No, Yeshi," I said. "I can't be the cause of you doing this."

"Only God is powerful," he said darkly. "We cannot govern the wind. I must leave this place as inevitably as you must." Then his voice softened and he whispered, "But you will grant me my only happiness if you allow me to stay near you. Forever."

I laughed at the over-the-top speech, but he remained serious, gazing at me with his singular intensity.

"I will be true," he added.

Coming from any other man I knew, these phrases would have sounded pompous or ridiculous, but Yeshi was like a man out of another time. His authority was quiet and unshakable, and I trusted him completely.

"But you . . . but your home is *here*, in the Himalayas," I argued weakly. "At your farm, in the valley. It's a long way from California." I stumbled over my words, confused. "I can't ask you to leave, Yeshi. I *want* to, but I can't."

He took my hand firmly, as if afraid I'd snatch it out of his grasp. "You're not asking me, Diandra. I'm asking *you*."

He let the words chime through the air.

"Those marriage papers never did get signed," I said with a smile.

"I want to start over with new papers," he said. "Papers that say you are my wife and I am your husband. Your *only* husband."

"But you're talking about leaving your farm and your family, Yeshi. Leaving Gaja. And your brothers . . ."

"My brother and I almost killed each other last night."

Vivid scenes of high drama came crashing back to me. One image stood out from the rest—that of Yeshi, half naked and bronzed in the dim light, the sword clasped in his hand as he stood above the crumpled body of his older brother, the blade only a breath away from the jugular.

"Diandra, I can't stay here anymore," he said quietly. "Not after what happened last night."

"This is all my fault," I whispered, squeezing my eyes shut and shaking my head to dispel the vision.

"It is no one's fault."

I was silent. Of course it was my fault. If I had not schemed and manipulated my way into his world, into his family, and destroyed the balance . . . Yes, I knew I had done this. But I could not bring myself to regret it. Because then I would never have known *him*.

"And even if it hadn't happened the way it did," Yeshi said, "I think I would have left the valley for good someday anyhow. But it *did* happen the way it did, last night, and now I must leave. And so I will. I will start a new life. Insh'Allah."

His topaz eyes sought me out directly, sincerely. I wondered if I had ever seen anything as clear or as beautiful as those eyes. My God, I thought. I'm so gone on him.

"Start this new life with me, Diandra."

I began to realize what he was saying to me. We were leaving the valley together. He was coming home with me. I thought of how it could be, arriving in California with Yeshi at my side. It *would* be strange, I thought, but oddly enough, it was not hard for me to imagine. How would we deal with our cultural differences? Would we make it together in the "real world"? Only in time would these questions be answered. But one thing I could not imagine was willingly letting go of this man. And it seemed that I did not need to. The happiness that now surged within me was so great I hardly dared to feel it.

"Say yes," he whispered.

I felt his arms around me, and it was beyond me now. His fierce sweetness was too powerful a force on my psyche, let alone my body. I had no choice.

"Yes," I said. *"Yes."*

Diana Mercury was born in Hawaii, grew up in Santa Barbara, California, and now makes her home in a cottage on a wooded hill above San Francisco Bay. Besides writing novels she has worked as a waitress, a chef for a meditation retreat, a belly dancer, and a ghost writer. She holds a degree in interior design and is passionate about old houses and gardens. She's traveled in Europe, South America, Canada, Mexico, and throughout the United States, taking creative inspiration from the beauty of nature and the diversity of human culture. The realm of the Lost Valley, however, is almost completely imaginary. Visit her at DianaMercury.com.